BLACKMAIL UNDER A DARK STAR

SPACE OPERA NOIR ON STAR CITY

BY GREG FOWLKES

Includes previews from the book

The Blood Red Sands of Mars:
Book One from the Murder on Mars Series

BLACKMAIL UNDER A DARK STAR

© 2017 The Fictional Press
www.TheFictionalPress.com

The Fictional Press is a small, independent press specializing in the publication of fictional works by emerging authors. If you are interested in bringing your fictional works to life in print as well as electronically, contact us! We can help!

www.TheFictionalPress.com

ISBN 13: 978-1-943403-44-8

Printed in the United States of America

BOOKS BY GREG FOWLKES

From the Wizard at Law Series:
The Laws of Magic
Trial by Magic

From the Murder on Mars Series:
Blood Red Sands of Mars
A Death at Station Alpha
A Corpse in Hut Town
Murder at the Mars Club

From the Fictional Detective Series:
The Fictional Detective
A Fictional Detective Trifecta

Star City Stories: Space Opera Noir Featuring Frank Sladek

The Uncorrupted Corpse

Tequila Visions

Cargo From Paradise

Ice Viking

TABLE OF CONTENTS

Prologue

Confessions of an Insterstellar P. I.

I don't have a problem with women, it's just that they seem to have a problem with me. Either they end up taking the first starliner leaving Star City—or they die.

My name is Frank Sladek. I'm a private investigator on Star City, a hollowed out rock circling a star sitting in the middle of nowhere that never made it to the big time. The thing is, being in the middle of nowhere is the same thing as being in the middle of everywhere which makes Star City the major transit hub for that irregular blob known as human space, the perfect place for passengers to make connections. Sooner or later, everyone traveling beyond their own star system passes through Star City.

Along with all those people passing through, come those who prey on them, the low-lifes, the pickpockets, the two-bil grifters and other criminal types working to part the honest people, and some not so honest, from their money. It's not so much gambling or prostitution or even most recreational drugs; those rackets are pretty much tied up by the people who run Star City. It's the other stuff like extortion or blackmail, that's where I come in, when people's secrets are in jeopardy of not remaining secrets any longer.

Most of the those who come to me protect their secrets are women. They're happy enough for me to help them out, but like I said, they never seem to stick around afterwards. One way or another . . .

BLACKMAIL
UNDER
A DARK STAR

Blackmail Under A Dark Star

I got the call while I was sitting in the Blue Moon. It was a name and number I didn't recognize which isn't that surprising. I don't do much in the way of advertising and most of my business comes by way of referral. This call was from a temporary comm unit, the kind that people in transit buy if they step off a starliner and plan on spending more than a few hours on Star City before getting back on another starliner for the next leg of their journey. They sell them by the day, the week, the month or whatever. If you're smart, you sell them back before boarding which saves you five credits or so. Otherwise you just toss them into a trash bin for someone else to fish out. The comms then get resold to people for whom the lack of identity is an advantage. For reasons lost in antiquity, these are call "burner" comms. I wasn't particularly surprised to get a call from a temporary comm, not in my business. Half my client base would just as soon not have their names known.

This call, if I could believe the ID, was from someone named "Fleur de Sol." I didn't recognize the name or the language for that matter, but then I didn't really care. My clients can call themselves anything they want as long as their money is good. I was short on work and long on time so I decided to answer.

"Mr. Sladek?" The voice was feminine, almost overwhelmingly so, warm and sensuous, yet innocent at the same time. The speaker had an accent that originated on a planet where the first settlers had spoken a language that was not some variant of Anglo-American. I didn't care. At least she was human and not a blueskin or a lizard man.

"This is Frank Sladek," I replied. I was trying to picture in my mind a body to go with the voice, but no one could be that good.

"You don't know me, Mr. Sladek, but a mutual friend suggested that you might be able to help me with a problem I have."

"That's what I'm in business for, helping people with their problems. Did our mutual friend have a name?"

"Lucinda."

She said it in the same way she might have said Betty or Miss Smith, but it stopped me cold for a moment. Lucinda was a part of my life that had departed on a starliner bound for better things. I won't say that I hadn't thought of her in months, because that would be a lie, but she was someone that was irrevocably in the past.

"Mr. Sladek?" The voice on the comm asked as if she was uncertain if I was still there. I guess I had been holding my breath.

"I'm still here. It's just that you caught me by surprise. I haven't heard from Lucinda for a while. How is she?" I asked, as if it were just small talk.

"She's fine, Mr. Sladek." Of course she was fine. Not only was she fine, she was famous. An artist in the truest sense of the word, she was so well known throughout human space that she was referred to by only the single name. She worked in that most ancient of mediums, pigment on a two-dimensional surfaces, and her landscapes of alien worlds, some real, most imagined, hung in the best galleries and museums on Crockett, Terra and any other planet where someone could afford them.

"That's good," I said. I meant it, too. Our relationship hadn't ended in acrimony. As they say, it had gone out not with a bang, but a whimper. She had fled to Crockett after discovering that those things that had drawn her to me in the first place, the sense of danger, the wildness, the living on the edge, were just a bit too real to live with for any length of time. That and the realization of the kind of things I did sometimes just to survive.

"Just what is it you want help with Miss—?"

"Fleur. Fleur de Sol." She said the name as if it should mean something to me. It didn't, not then. "I'd rather not say over the comm. If we could meet?"

"Yes, that can be arranged." I realized I was being clumsy. Thinking about Lucinda again was affecting me.

"I'm singing tonight." So she was a singer, I thought. "Perhaps you could come to my dressing room after the concert. I could send you a ticket—"

"That would be fine, Ms. De Sol."

"Please, Mr. Sladek. Fleur," she corrected with a warmth that sounded like it actually meant something.

"Fleur."

"I'll be waiting for you then." The comm beeped off. A second later there was a ping indicating that a ticket had been deposited. Out of curiosity I glanced at it. It was for a seat, center orchestra, third row at the Opera House. Maybe Fleur had been right when she had assumed I would recognize her name. Of all the entertainment venues on Star City, the Opera House was the most prestigious. Only "serious" performers were allowed to grace its stage.

A quick search on my comm confirmed that my suspicions had been correct. Fleur de Sol was well known in music circles as a singer of the classical repertoire. In my defense, my taste in music runs towards the jive samba, but I really should have known who she was. She had performed in some of the best concert halls on Crockett, Midgarth, and New Albion. She had even sung at the rebuilt La Scala on Terra. And now she was to sing on Star City.

Star City is a hollowed out asteroid circling a brown dwarf star that is literally in the middle of nowhere. By coincidence this means that it's also in the middle of everywhere, a tiny piece of rock orbiting a pin-prick of almost light placed at the geometric center of human space. Its sole function is to serve as a transit point for the grand starliners that travel between planetary systems, a place for passengers to make connections. It's been said that half the traffic in the human sphere of influence passes through Star City. It's not quite true, but it's close.

One benefit of this is that nearly anyone who is anyone sooner or later ends up spending time on our little rock, including performers and artists of all types. And given that there is a nearly captive audience of quite wealthy people killing time while waiting for the next starliner, it is quite natural that many of these performers take advantage of the situation and play one of the numerous venues Star City offers. Apparently, Fleur de Sol was one of those performers, engaged to play that night at the Opera House.

That evening I put on my best suit and took a tram up to the fancy end of Star City. The Opera House is located in what is termed the "culture district." It's two blocks over from the Museum of Art and within easy walking distance of the Rigel Royal, the Casino and most of the other top tier hotels. This is of course by design. These institutions cater not to the permanent residents of Star City, but to passengers in transit. That's where the money is.

The usher who took my ticket gave me a suspicious once over, but when the ticket checked out he politely escorted me to my seat. I'm no expert in such matters, but my guess is that it was one of the best seats in the house. Judging from the finery of the people in the adjacent seats my ticket would have cost about what a bartender at the Rigel made in a month. After tips. I was starting to feel conspicuous and definitely underdressed.

The main hall of the Opera House seats just over two thousand. I had gotten there early, so I had a chance to watch as it filled up. By the time the lights went down, it was clear that the hall had sold out. I didn't know what Fleur de Sol's cut of the take would be, but at what they were charging a ticket, it didn't really matter. My normal fees for a job would be covered by her take from a single row in the balcony.

To my surprise, there was no orchestra in the pit. I was wondering whether she would be performing to a recorded accompaniment, but when the curtain rose it revealed a piano of the kind known as "grand" on an otherwise empty stage. It was an acoustic piano with no apparent electronic augmentation. A rather dignified woman who looked to be in her late fifties was sitting at the bench. She was wearing a severe looking dress and seemed to be staring at a point in space somewhere at the back of the hall ignoring the presence of the two thousand or so people in the seats around her. There was no way that I could associate that woman with the voice I had heard on the phone.

This proved to be the case as a moment later, Fleur de Sol walked out to the center of the stage. I recognized her from our conversation on the comm, but that had not done her justice. She was dressed in a black floor-length gown which had the kind of simplicity that costs real money. While in person it was clear that Fleur de Sol was not as young as she once had been, on stage at least, she had the sort of presence that younger women can never match. I found myself standing with the rest of the audience, applauding before we had heard a note.

After the applause had died down and the audience had resumed their seats she gave a nod to her accompanist. A few chords sounded and then she began to sing. Now as I said earlier my taste in music runs to the jive samba, but I could see how Fleur de Sol had gotten the reputation she had. It wasn't just her purity of tone, but the emotion with which she was able to fill the songs that she sang. And she was carrying the performance on the strength of her voice. The accompaniment, while tasteful and accomplished, was minimal.

The notes that had been sent to my comm said that the program had been selected from the "classical" period of Earth. I don't know what makes a song classical. Is a piece that is a five hundred years old less classical than one that is a thousand? I didn't recognize the material, though every once in the while I would catch a hint of some familiar tune. It didn't matter, nor did it seem to matter to the audience. We were all entranced.

She sang for nearly an hour, and then there was a short intermission. She returned, sang for another forty-five minutes and then left the stage. Of course she came back for the obligatory encore which was followed by a second and then a third. She left the stage a second time to a standing ovation that dragged on so long the audience started to shuffle nervously thinking that the performance might actually be over.

Then Fleur de Sol returned one last time. As she passed her accompanist she whispered something to that lady and then took up her position once more. A few notes sounded from the piano and then she began. It wasn't a classical piece this time, but a popular tune that had been current on Earth maybe a hundred and fifty years ago and which had been bouncing around human space ever since with periodic revivals as it traveled from planet to planet. It's been recorded hundreds of times by nearly as many performers in settings ranging from solo without accompaniment to having the backing of a full orchestra. Unless you're deaf you've heard it dozens of times. I know I have. But never have I heard it performed better than I heard it that night at the Opera House. I decided then and there, that whatever Fleur de Sol's problem was, I would do everything within my power to help her.

That was the final song of the night. The house lights came up, Fleur de Sol bowed gracefully. An extravagant bouquet of flowers was presented by the manager which she accepted with consummate grace. More flowers were tossed on the stage at her feet. She bowed once more and then withdrew for the last time.

After a few minutes the audience seemed to accept the fact that it was over and started to file out. I waited until the hall was almost empty before I cornered an usher and asked the way to dressing rooms. He eyed me dubiously with the look that is usually reserved for the maitre'd at a second class restaurant. I asked him to check. He was about to refuse when I casually let him catch a glimpse of the needle gun I had tucked in a shoulder holster.

That convinced him to place a call.

"Mr. Sladek?" he asked after he had hung up.

"Yes."

"It seems you are expected." Instructions on how to reach back stage followed. I thanked him and left.

The word must have been passed ahead, because the guy manning the door to the backstage space just looked me over and let me through. As with most theaters, backstage is a maze of rigging, props, and dim corridors leading off who knows where. I got lost twice, but crew members helpfully got me on the right path. I guess they figured if I had gotten backstage, I was ok.

There was a guy standing in front of Fleur de Sol's dressing room, the kind of guy who gets hired for security because he looks like he could twist you into a pretzel, except this one looked like he really could.

"Sladek?"

"That's me," I said nonchalantly.

He opened the door and waved me through.

Now I've been in a few dressing rooms in the course of business over the years, but never anything like this. It was nearly as big as my apartment and much better furnished. It seemed empty at first, but then I heard some rustlings behind a screen that blocked off one corner.

"Mr. Sladek?" came a cheerful voice from behind the screen. "I'll be with you in a minute. Pour yourself some champagne if you like. There's food on the table, too, if you're hungry."

There was a bottle in an ice bucket on the table. I recognized it as some of Crockett's finest. I'm not a big fan of sparkling wines normally, but what the heck, I thought. I poured a glass and eyed the collection of cold meats, fruits, and salad fixings. All of it looked like it had come from real animals or plants instead of a vat. I put a few pieces of cheese and cold cuts on a plate to be sociable.

When Fleur de Sol appeared from behind the screen the gown was gone and had been replaced by a simple dressing gown. She had removed what had obviously been a wig that she had worn on stage. Her natural hair was cut rather simply and short, and had a few streaks of grey. The stage persona was gone, but the vitality, the presence, was still there.

She gave me the once over and I shifted uncomfortably under her gaze. She poured herself a glass of champagne and turned to face me.

"You're not quite what I had expected, Mr. Sladek. Marcus portrayed you somewhat differently, I think." Marcus, that's Marcus Fitzroy the author, is said to have based one of the characters in *The Sun Never Rises* on me. Personally, I've never seen the resemblance.

"Marcus has been known to exaggerate. Just look at his fish story."

I thought she was going to spew the wine all over the room. "Oh, that's rich. I don't think I've ever heard it referred to quite that way before." The novella in question, *The Old Man's Fish,* had won Marcus the Crockett Medal of Literature the year it was published. From what I understood, that was a big deal. "You really don't care what anyone thinks of you, do you, Mr. Sladek?"

"Not many, at least."

"And Lucinda, is she one of the ones who you cared about?"

I took my time answering. Fleur de Sol's acquaintanceship with her had brought some old memories to the surface.

"I'm sorry. You don't have to answer that, Mr. Sladek."

"No, that's alright. And, yes, she was one of those who I cared what they thought about me. Obviously, it wasn't much."

"I can tell. And Marcus?" she asked.

"Marcus was I guy that I got drunk with. Him more than me. I helped him out of jam once." I didn't mention that he'd saved my life.

"That sounds about right, though most people wouldn't think of the most important writer of the decade in those terms."

"Why the third degree, Ms. De Sol? That is right, isn't it?"

"You'll have to pardon me, Mr. Sladek. I'm about to ask you to do something very important and sensitive for me. I need to know what kind of man you really are. There are some things that I won't take even Lucinda's word for. And you can call me Fleur. It's simpler."

"OK. If you don't mind my asking, is Fleur de Sol your real name?"

"Lord, no. I was born Zelda Gilkins. I changed it of course as soon as I had even the hint of a career."

"It's not so bad, really. You can call me Frank if you like."

"I'll do that, Frank. But don't you dare call me Zelda."

"It's a deal, Fleur. Now just what is this problem you need the help of a two-bit Star City shamus with?"

She seemed to gather herself together for a moment. She topped off her glass of champagne and sat down in one of the dressing-room's over-stuffed chairs.

"The long and the short of it is, Frank, that I'm being blackmailed. It's been going on for some time, and I want it stopped. Now and permanently. Lucinda seemed to think that you were the kind of man that could do that. Was she right?"

"You and Lucinda seem to be quite close."

"When you get to be a celebrity of my stature there aren't many people you can relate to, Frank. Lucinda is one of those. She and I share the same relative place in the galaxy. We talk to each other simply because we are lacking in anyone else who understands that. But let's get back to the matter at hand. I'm being blackmailed by someone who I believe to be quite dangerous. I want that clear up front, Frank. Are you the kind of man that can deal with danger?"

"I've been in a few dicey situations over the years. I don't go out of my way to look for trouble, but it seems to find me just the same."

"And could you kill a man if you have to?"

"Lucinda may have given you the wrong idea about me, Fleur. I'm not a hired killer," I replied coldly.

"But you could kill a man if you had to, Frank? Couldn't you? If it came to that?"

"I have, more than once, if that answers your question."

"I think it does, Frank. And I think Lucinda was right in what she told me about you."

"Just what was it that she said?"

"That you could be trusted implicitly, but that you had your own way of looking at the world, a more primal way, without regards for the conventional views of what constitutes justice or morality."

"That's not necessarily the way I would have put it, but it pretty much sums things up. I've never gone out of my way to kill someone, but I've never been shy about defending myself, or my friends, either. Do you have a problem with that?"

"No, Frank. In fact, that's what I'm counting on."

"OK. That's settled. Is it important that I know what you're being blackmailed with?"

"No, not the details," Fleur answered. "Let's just say that it involves certain youthful indiscretions on my part."

"I wasn't aware that indiscretions were a draw-back in show business," I said.

"You are a wonder, Frank. You know there are *some* of my colleagues who would take offense at your terming what I do show business. Public perceptions are perhaps more important in my particular corner of, as you say, show business, than others. If certain facts came to light, it would affect my earning potential, I admit, but I've made plenty of money over the years and managed to keep most of it. And I'd probably still be able to make a living for the few years that I have left as a performer no matter what came out about my personal life. But what would happen to me isn't really what's important. It's that someone who was close to me at one time would be hurt far more than I would."

"I see."

"I don't think you do, Frank. The nature of my indiscretions wasn't moral, it was political, and the other person who was involved is now quite an important political figure. He's also a very good man, Frank. Believe me when I say his home planet would be the worse for his absence."

"OK. Let's just say you and him did something when you were kids that could cause some political embarrassment and leave it at that."

She looked at me, then, and flashed a smile that could have lit up the Opera House. "You are a gem, Frank. I wonder if Lucinda didn't make a mistake—"

To avoid any awkwardness I cut in, "So, to cut to the chase, who's blackmailing and how?"

"That's part of the problem, Frank. I don't know."

"You don't know who's putting the touch on you?"

"No. All of the communications have been anonymous. Notes in flowers. Packages left at the stage door with recordings inside. That kind of thing. You have to understand that I get hundreds of such gifts every time I perform."

"So how do you know this person has the goods on you?"

"Because, there are things that are mentioned in the notes that only someone who had the 'goods' could know."

"And you think this person is here on Star City?"

"Yes. I'm sure of it. I'm in the middle of a twelve planet tour. At each planet I've stopped at, I've gotten a note demanding money. And each time, I've paid. But the notes keep coming. When I got to Crockett, I mentioned my problem to Lucinda. She knew that my next stop was Star City. That's when she mentioned you. When I got here—well, I found this in some flowers that were waiting in my hotel room."

She handed me a card. It was the typical sort of thing you get handed at a florist. There was a message on it. It had been written in pencil in block letters, the kind of thing that is impossible to trace. The message was simple: "$100,000C By Friday. Instructions to follow." Friday was six days away.

"A hundred grand in dollars Crockett. That's a lot of money. Can you raise it?"

"Yes. But I don't want to, Frank. I want this to stop. I can't keep going on like this. It's starting to affect my singing I'm so worried."

"We wouldn't want that, Fleur." I could tell that that was what mattered, more than her reputation, more, even, than her life. Lucinda had been like that. I didn't really want to follow that train of thought. "How'd the flowers arrive?"

"By delivery boy, I suppose. I asked the desk clerk, but he couldn't be of help. No one thought anything about it. There were dozens of flower arrangements waiting for me when I arrived."

"I take it this tour was planned well in advance?"

"You really don't know anything about the concert business, do you, Frank. This tour has been planned for over a year. You just don't throw these kinds of things together at the last minute."

"And this information has been public?"

"Of course. It takes time to sell out halls at the prices that are charged. Word went out nearly as soon as the details were finalized."

"So there was plenty of time for the black-mailer to make arrangements."

"All the time in the galaxy, Frank."

"Not much to go on, Fleur."

"But you can help me, can't you, Frank?" There was a tremor of uncertainty in her voice that was so different from how she had sounded on stage.

"I'll look around, Fleur. One good thing, this guy is an outsider. He's not from Star City. We know about when he got here and where he came from. That gives me something to go on. I'll poke around a bit, and stir things up. They tell me that's what I'm good at. I'll let you know what I find tomorrow."

"Thanks, Frank, I appreciate it."

"It's getting late. I'd better get going. I'll be in touch."

"But you haven't told me how much you charge, Frank."

"No, I haven't," I said at the door. "But it will be a lot less than a hundred grand."

I left then and took the tram home. On the way, I had a funny feeling like I was being tailed. If I was being followed, whoever was doing the job was good, because I couldn't spot him. Once I got to my apartment, I spent some time on the balcony with the lights out to see if I could spot someone in the street below, but all I saw was a procession of drunks stumbling in and out of the Blue Moon across the way.

In the morning, I got down to business. The passenger manifests of starliners docking at Star City are a matter of public record. Anyone can log onto the cloud and access them. I did just that, looking for all the people who had traveled from Crockett, the last stop on Fleur's itinerary, and who hadn't yet made a connecting flight. Of course, Crockett to Star City happens to be one of the most heavily traveled routes in human space and I ended up with a list of about three thousand names.

The next step, looking for those passengers on the list who had also arrived on Crockett from the previous stop on Fleur's tour, was a little harder. Technically, I wasn't authorized to access that information, but long ago I had made certain contacts within Star City's administration. Cindy wasn't one of the higher ups, but she was something much more useful from my point of view, a clerk in the records department. It's surprising what dinner and a few drinks in a nice restaurant will get you. One of the things it had gotten me was the password into the Security Service computers. OK, not a high level password, but one that is good enough to get me into the system they use to check passengers for security risks.

This allowed me to narrow my list down to under a hundred people. I also was able to get thumbnail biographies of each of the people on my list. I spent the rest of the morning using the bios to prioritize the list. I had a crude profile of what I expected the blackmailer's past to be like. For example, the retired school teacher from a planet named Nebraska was probably not a prime suspect, while the financial consultant named Gaston LeClerque probably was worth a closer look.

None of this is particularly glamorous, but then I don't get paid for glamour. In my line of work, the clients are much more interested in results. What I ended up with was a list of eleven names of likely suspects. It wasn't a small list, but at least it was small enough for it to be feasible for me to check into them more deeply.

Sometimes, looking into a potential suspect can be pretty easy if you go about it the right way. Take Gaston LeClerque. He was staying at the Rigel which wasn't surprising. It's a big hotel, not cheap, but not quite first class. Lots of business people and tourists stay there, usually only for a couple of days.

It was late morning. I figured that if LeClerque was really a financial consultant he'd be busy consulting. I placed a call to the hotel's front desk. When the clerk picked up the name on her display read was Edwerd Smythe from Svalbard Commercial Bank, LLC. I have no idea where Svalbard is or whether they have a commercial bank, but in my line of work it sometimes pays to appear to be someone else. Strictly speaking, of course, this is illegal, but for a comm call, who's going to care?

"Royal Rigel Hotel," the clerk announced. I pictured her as in her mid-thirties, not unattractive, but with that drained look you see on people who work at a job they don't really like. She sounded bored, which was good for me.

"Is Mr. LeClerque in? He's staying in room 1347 I believe." I'd gotten the room number from his transit information.

"I'm sorry, Mr. Smythe, I believe he's at a meeting. Would you care to leave a message?"

"Is that the meeting with Transport and Commerce Bank?" I asked, trying to match the boredom in her voice.

"No. I don't think so. He asked for directions to Interstellar Insurance before he left the hotel."

"Oh. Good," I said, trying to sound relieved. "Then I can catch him before the T&C meeting. Thanks, you've been a big help." Then I broke the connection.

That little exchange more or less confirmed that LeClerque probably was a financial consultant, and it did so without in anyway exposing the fact that I was poking around. It didn't necessarily eliminate LeClerque, but it did push him to the bottom of my list.

With a dozen more calls and a few e-mails I was able to do the same for seven more of the names on my list, and I'd done it without ever having left my apartment. I was feeling pretty good about myself.

That left me with four names to check out. Other than the fact that their travels had paralleled Fleur's itinerary, there wasn't much to distinguish them, certainly nothing that screamed blackmailer. I'd gotten about as far as I could through official records. The investigation had reached the point where some legwork was called for.

One thing that had caught my eye was the fact that one of the four was staying at the Landfal Hotel. Now the Landfal wasn't really disreputable, but it was a few notches down from the Rigel. The management wasn't so much discrete as indifferent as long as the cops weren't called in. It seemed the perfect place for Gork Jacsen to use as a base if he was, in fact, the blackmailer.

I went to my closet and put on the suit I use for occasions like this. It's a nondescript gray; it fits me well enough, but is cut just a little bit unstylish. In other words, it lets me look like an unimportant mid-level businessman, the kind you'd just as soon avoid in case he tried to sell you an insurance policy or something.

Half an hour later I was sitting in the lobby of the Landfal pretending to scan a newsfeed on a reader. My back was towards the front door and I had a good view of the elevators and the front desk. To all appearances, I was just another bored business type waiting on something or someone.

I had sat there through the lunch hour with no sign of Jacsen. This is the real reason why private detectives charge so much. It's the boredom. I was debating whether to pack it in when a heavy-set man sat down in the chair next to mine. He was in his late fifties, and from the way he sat I could tell that he was still more muscle than fat, though how long that would continue to be the case was anyone's guess.

Without so much as giving me a glance he asked, "Anything I should know about, Frank?"

I'd recognized him as he'd sat down. His name was Rik Lane, and he was the Landfal's house detective. We knew each other on a professional basis, and as far as I knew he didn't have a problem with me.

"Not so far as I know, Rik. I'm just trying to get a look at one of your guests."

"Which one?" he asked indifferently. If someone across the room had been looking in our direction they would have had no idea that we were having a conversation.

"Gork Jacsen."

"What a name," Rik responded. "Not local, I take it?" With a couple of hundred human planets and a thousand years of divergence, you run into some pretty odd names shuffling through Star City. The locals barely notice.

"No. From somewhere the far side of Crockett, I think. At least that's where he came from last."

"So what's the interest?"

"I've got a list of people who may or may not be up to something affecting my client. I'm just trying to eliminate some of them."

"So this Jacsen isn't involved in anything that I need to worry about?"

"As far as I can tell. If things change, I'll let you know."

Lane got up and turned to look at the front door. "Have a nice day, Frank." He turned back and started towards the elevator.

"You have one, too, Rik," I said to his back. I sat around for ten more minutes without a glimpse of Jacsen and then left.

I did the same thing with about the same results in two other hotel lobbies. In neither one had the house dick spotted me, or if they had, they had decided it was none of their business. The one thing that bothered me was that as I was walking from the second to the third hotel I got that feeling again, the one about someone following me. Out of curiosity, I doubled back twice and spent a lot of time looking at reflections in shop windows, but I never was able to make him or decide if he even existed.

It was late afternoon by the time I got tired of sitting around in hotel lobbies. My butt was sore and I was hungry. I needed a drink, too. Fortunately, Star City is well equipped to cater to my needs.

Around the corner from the third hotel was a diner. I'd never been in it before, but it had the right kind of ambience, not too bright, not too loud, and not too clean. There was a counter running down one side with booths down the other. I grabbed a stool and the waiter behind the bar shoved a menu at me. While I was looking over the menu I ordered a glass of brown with a beer chaser. The glasses were clean, the brown came from the same vat that all the other liquor on Star City comes from and the beer was reasonably cold. I was a happy man.

I ordered a meat sandwich with a side of fried stix. I'd thought about the "chicken," but in my experience it all tastes like chicken. I know that all the protein us locals eat on Star City comes from the same set of vats down at the back end of the city, and that it's only the seasonings and chemicals they add in the final processing that distinguish one from the other, but I try to maintain the illusion that it matters.

While I sipped my beer I tried to think out my next move. The hotel stakeouts had proved a bust, and I was still left with four names on my list. I was still thinking when the waiter brought my sandwich. The stix were a little soggy, but the cook had added a gravy to the meat that was quite tangy. I told the waiter to pour me another beer.

It was 1900 when I left the diner. It was that time of year when they were turning down the overhead glow tubes early to provide us residents with an ersatz autumn. Personally, I think that they do it just to save energy. The city was bathed in an artificial dusk and the street lamps were casting shadows. There were still plenty of people around at that hour, in that part of the city mostly tourists and travelers.

The crowds got thinner as I headed down city towards my apartment. The closer one gets to New Minglewood, the more dangerous it gets, and I live right on the borderline. It didn't bother me. I'd grown up in that part of town and thought of it as home.

I'd just left the Souk when it happened. I heard a sound behind me, then a flash of light in the back of my head. . .

The first thing I remember when I came to was a slap to the face. Not hard, mind you, but enough to jar me. The next thing was a slap on the other cheek. I opened my eyes. I recognized the face. I thought he was going to slap me again, but when he saw my eyes were opened he stopped, his hand in mid-air.

"Hey, Sladek. Sleeping it off? Or do I need to run you in for vagrancy?"

Like I said, I recognized the face. It was that of a cop named Rossetti. He was a detective with the homicide squad and he usually partnered with a detective sergeant named Latimer.

Latimer is ok and by Star City standards honest. I can't say the same for Rossetti.

"I was mugged. Somebody hit me from behind."

"He's right, detective." This was from a uniformed cop who was shining a flash stick at the back of my head. "I can see the blood. He probably should go to the hospital."

"Pretty sad, Sladek. The big private dick gets jumped by some guy coming out of an alley. Who was it, Frank? Sleep with someone's wife?"

"I don't know, Rossetti. I never got a look. I heard a sound and then the lights went out."

"Should I call for an ambulance, detective?" the uniform asked. He was young and actually had a look of concern on his face.

"No, that won't be necessary. Sladek here has got one of the hardest heads around. Besides, I'll take him down to the station. Latimer wants to see him."

The two of them stuffed me into the back seat of Rossetti's unmarked police cruiser. Rossetti patted me down, probably from habit, but didn't find anything because I wasn't packing. I didn't have a clue as to what Latimer wanted with me. At least things couldn't be too bad. Rossetti hadn't put restraints on me.

At the station Rossetti put me in an interrogation room and told me to stay put. Like it mattered. The door was locked from the outside. I sat there for a while and then a police medic came in. He made some clucking noises as he poked around the back of my skull, wrapped a bandage around it and gave me a couple of pills to take that toned the pain down to a dull ache.

Another half-hour or so went by before the door opened and Rossetti came back, this time with Latimer. Latimer is a big guy, beefy with plenty of muscle to back it up. What he has that Rossetti lacks are some brains.

"What have you been into, Frank?" Latimer said first things. There wasn't any need for introductions. I'd been across the table from Latimer in that room or ones similar to it enough times that we could skip the formalities.

"I haven't been into anything, Latimer."

"You want me to believe that you got mugged just like any ordinary citizen?"

"It happens," I protested.

"Bullshit." Latimer isn't particularly inventive with his language, but he can be emphatic. "We know you visited that singer. Fleur de Sol. A little out of your league, isn't she, Frank?"

"We have a mutual acquaintance. We were just reminiscing."

"Sure you were, Frank. And I'm the pope of Las Vegas. Tell me what's up, Frank."

"I can't."

"You can't, or you won't?"

"Same thing, isn't it, Latimer?"

"Sladek. You're a big pain in the butt. I should tell Rossetti that next time he finds you lying in the gutter he should just leave you there."

"Fine with me. I didn't ask to be brought here." OK, I know I was sounding like a twelve year old kid, but Latimer can do that to me sometimes.

"Look, Frank. We know you saw de Sol, so that means she's probably your client. The thing is, Ms. De Sol is a big time celebrity. The people who run things would prefer that nothing happens to her while she's on Star City. And that includes her being bothered by a two-bit gumshoe." We both knew who he meant by the people who ran things, and he wasn't referring to the people on the top floor of city hall. Star City exists to provide services to people in transit, and that means the hotels and casinos, not necessarily in that order. It doesn't really matter as they're all the same people, anyhow.

"She *called* me, Latimer."

"Why?"

"Like I said, we have a mutual friend."

"Sure you do, Frank. You and one of the highest paid entertainers in human space. Who's your friend?

I hesitated a moment, then answered, "Lucinda." There was enough truth in that statement that Latimer might actually believe it.

"Are you conning me, Frank?" Latimer asked. I could see he was trying to decide if it just might be true. He knew the artist and I had been an item before she had left for Crockett. He could understand Lucinda and Fleur knowing each other. Besides, they were both women, and dames had always been hard for Latimer to figure out. Him and me both.

"Would I do that?" I answered in my best smart-alec voice.

That settled it with Latimer. "Rossetti. Get this bum out of here. And see that he gets home in one piece. We don't want to have to scrape him out of the gutter again. At least not until tomorrow."

Latimer slammed the door on his way out. Rossetti just smirked. But he did see that I got a ride home in a squad car to my apartment in the Aldeberon Arms. If the neighbors noticed, they didn't let on. That's one of the things I like about the place.

I assured the officer that I didn't need help getting up to my apartment. The elevator was non-functional again, and by the time I was on the third flight of stairs, I wasn't so sure, but I made it safely. Once inside with the door locked, I turned the lights on and went to the balcony. The squad car was still in the street down below. I waved to show I was alright and it drove off.

I had a pounding headache when I woke up in the morning. A quick trip to the autodoc the next street over confirmed that I had a mild concussion. It dispensed two more pills for me to take and suggested I take it easy for the next few days and refrain from alcoholic beverages. Of course it says that every time I use it; something about my liver function. On the way back to my apartment I picked up an order of scrambled eggs and fried potatoes to save me the work of making breakfast, the one never having seen the inside of a bird and the other never having been in the ground. Frankly, I find the way people on planets get their food somewhat disturbing what with the reliance on nature rather than good old fashioned chemistry. It just doesn't seem hygienic.

Back at my place, I washed down breakfast with "juice" in deference to the autodoc's instructions. The headache had subsided to a muted throbbing in the background and I was able to think again.

I was trying to think of my next move when my comm alerted for an incoming call. The ID informed me that it was Fleur de Sol. My morning was looking up.

"Good morning," I announced as cheerfully as was possible under the circumstances.

"Mr. Sladek. What has happened to your head?" I realized I still had the bandage that the police medic had put on the previous night.

"I was slugged from behind," I explained.

"It didn't have anything to do with me, did it?" Fleur asked. "I'd hate to think I was responsible for your being injured."

"It was probably just some mugger. I wasn't in the best of neighborhoods at the time."

"Are you sure, Mr. Sladek?" Fleur said uncertainly.

"Well, it's not like I haven't made a few enemies over the years, but most of them tend to use more lethal weapons." I didn't add that most of my enemies were no longer amongst the living.

"You must be careful, Frank. I would hate for you to be hurt, especially if it was on my account."

"Trust me Fleur, I'll be cautious. Is there something I can do for you?"

"I just called to see if you had made any progress."

"Some. In fact you can help me out. I've got images of some people of interest. I wonder if you could take a look at them and see if there is anyone you recognize?"

"Of course, Frank. I'm more than happy to help any way I can."

I sent the images of my four top suspects to her comm.

"There's one of them, the first one, that I think I've seen before," Fleur announced after taking a few moments to study the pictures. The first one was of the man I knew as Gork Jacsen.

"He's using the name Gork Jacsen," I said. "Does that ring a bell?"

"I'm afraid not, Frank. I know I've seen the face before, but the name isn't familiar. I think he might have been at one of my concerts on Crockett. Or maybe it was a reception. Do you think he's the blackmailer?"

"He might just be a big fan, but he seems to have been on every planet of your current tour. I think Mr. Gork Jacsen may be worth checking into. I'll let you know if I find out anything, Fleur."

"Thank you. And Frank—please be careful. I'd never forgive myself if anything happened to you on my account." The strange thing was that she sounded sincere.

I found it odd that I had gotten conked on the head after talking to Lane about Jacsen. As far as I knew, no one knew that I was looking into the other three men on my list.

I decided it might be worth my while to pay another visit to the Landfal. I showered, shaved and put on a clean shirt. I don't normally carry a weapon, but I put on a shoulder rig and slipped a needle gun into the holster. I topped off the ensemble with a jacket that I knew was just bulky enough to make the fact that I was packing a gun less than obvious.

I entered the lobby of the Landfal from the side entrance, pausing long enough to scope out the lobby. Rik Lane was standing next to a pillar, his eyes focused on a pair of blueskins sitting on a couch off to the side sharing an air bottle. They were dressed kind of loudly for blueskins. If I had Lane's job I'd be keeping my eye on them, too.

I edged my way up behind Lane and then stuck the knuckle of the index finger of my right hand in the middle of his back. With the right pressure, that gives a reasonable impression of a 25 kJ laser pistol. I know it's a gag as old as the hills, but that doesn't mean it doesn't work. Lane tensed, but didn't turn around.

"Hi, Rik. Someplace we can talk?"

"Sure, Frank. Just no rough stuff."

"Not from me, Rik. You can turn around now. I'll keep my eye on your blue buddies over there."

Lane turned around and I showed him my empty hand. He gave a tight little chuckle. He also didn't catch on to the needle gun resting under my armpit.

"Look, Frank—"

"Oh, I'm not sore, Rik. I just want to know if you tipped off Jacsen that I was looking for him."

"It's like this, Frank. He paid me twenty to let him know if anyone came around checking him out. You know this job doesn't pay that great."

"Well, you made a mistake, Rik. I'd have given you twenty five for that info and for not letting him know about my sniffing around."

"Heh. Guess it's my loss then," Lane said. "But no harm then, eh Frank?"

"It's just this, Rik. Some guy sneaked up behind me as I was walking home last night and tried to bash my head in. Now, I don't know if it was Jacsen or not, but it *is* quite a coincidence."

"I'm sorry about that, Frank. I didn't think the guy meant any harm. He didn't seem the type. You got to believe me."

"Sure, Rik."

"This Jacsen. You think he's trying to pull a con?"

"Or worse. That's what I'm trying to find out, Rik. But you might want to keep an eye on him. I wouldn't want to see the Landfal get a bad name."

"Thanks for the warning, Frank. I'll keep it in mind."

"I'd appreciate it, Rik, if you wouldn't tell Jacsen about our conversation. I figure you owe me that much at least."

"Sure thing," Lane said nervously.

"Oh, one other thing, Rik."

"What's that, Frank?"

"Your two blueboys just got up and are following a guy with a valise towards the elevators. It looks to me like they might be planning to hold him up between floors."

Lane looked around in a panic. I took advantage of the distraction to fade into the crowd. Hell, for all I know, the two blueskins *were* up to something.

Once outside, I noticed that there was a little sidewalk café on the corner across the street from the Landfal. From the right seat, you could get a good view of both the front and side entrances to the hotel. As it was just before noon, I went over, sat in that table and ordered a cup of joe and a sandwich, just another businessman enjoying a leisurely lunch.

I was wondering how long I could stretch out my second cup of joe without annoying the waiter when I spotted Jacsen leaving by the side entrance. He stopped just outside on the sidewalk, looked around as if he was trying to get his bearings, and then took off down the street. I'd been in his shoes often enough to know that what he had really been doing had been checking for a tail. I left enough on the table to cover the check with a nice tip for the waiter and got up to follow.

The thing was, I was pretty sure that walking in the direction he was, Jacsen was heading for the nearest tram stop which was about three blocks over and one block up. I also knew, as a native, that there was also a stop on the same line three blocks over and three blocks down. Assuming that Jacsen was heading down city and not up, there was a good chance that by walking quickly I could hit the second tram stop in time to be waiting on the platform when the downward bound tram arrived.

I was cutting it close, but I made it. Jacsen had taken a seat at the back of the car. I hopped on and took a seat up front. It wouldn't matter that I couldn't see him; I'd be able to spot him when he got off.

We travelled a couple of kilometers down the line. This was well away from the part of the city that caters to travelers and tourists, but not yet down in the warehouse district. It was mostly residential, with some commercial geared towards the locals. Jacsen got off and headed spinward. I waited until the tram was just leaving and followed.

It was obvious after a few blocks that Jacsen had spotted me. He doubled back and then headed back up city again. We played cat and mouse this way for about ten blocks before I gave it up. I wasn't really that interested in where Jacsen was going. What I really wanted to know was if he was the blackmailer, and by that point I was pretty sure that he was my man. There was no question that he was a pro. He'd spotted me pretty quickly and played me just enough to make sure that I was on his tail. I let him slip away thinking he had lost me and headed for the tram home.

On the way back to my apartment I received a call from Fleur. There was a note of desperation in her voice that hadn't been there before.

"Frank. He's contacted me again. He wants another payoff and he wants it tonight. I don't know what to do."

"Take it easy, Fleur. We knew this was going to be coming sooner or later. Just what did he say?"

"He wants a credit stick with fifty thousand dollars Crockett. He wants me to leave it under a bench in a place called Orton Park just after midnight. He said I was to come alone and that no one was to follow me."

Orton Park was a remnant from the days when the builders of Star City still had plans that reached beyond finding new ways to fleece the tourists. It was a small pocket of green about a third of the way down the length of the city in a lower middle-class residential zone. It was supposed to be a half block oasis for the locals, and during the day that's pretty much what it is. After dark is another thing. Anybody with any smarts stayed out of it once the glow tubes dimmed. It wasn't New Minglewood bad, but it was dangerous enough. I didn't like the idea of Fleur going there. There were just too many dark shadows for someone like Jacsen to hide in. I told Fleur as much.

"But Frank, he said that if I paid him this time he'd send me all the evidence that he has. He said that it would be over."

"Do you believe him, Fleur?"

"I don't know, Frank."

Besides the choice of a meeting place, there was something else about the setup that bothered me. Jacsen seemed to be breaking his established pattern. Maybe my coming on the scene had spooked him and he was just in a hurry to get away, but there was a chance he had something else planned.

"The other times that you've paid him, how has it been arranged?"

"Usually he'd call with a bank account number for me to transfer the money to. It was always an off planet account, something that couldn't be traced easily. Once I was to send it to a number at an address he gave me. It was a place that accepted packages for other people."

Both methods were common enough and could be anonymous and untraceable if one was careful and didn't wait too long to empty the account or pick up the goods. I could name at least a dozen places on Star City that offered the same kind of service both openly and under the counter. Jacsen would have had no problem finding one.

"So he's never had you drop off the payoff in person before?"

"No. That's why I'm worried, Frank." Fleur had a right to be concerned. I didn't like the setup. Jacsen had already proved himself willing to use violence. My head was evidence of that. It was possible that Jacsen realized that I was getting too close to him. I didn't have any proof on him yet, but I did know who he was. He might be planning to call it quits and decided it was time wrap up all the little details, like taking care of Fleur and myself so that there wouldn't be any witnesses. That was why I didn't like the setup in the park.

"Can you get the money?"

"If I have to."

"Look, Fleur. It's your call; I'm only someone that works for you. We can play this out like Jacsen means to keep his end of the bargain, or we can set a trap for him. Or I can meet him in the park in your place and try to reason with him."

I'm not sure that what my idea of reasoning with him entailed would be something that Fleur would have approved of, but it was an option.

"But what if things go wrong? What if he doesn't agree? He might see that the information got out. I can't risk that, Frank."

"There's always a chance that that might happen, Fleur. These things seldom go off as planned. On either side."

"I think I have to take the chance and pay him, Frank."

"I understand, Fleur. If that's the way you want to play it, that's the way it will be. But there's something I want you to do. Just before you make the drop, send me a message, then, after you are out of the park and on your way back to the hotel send me another message. I'll be close by. If I don't get the second message, I'll come to the rescue."

"But he said to come alone, Frank."

"This is my city, Fleur. I can hide where Jacsen won't spot me."

"If you think it the right thing, Frank. I'm in your hands."

"I won't let you down, Fleur. Lucinda would never forgive me." I don't know why I added the last bit.

By the time I got back to my apartment there was an hour or so until they turned down the glow tubes. I wanted to be in place before dusk, but I had a couple of preparations to make first. The first was to write down what I knew about Jacsen and what was going to happen that night. If things went bad I didn't want the rat to get away with it. I put it all on a memory stick and shoved it in my pocket. The second was to open the safe in the back of my closet and pull out a 25 kiloJoule laser pistol as a backup to the needle gun I was carrying in a shoulder holster. It doesn't have much of a punch or range, but it's small and flat and easy to conceal.

The third thing I did was to go across the street to the Blue Moon and have a shot of brown. I didn't need the Dutch courage, but I needed an excuse to talk to the bartender. I slipped him the memory stick and told him that if I didn't contact him before closing to pass it on to Latimer. I left a Crockett fin as a tip on the bar.

I'd have a long wait in the dark, so I stopped at the diner on the corner for a meat sandwich and a container of joe to go. I've done this often enough that the guy behind the counter didn't even blink.

Orton Park is a little square about fifty meters on a side. Three of those sides are fronted by streets, the fourth side butts up against a pair of apartment buildings four stories tall. There's a narrow alley that runs between the two buildings to provide access for the waste collection wagon. Once the glow tubes dim, it's a very dark alley. There's a fence at the end of the alley next to the park, but generations of kids have made an opening through it so it's easy enough to slip into the park from the alley.

I got into place in the alley behind a trash container just as the glow tubes started to dim. This process takes about a quarter of an hour. I've never understood whether there is some sort of technical reason for this, or whether it's done for effect. Frankly, I've never cared.

I waited. Then I waited some more. Around 2100 I finished off the sandwich. The joe lasted a little longer. At 2300 I went to the end of the trash bin and took a leak, and then I went back to my hiding place.

I had a good view of the park. There are two paths that wind through the park and cross in the center. There's a kind of clearing where they meet. That's where the bench was. The rest of the park was given over to trees and overgrown shrubbery.

With the glow tubes off, the lights from the adjacent streets provided the only illumination, but the trees and shrubbery meant that most of the park was in dark shadow. There was just enough light coming down from the lights on the other side of the city three kilometers overhead that you could sense the outlines of the trees as a darker black. I hadn't spotted Jacsen when he had entered, but I had heard him moving around and was able to catch a glimpse of him. He was hiding behind a bush just off the clearing. This was about half an hour before midnight.

Right on time Fleur sent me her message. I saw her walking up the path from the street opposite me. There was enough light coming in along the path that she was silhouetted against it. I could tell that she was nervous because she was glancing back and forth to either side.

She made her way to the clearing, more or less feeling her way. She bent over and left the credit stick, then turned to leave the same way as she had come. I'd made my way through the opening in the fence, and stood just inside the park.

That's when I saw Jacsen stand. He was holding something in his hands. I couldn't really see it, but I knew what it was, a laser pistol. He was taking aim to shoot Fleur in the back.

"Jacsen," I called out, at the same time releasing a burst of three darts from my needle gun. I was too far off for them to be accurate, and I could hear the sound of the needles tearing into the shrubbery, but it was enough to make Jacsen miss. The flash of the laser lit up the clearing for a microsecond. Fleur began to run.

I moved forward and fired off a snap shot in Jacsen's direction. I didn't really expect to hit anything, but I wanted to keep him distracted. I wasn't sure what kind of weapon he was carrying or how long the capacitor would take to recycle. That's one problem with a laser unless it's a military one with a separate power pack; there's a finite time between shots that can be anything from five to thirty seconds.

There was another laser flash, this time in my direction. Jacsen's laser had taken fifteen seconds to recycle. I let off another burst in his direction. By now Jacsen had figured out that I was armed with a needle gun and could pump off shots a lot quicker than he could. I heard the rustle of bushes and then the slap of shoe leather against the path as Jacsen beat a retreat. I stood motionless for a couple of minutes until I was sure that he was gone. Then I went over to the bench, I picked up the credit stick, stuffed it into my pocket, and followed the path Fleur had taken.

When I finally caught up to her she was walking blindly down the street. Her eyes were staring straight ahead, and when I placed my hand on her shoulder she was trembling.

"He tried to kill me," she said as she turned to face me.

"Yes, I was afraid of that. That's why I was watching."

"No one has ever tried to kill me before, Frank. Why did he do that?"

"He realizes that the game is up, that he's been identified, so he's trying to end it. It wasn't personal. He was just trying to tie up loose ends."

"Murder isn't personal, Frank? What kind of world does he live in?"

"Not a very nice one, I'm afraid. It's alright. I'll take you back to the hotel."

"I don't want to go there. I don't want to be alone tonight."

"Alright. We won't go back to the hotel. We'll go to my place. It's not that far. How's that?"

She just nodded, clinging to me for a moment before she pulled herself together. "I'd like that, Frank."

I steered her to the stop for the circumferential tram, choosing the one that took the long way around the inside of the cylinder that was Star City. I wanted time to spot Jacsen if he was following us. If he was, he was doing a good job of it, because I didn't see him. A short ride on the up tram and we were within walking distance of my apartment.

We reached the Aldeberon Arms without incidence. The trip, short as it had been, had left Fleur in a dazed state. By some miracle, the elevator was working. It was just as well, as I'm not sure how I could have gotten Fleur up three flights of stairs to my apartment if it hadn't been.

Once inside, I sat her on a chair in the living room and went into the kitchen where I poured her three fingers of brown, adding a couple of cubes of ice to cut the taste. I did the same for myself. It had been a close thing.

Fleur stared at the glass for a moment when I handed it to her, then took a large swallow. The raw taste of the liquor caught her by surprise. She coughed, and then looked at me with wide eyes.

"That's terrible, Frank. What is it?" The liquor had had its effect. She was almost smiling.

"Brown. It's a locally produced alcohol. It comes out of a vat and then they add flavor and color. It's supposed to be like whiskey, but it isn't."

"That's an understatement. Do you actually drink this stuff?"

"When I can't afford anything better. Which is most of the time."

She looked around at the place, seeing it for the first time. "You seem to be doing alright for yourself, Frank."

"The rent is cheap. This used to be a nice building back when New Minglewood was supposed to be a park. It's a slum now, the worst of Star City. That's it just a block over. You can see the edge of it over the Blue Moon's sign. When the neighborhood went, the rents dropped. That's how I can afford it. I don't mind the neighborhood much, and having a bar across the street is convenient."

"This isn't quite what I had envisioned for you," Fleur said with a gesture of her hand. "It's actually—"

"Tasteful?" I supplied.

"Yes. Tasteful, that's the word. Who's your decorator?"

"Oh, I've picked up a good piece, here and there. Used of course. Most of the furnishings I've gotten because someone else was throwing them out. They're cheaper that way, but you can do alright if you time things right."

"You continue to amaze me, Frank. I think I'm starting to understand what Lucinda saw in you. Is that one of hers?" She was pointing at a painting that hung on the wall over the sofa. It's an alien landscape, strangely contoured in mostly oranges and reds. I don't know if it is an image of someplace real or was just a product of Lucinda's imagination. She gave it to me when she first started sleeping over.

"Yes, that's one of hers," I answered flatly.

Fleur stood up and began to look the place over. She still had her drink in her hand and was sipping gingerly from it from time to time. I took that as a good sign. She stopped at the bookcase, reading the titles. She pulled one out and examined it. It was a copy of Marcus Fitzroy's *A Farewell to Holm.* It's a signed first edition. She looked at me questioningly.

"I met Marcus in the bar across the street. He was drinking a lot in those days, amongst other things, and hadn't published anything yet. We hung around for awhile until things got too dangerous for him. I helped him get off Star City."

"This is a first edition, Frank, and signed. It's quite valuable, at least on Crockett."

"Oh, I know. Marcus sends me copies of all his books. I think of them as my retirement fund."

"Do you think of Lucinda's painting in the same way?"

"Things would have to be pretty low for me to sell it." To break the mood I added, "I've got a signed copy of Jack Feldman's book, too. Of course that's worthless. He gives them away to everyone who will take one. I'm sure I can get one for you if you want."

Fleur laughed at that. Feldman had had his moment of fame fifteen years earlier and had been living off it ever since. "I think I'll pass on that, Frank."

"Lucinda mentioned another picture, a portrait. I got the impression it was of you." Lucinda had become famous for her alien landscapes, surreal visions of places that might or might not actually exist. She's rarely painted pictures of people, and then never for sale or exhibition.

"It's in the entryway, just across from the door." I keep it there to remind myself of who I am.

Fleur went to examine it. When she came back there was an odd expression on her face. "I didn't really believe Lucinda when she told me about it, but I see she wasn't exaggerating."

The title Lucinda had scrawled on the back of the canvas reads "Portrait of Frank Sladek," but the full length figure on the front is quite disturbing and not exactly human. It was Lucinda's parting gift.

"I've never been sure if that is what she really thought of me or if she was just mad at me at the time."

"I don't think she was mad at you, Frank. At least that's not the way she tells it now."

That, of course, leaves the other option, that she saw me as an inhuman monster, which might explain why she left.

To break the silence I said, "She left me another painting. It isn't nearly as—unusual. She hung it over my bed. If you'd care to take a look—"

"I thought you'd never ask, Frank," Fleur quipped, coquettishly. All the warmth and femininity had returned to her voice.

I hadn't intended my offer as anything more than an invitation to view the painting, a rather inviting alien seascape of phosphorescent waves lit by three moons, but, well, one thing led to another.

I woke in the morning to Fleur's snoring. It was dainty, melodious snoring, but snoring all the same. I didn't mind. I knew that in three days she'd be catching a starliner for the next leg of her tour. There was no possibility for any sort of entanglement, and no illusions of anything more on either of our parts.

She stretched languorously, like a cat, and then opened her eyes with that momentary look of disorientation you get when you wake up in a strange bed. She pulled the sheets up around her and then realizing what she had done cast them off. She might have been a few years older than me, but she had taken good care of herself. I suppose as a singer she had had to.

"Care for breakfast?" I asked.

"You cook?"

"When I have to," I replied.

"What time is it?" she said, suddenly in a panic.

"It's 0900."

"Oh, lord. I've got a rehearsal in a little over an hour and a half. I have to get back to the hotel and get ready." She was suddenly very professional and in a hurry.

"Let me get dressed, and I'll escort you to the hotel."

A shadow crossed her face for an instance, then she began gathering up her clothes from where they lay on the floor. "Can I use your bathroom, Frank?"

"Feel free," I said and then added, "You might find some useful things in the upper right drawer." That was where I stuffed the detritus of other female companions who had spent the night.

She looked at me with one eyebrow raised and then dove into the bathroom. A second later I could hear the sound of running water in the shower.

I cleaned myself up as best I could and then dressed. I reloaded the needle gun and grabbed a small laser pistol that I knew would hide flat in my jacket pocket. I was ready to go when Fleur emerged from the bathroom.

Fleur wanted to call a taxi, but I assured her the trams would get us there faster. They were also more public providing, fewer opportunities for Jacsen, but I didn't mention that.

Her suite at the hotel was twice the size of my apartment, and much more luxurious. When we got inside, she was all business again.

"I've got to change and get ready, Frank. Why don't you order something for breakfast for the both of us? Just have them put it on the room. And tell them to hurry. We've only got about 45 minutes."

I did as she asked, ordering eggs from real chickens and bacon from real pigs for myself and "whatever Ms. De Sol normally had" for Fleur. I also ordered real coffee, though I would have been just as happy with joe.

We made it to the rehearsal just in time. I hadn't realized until then that Fleur's performance was to be with the entire Star City Philharmonic as her backing. I took a chair in the orchestra seats where I could watch the stage and still keep an eye on the exits. Jacsen didn't show, but Fleur sang wonderfully, perhaps even better than in her solo concert. It seemed as if she had a heightened sense of life about her.

After the rehearsal, Fleur invited me to lunch. As I didn't want to let her out of my sight, I accepted. Lunch turned out to be at the Café Stellar, the roof top restaurant on top of the Casino. I'd only eaten there once before, with Lucinda, Marcus, and Jocelyn, the woman who later tried to kill Marcus and me. Fortunately, the food is excellent, prepared by master chefs from the best ingredients in human space. Fleur hadn't had a chance for more than a few pieces of fruit before rehearsal, so she was ravenous. I was hungry, too.

It seemed too perfect an occasion for it, but reality is hard to ignore. As we sipped our after lunch coffee we were both thinking of the events of the previous night.

"What are we going to do, Frank?"

It was too serious a situation for me to respond with something as fatuous as "About what?" Instead I said:

"I've been thinking about that. So far you've been playing by Jacsen's rules. But things have changed now. You know who he is, and he knows that you know who he is. He also knows that there is a third player in the game, me. I've messed up his little game. Now I think the time has come to change the rules of the game on him while he's off balance."

Fleur looked at me. I wasn't sure she liked what she saw. "Just what are you proposing, Frank?"

"Jacsen knows that the game is up. He's trying to find a way out. What I'd like to do is offer him that way, but on our terms, not his."

"I don't understand."

"I'm going to contact Jacsen to arrange a meeting, just between me and him without your involvement. I'll tell him that he can have ten thousand if he turns over everything he has and leaves Star City on the next starliner. If he doesn't agree, I go to the police."

"If we go to the police, everything will come out. I can't risk that."

"You underestimate Star City's police forces ability to hush things up when it serves their interests. They could make Jacsen disappear without a trace. Jacsen knows that. He'll agree."

"But will he keep his end of the agreement? How do you know that he won't double-cross you?"

"That's up to Jacsen. Just keep one thing in mind, the double-cross is Star City's national sport." I said it as a joke, but it's still true.

"Frank, be careful. Jacsen is a dangerous man, and treacherous."

I sipped the last of my coffee, and then said, "I'm counting on that, Fleur."

She looked at me, realizing for the first time that Lucinda's portrait might just have captured the real me.

I left a message at Jacsen's hotel setting terms, a time, and a place. A text came back almost immediate accepting. The rest of the day I kept close to Fleur just in case. That night I shared her suite, but not her bed. It was nothing personal she assured me; she just liked to sleep alone the night before a major concert. I chose to believe her.

Her concert was at 2000. I had scheduled the meeting with Jacsen for 1600. By then Fleur would already be at the concert hall preparing. There would be lots of people around her and plenty of security. I got her settled into her dressing room and then left.

At my apartment, I changed into something more appropriate, dark and loose enough to give me freedom of movement. From the safe in the back of my closet I pulled a 60 kJoule laser pistol I'd taken off of a guy that had tried to shake me down once. It was one that I'd never used before and there would be no way to trace it back to me. Latimer has frisked me often enough to know that I favor a needle-gun.

I had a shoulder holster that fit the laser. I checked the rig to make sure I could draw it without it sticking. The needle gun I tucked into my waistband in the small of my back. The little 25 kJoule laser I left in my jacket pocket as insurance.

You'd think that on a place as small as Star City with a population of two million that there wouldn't be many places that were devoid of people, but you'd be wrong. I'd set as the meeting place the warehouse complex where they store excess baggage for people in transit. It was close enough to the head end where the starliners dock to be convenient, but isolated enough for my purposes. There would be plenty of activity, but it would all be in the form of robotic baggage handlers.

I took the tram to the nearest station, and then approached the rendezvous point from the downward side. The complex is supposed to be secure, but the robots have to get in and out some way, so it wasn't hard to slip in in the shadow of one of them. I figured that Jacsen wouldn't have had any trouble getting in, either. I was pretty sure that he would have gotten there before me to check out the setup. In fact I was counting on it. I wasn't disappointed. The complex is arranged as a grid of corridors that are flanked with storage cubicles stacked five high. Everything is numbered with an identifier based on the location within the grid. When I arrived at the intersection I had specified, Jacsen stepped out of the shadows. He was holding a laser in his right hand. I had expected that.

"Hold it right there, Sladek."

"I'm holding," I said, my hands open and at my side to show they were empty. We were about ten meters apart, long range for a needle gun, a piece of cake for a laser.

"Do you have the money?"

I reached in with my left hand and produced a credit stick. "It's right here."

"You're a fool, Sladek

"I've been called worse."

"What's to keep me from shooting you right now?"

"Nothing."

"That's what I thought."

He started to raise the pistol in an arc that would have ended up aiming at the point right between my eyes. He never got the chance to finish the motion. Star City takes security seriously, particularly when it comes to the passengers of the starliners and their possessions. The baggage complex has an automated security system armed with lasers that are cued to shoot anyone trying to fire a weapon. It's very accurate.

I went to check Jacsen's body. Lasers had hit him in the head from two directions. I went through his pockets, but if he had the information he'd been blackmailing Fleur with, I couldn't find it. I wasn't surprised.

I knew better than to hang around. The police would have been notified the moment the security system had fired.

My next stop was the Landfal.

Rik Lane was in the lobby when I got there. I slipped him a fifty. I didn't have to ask him to look the other way.

I'd swiped Jacsen's room key when I frisked his body, so I had no trouble letting myself in. Hotel rooms, particularly at a mid-level place like the Landfal, only offer so many places to hide things. Jacsen had been careful, but not particularly original. I found a water-proof pouch resting inside the toilet tank. It wasn't marked, but I figured that it had to be what I was looking for.

Back down in the lobby I dropped the key in the slot provided for that purpose, just as if I was a guest checking out. I was about to leave when I bumped into Latimer and Rossetti.

Rossetti asked, "What are you doing here, Sladek?"

Latimer wasn't interested. All he said was, "Funny thing, Frank. We found a dead guy down in the baggage yards. The security system had nailed him. He was a guest here. Name of Gork Jacsen. You wouldn't know anything about that, would you?"

"Jacsen? Never heard of him. An out of towner?"

"Yeah. Seems he didn't know about the security robots at the baggage yard. Tried to shoot a laser."

"Gee. That's too bad. Who was he shooting at?"

"No idea. Whoever it was didn't stick around."

"Can't blame them. Not if someone was trying to shoot at them."

"You didn't answer Rossetti's question, Frank," Latimer remarked, his eyes focused on my face. Rossetti was fuming in the background.

"No, I guess I didn't," I replied, shaking my head.

"It wouldn't have anything to do with Ms. De Sol, would it?"

"You know that I can't reveal my client's business, Latimer."

"Speaking of Ms. De Sol, how is she?"

"She's fine, Latimer. In fact, she's scheduled to sing in a little over an hour. If there's nothing else, I'm kind of in a hurry. She was kind enough to give me a ticket for the performance."

"No, you can go. We know where to find you if we want you. Enjoy the concert, Frank," Latimer said, and then motioned Rossetti towards the elevators.

I knew I hadn't fooled Latimer, but he hadn't cared. Like most people on Star City Latimer had a flexible sense of what constituted law and order. What mattered to him was that the privacy and security of one of Star City's VIP guests had been assured. That would make his bosses happy which was enough for him.

I barely had time to get back to my apartment, change into a formal rig, and make it to the concert hall. I was just sitting down as the curtain rose.

It was a less intimate show than her earlier performance, but Fleur still sang with a power and emotion that left the audience drained yet feeling as if they had been touched personally by the artist. There were three encores with the orchestra, and then she came back for one more song accompanied only by a piano. It was a song about love and loss, something about a soldier who had gone off to some war a thousand years earlier. She couldn't see me, but I got the impression she was singing it just for me. Of course, half the audience probably felt the same way.

I waited for the crowd to thin and then headed for Fleur's dressing room. Her maid let me in and then left. Flowers and notes of congratulations filled the room marking yet another successful date on Fleur de Sol's tour.

"Is that you, Frank?" Fleur called from an inner room.

"Yes, it's me. You sang wonderfully."

"Thank you, Frank. There's some champagne in a bucket if you'd care to open it."

I fumbled with the cork while I waited. You'd think in a thousand years they would have come up with something better, but that's tradition for you. I finally got it to pop without losing half the bottle and poured two glasses. By this time Fleur had emerged, draped in a robe of some silky material.

"I'm glad you're safe, Frank."

"So am I," I said, handing her one of the glasses. I reached into my pocket and pulled out a memory stick. "I think this is what Jacsen had on you."

"And Jacsen?" she asked uncertainly.

"He won't be bothering you." I explained what had happened leaving out the more graphic details.

"You knew that was what was going to happen, didn't you, Frank?"

"Yes. Pretty much. At least that was the way I planned it. Jacsen could have played it straight. I'd have kept my end of the bargain. He would have been ten grand richer and free and clear. But he didn't. It was his choice."

Fleur took a long hard look at me before saying, "I understand, now, why Lucinda left you. Don't get me wrong, Frank. I'm grateful for all you've done. More than I can ever say. But there is something about you that frightens me in a way I can't describe."

There wasn't much I could have said in response to that, was there?

Fleur dressed then. The concert promoter was putting on a dinner in her honor. I found that I was invited as her guest. It was a strange occasion. None of the guests had any idea of what had happened, they were only happy to be in the presence of celebrity. We both ate and drank a great deal.

We ended up in Fleur's room at the hotel afterwards, two tired people seeking comfort in the others presence. It was good-bye.

I saw Fleur to the starliner in the morning, off on the next leg of her tour. After she had boarded I went up to the Promenade to watch the starship depart. It occurred to me that I'd never done that for anyone else before, not even Lucinda.

As a parting gift she had handed me a recording that one of the sound engineers had made of her first concert on Star City. I play it now and again when I'm not in the mood for some jive samba. I'll probably never hear her again live, but then, this being Star City, you never know.

THE
BLUESKIN
GIRL

THE BLUESKIN GIRL

I was walking home from a job, taking the long way around to avoid New Minglewood, when I spotted the body in the gutter. I'd been shadowing a guy for a client, a bookkeeper who seemed to be spending his money a little too freely. I'd seen him spend plenty of money, but I hadn't seen anything to indicate where it was coming from, so I'd headed home after a night of sipping weak drinks which may or may not have had alcohol in them.

Ordinarily I don't have much use for blueskins, but when I saw her body give a shudder as she gasped for oxygen, I knew I couldn't just leave her there. I guess I'm just not that kind of man. Not that I haven't left my share of bodies lying in gutters, but those are mostly bodies that I've put there, and their abandonment has more to do with avoiding embarrassing answers to awkward questions from policemen, than to any failure of my moral compass.

I checked the gauge on the oxygen bottle at her waist, and as I'd thought it was empty. Blueskins were originally humans that had been genetically modified to survive on Asimov III, a planet whose atmosphere has a much higher oxygen content than that found on Earth, or Star City for that matter. The problem is, that when they get to anyplace with a normal oxygen level, they need a supplemental supply, hence the oxygen bottle.

I had to do something, and do it fast. She might not die, but being deprived of oxygen long enough would leave her brain dead or something close to it.

I knew there was an autodoc a few blocks away. Assuming it was functional and fully stocked, I should be able to refill the girl's oxygen tank there. I could walk there and back in a matter of minutes, but could I leave the girl lying there while I was gone? Blueskins weren't looked upon fondly this close to New Minglewood. I didn't know how this particular one had ended up in the gutter, but there was a fair chance that she wouldn't be alive by the time I returned.

I didn't see any other option than to try to get her to the autodoc. I slapped her face gently trying to rouse her, but I didn't evoke even a stir. It was strange how her skin, despite the color, felt like that of a normal human. I got my arms underneath her and picked her up, tossing her over my shoulders. Blueskins don't run to much body fat, at least where the oxygen levels are Earth normal, but the girl seemed to weigh hardly anything. Even so, I was winded by the time I reached the autodoc.

Fortunately, it was unoccupied. I pushed my way inside and sat the girl on the chair proved for patients. I shoved a credit stick into the slot provided. Autodocs are cheap, but not free.

"Please leave the booth. Only one patient may remain in the booth at a time." The voice wasn't belligerent, autodocs were designed to have a warm bedside manner, but it was firm.

"The patient is unconscious," I tried to explain. "She's a blueskin, she's dying."

"Please leave the diagnosis to me. Please leave the booth. You may return after the scan has been completed."

There didn't seem to be any choice. I exited the booth, and the door closed behind me. Several minutes passed before it slid open again to let me reenter.

"The patient is suffering from hypoxia. This is a lack of oxygen."

"I know that," I said, aware that I was arguing with a machine.

"DNA analysis indicates that the patient is from genetically modified stock. The colloquial term is 'blueskin' due to the condition which results when there is insufficient oxygen to bind to the hemoglobin in the blood. I have administered a drug that will temporarily correct the condition. I am also refilling the oxygen tank. It is recommended that in the future it not be allowed to run empty."

"Is there any permanent damage?"

"Has the patient authorized you to receive confidential information?"

"I'm the one paying for this consultation. That's my credit stick in the slot."

The autodoc pondered this for a few seconds.

"Tests do not reveal any permanent damage, though you should know that the capabilities of this device are limited."

"That's good enough for me."

"The patient also has consumed several recreational pharmaceuticals, most notably the one known as 'blank.' Their use by one in her condition is contra-indicated."

I shouldn't have been surprised. Blank was a common enough street drug. Its major effect was to block access to memories, at least temporarily. The girl probably had enough of those that she wanted to forget.

"The consultation has been billed to your credit stick. Please exit the booth as there is another patient waiting. Have a nice day." The door to the booth slid open.

The girl was starting to come around. I got her to her feet and managed to navigate her out onto the sidewalk. The guy that had been waiting gave me a dirty look as the door slid closed after he entered the booth. A lot of people don't approve of blueskins or those who associate with them.

That left me alone with the girl. She could barely stand up If I held onto her arm. If I left her to her own devices, I might as well just have left her in the gutter where I found her. Instead I took her home.

I live in a fourth floor apartment facing the street in a place called the Aldeberon Arms. It had been swank a few centuries earlier before New Minglewood had degenerated into Star City's worst slum. The joint has seen better days, but the apartments are cheap and quite large by Star City standards. I've had mine for a dozen years.

Fortunately, it was late, and there wasn't anyone hanging around the lobby. I may not have the best reputation, but I didn't necessarily want to be seen hustling a blueskin girl up to my apartment. People might talk. I was lucky, too, in that the elevator for once was working. I'm not sure I could have gotten the girl up three flights of stairs. No one was in the hallway when we got off the elevator, either. People that close to New Minglewood tend to mind their own business.

Once inside, I steered her to the couch in the living room. She curled up and went to sleep. I checked her breathing, but she seemed to be doing ok. As an afterthought, I covered her with a blanket. Then I went to bed.

She was still asleep when I got up the next morning. Her breathing was shallow but steady. Sometime during the night, the blanket had slipped off her. As I reached down to cover her up again I noticed how thin she was. Blueskins never run much to fat, but she was exceptional in that regard. One of the modifications to their genome had resulted in their lungs being smaller than a normal human's. Her breasts were small, hardly visible underneath her thin dress as I draped the blanket over her again. I checked to make sure that the tube from her oxygen tank was secure and then went and made breakfast.

I scrambled some protein and fried up a dozen pieces of what is euphemistically known as "bacon" on Star City. I know it's not the real thing, but I grew up poor on Star City, and to me it's home cooking. The "rye" flour that was used to make the bread I toasted never saw a field, either, but who cares. Don't even ask where the orange colored juice came from.

Maybe it was the smell of hot grease that woke her or maybe it was the aroma of joe brewing. I heard her stirring in the living room. I plopped the food on a couple of plates and carried them into the living room and dropped them on the table I use for eating.

"Breakfast."

I'm not sure what confused her most, the fact that she was alive, or that someone was serving her breakfast. I pointed at the chair by her plate. She got the idea, and sat down, trying to adjust her skimpy dress to cover her as best she could.

She was a dainty eater, but she finished what was on the plate, taking her time and catching her breath between bites. Finally, when she was done she asked, "What happened? I mean last night?"

"I found you lying in the street. Your oxygen bottle had gone empty. I filled it at an autodoc. You were still pretty out of it, so I brought you here and put you to sleep on the couch."

"Why?" She was as suspicious as she was puzzled.

"I couldn't just leave you lying there, could I?"

We both knew that I could have. The question was why I hadn't.

"Thank you." She said it like it was a foreign concept, but then I guessed that she hadn't had much to be thankful for in her life.

"You're welcome."

"If you want, we can—" She didn't say it, but we both knew what she meant.

"That won't be necessary," I answered.

"Why? Because I'm a blueskin?" She asked that with the first hint of emotion I had heard in her voice.

"That's not it. I just make it a rule to never sleep with women who feel they have to because they owe me something. I guess I'm funny that way."

"Do you sleep with women who don't feel they owe you?" It was a strange question. I guess I'd never thought that much about it.

"Sometimes," I answered. Defensively I added, "I get by."

I think that scared her a little, because she replied, "I'm sure you do."

"Look, I've got a couple of errands to run. Are you going to be alright on your own?"

"I'll be OK."

I headed out. I wanted to see where the bookkeeper went on his lunch break. It was 1400 hundred by the time I got back. The blueskin girl was gone. I wasn't surprised. As far as I could tell, she hadn't taken anything. The blanket had been folded neatly and put on the couch.

I never saw the blueskin girl after that except for the once.

It was early afternoon and I had cut through the Souk on my way home. I'd been doing surveillance on a woman for her husband. She'd had lunch with a friend, and let's just say that the husband wasn't going to be happy with my report.

I noticed that a crowd had gathered on the street up ahead. In that part of Star City, that's usually not a good sign. That was confirmed when the meat wagon from the medical examiner's office pulled up. Out of curiosity, I joined the crowd of gawkers to see what had happened.

That's when I spotted the blueskin girl. She was lying in the gutter just like the first time I'd seen her, only this time she was dead. Judging from the blood spattered on the pavement, it wasn't because she'd run out of oxygen, either. Nobody had bothered to cover her up. Maybe a sheet hadn't been handy, but I doubted it.

Latimer was the detective working the case, though it appeared that he was just standing there waiting for the M.E.'s crew to haul the body away. His partner, Rossetti, was working the crowd asking if anyone had seen anything. As usual, the answer was no.

Latimer and I have what you might call a complex relationship. I have a habit of reporting murders that Latimer has to investigate. We don't completely trust each other, but then we don't not trust each other, either. We both accept that the other is as honest as you can be on Star City and leave it at that.

I sauntered over to where Latimer was standing. He caught sight of me out of the corner of his eye and asked, "What are you doing here, Frank?"

"Just passing by on my way home. Thought I'd see what all the excitement was about."

Latimer just grunted.

"What happened?"

"From the blood on the end of it, I'd say someone took her oxygen bottle and used it to bash in the back of her skull. Of course no one saw anything." It was the middle of the day on a busy street.

"When did it happen?"

"Not too long ago. The body is still warm. Someone commed it in about half an hour ago. Couldn't have happened much before that." Latimer got a look like two synapses had just connected inside his brain. "Why the interest, Frank? Do you recognize the girl?"

"You know they all look alike," I answered with a shrug. They don't, of course, but it's the conventional thing to say.

"Yeah. Sure. You wouldn't be holding anything out on me, Frank, would you?"

"Why would I?"

"No reason, I guess." He didn't seem that interested.

We stood there and watched while the guys from the meat wagon zipped the body into a bag and carried it to their truck on a stretcher. They did it in a professional, dispassionate manner, but they might just as well have been street cleaners.

Rossetti came over while we watched. "No one saw nothing." Not very literate, but succinct. He had ignored me like I was a light pole, which suited me fine. He asked Latimer, "What's Sladek doing here?"

"Just passing by, Rossetti. Just passing by." I answered. There's no love lost between the two of us.

"That's Detective Rossetti to you, Sladek."

"Can it, Rossetti. Frank and I were just talking." Latimer has about as much use for his partner as I do.

They buttoned up the meat wagon and it drove off towards the morgue.

"If you hear anything, you'll let me know, won't you, Frank?"

"Yeah, sure. Be seeing you."

I went on my way. Latimer would file a report and that would be the end of it. There wasn't much interest in investigating the death of a blueskin working girl. If someone confessed, they might choose to prosecute, but then again they might not bother.

As I walked the rest of the way home, it occurred to me that I didn't even know the dead girl's name.

That should have been the end of it, at least on my part. Somehow, though, I couldn't let it drop. I felt the need for some answers, and the only way I know of to get answers is to ask questions.

The next day I went back to where the blueskin girl had been found and tried to canvas the local shopkeepers to see if they'd seen what happened. I had about as much luck as Rossetti had had; no one had seen anything and no one knew anything about the girl. Finally, I quizzed the proprietor of a noodle shop across the street. You know the kind of place, a counter with a half dozen stools where, for a credit, you can get yourself a bowl of hot noodles served with something pretending to be animal, vegetable, or for all I know, mineral on top, all covered with a spicy broth. It might or might not be nutritious, but it was hot and filling. The man behind the counter was an old guy maybe a head shorter than me. His skin color and the shape of the folds around his eyes made me think that he'd been born someplace far from Star City.

When I asked him if he'd seen anything he waved the big ladle at me that he used to pour the broth over the noodles and said, "Mista', why you make trouble." From his accent he came from one of those planets where the local language wasn't some variant of Terran. There'd been a number of those colonized in the first wave of human expansion.

"Why you ask questions about dead girl?   Answers do no good. Just cause ev'ry body headaches."

"What are you afraid of, pops?" I asked.

"Not pops, mista'. Sing Lee. Me not afraid. Just don' wan' no trouble. Blueskin girl dead. Questions not bring her back."

"Maybe not, but you know something, Sing Lee. Maybe this will help your memory." I dropped a Crockett double sawbuck on the counter. Sing Lee looked at it greedily. It was probably as much as the profit the noodle shop made him in a day. He didn't pick it up, though. There was a hint of fear in his eyes. I decided to put a little pressure on him.

"You seem to be hiding something, Mr. Lee. Maybe you won't tell me what it is, but I bet if I tell him, Sergeant Latimer can sweat it out of you uptown."

Sing Lee's eyes got big. He'd probably seen me talking to Latimer the day before. Maybe he thought I was an undercover cop, maybe just an informer, but either way he was thinking I could make my threat happen.

"Who you, Mista'? You no police."

"I'm just a concerned citizen, Mr. Lee."

"Like hell," he responded. For an old guy he was pretty feisty, but he was smart enough to know when his options had run out. "Why you care 'bout blueskin girl, anyway?"

"My name is Frank Sladek, Mr. Lee. I'm a private investigator. I could show you my license, but that wouldn't mean much. I knew the girl slightly, and it happens I just don't think it's right that she's dead and no one seems to care. You can believe that or not. I can tell Latimer about you, but I'd rather not. Answer my questions, you can keep the double sawbuck and I'll keep my mouth shut about this conversation."

"You buy noodles." It wasn't a request but a condition. I flipped a credit coin onto the counter next to the twenty.

"Chick or veg?" Lee asked, all business. We both knew where the "chicken" came from, a vat at the down end of Star City.

"Veg."

He put some noodles in a bowl, dumped some cubed vegetables of various colors on top and poured a ladle of broth from a big pot over the combination before sliding the bowl across the counter towards me along with a pair of chopstix. He picked up the coin and stared at me.

I used the stix to pick up some noodles and sucked them down making appropriate slurping noises. The old man looked somewhat mollified.

I ate a piece of vegetable, I'm not sure what kind. Trying to look like I was just a guy having lunch and shooting the breeze with the counter man I asked "Did you know the girl?"

"See her sometime. She work street. Sometime she come buy noodle."

"Had she been around long?"

"Not long. Maybe year, little more."

"Do you know her name?"

"She call herself Lili Blue," he answered. We both knew that wasn't her real name, not if she was a working girl. Half the blueskins on Star City tacked on Blue or Blu or Blau or some sort of variation to their name. I'd known of one smart blueskin punk who had called himself Johnny Azure until he got knifed one night in New Minglewood. It wasn't much, but at least it was something I could ask around with.

Next came the sixty-four credit question. "Did you see what happened?"

Sing Lee looked around to see if anyone was watching.

"Sure. Sing Lee right here like always. Lili across street, standing, hoping some tourist come by see her. No tourist. Guy, big, like wrestler. Start talking to Lili like he want her to come with him, but she no want go. Guy he grab her oxygen and pull out the hose. Lili look scared, like no breathe. Start to make funny noise. Guy with oxygen get mad, hit her over head with bottle. Hard. All over. Lili dead. Guy walk away. Sometime someone call police. The rest you know."

"This guy, did you recognize him?"

"Never see before." Lee shook his head.

"Could you describe him?"

"Sure. Big. Mean. Maybe carry gun. Sing Lee get busy making broth, turn away so no see." The ladle in Lee's hand started to tremble.

"Could you be a little more detailed?"

"Big. Maybe brown hair. Nice clothes. Expensive. Wear jacket funny color. Red."

It was becoming clear that I wasn't going to get much more out of Sing Lee. All that stuck in his mind was that he was big, but then he was short enough that most people would look big.

"Was he taller than me?"

"Sure. Maybe this much taller." He held up his hand and showed me his index finger and thumb spread apart as far as they would go, maybe ten centimeters. Not a giant, then, but bigger than average. Big enough to be hired muscle. The expensive clothes probably meant that he worked regularly and wasn't just a hired thug.

"Did he look like a pimp? Like an enforcer?"

"Look like bad man to get mad at you, that what he look like."

"I get the idea, Mr. Lee. Thanks for the information."
Lee turned and went back to playing with his pots. I finished the noodles. They weren't half bad, but then I was born and raised on Star City and hadn't touched food that didn't come out of a vat until I was in my twenties.

As I got up to leave, Sing Lee said, "You come back anytime. Just noodles, no questions." Just another satisfied customer.

As I walked away I wondered just what the blueskin girl had gotten herself into. From Sing Lee's description, the heavy sounded more like professional muscle on a job rather than a disgruntled john whose attempt at a pickup had gone wrong. But why the interest in a blueskin street walker? It didn't make sense.

There's not that much of what could be called organized crime on Star City. When the ones who make the laws are the same people that run the casinos, nightclubs, and joy parlors there aren't that many illegal activities to build a business on. That didn't mean there weren't some players on the fringes, particularly those that dealt with certain pharmaceuticals that the big guys considered too disruptive to be good for the business of parting travelers from their cash. Mostly, though, they operated in the shadows, keeping a low profile and trying to avoid the notice of both the police and the powers. Killing a girl, even a blueskin girl, in broad daylight wasn't keeping a low profile. I was missing something, but I didn't know what.

One thing I've learned as a private dick is that if you aren't getting anywhere working one angle, you try another. You keep poking and prodding at a problem until you stir things up. Sooner or later the people who are behind it all will take notice. Then things get interesting.

If what Sing Lee said was true, then the blueskin girl had been plying her trade in the neighborhood. That meant she had to have someplace to take her johns when she scored. Star City is pretty liberal about sex, but even here, doing it in the open is discouraged, and most johns want a little more comfort and privacy than is offered by ducking into some alleyway. That meant that there was probably a hotel nearby that rented accommodations for very short term occupation. If I could find it, it might give me some more information as to why the blueskin girl had been killed.

Finding the place wasn't going to be as easy as looking for a sign. That sort of hotel tends not to advertise. The girls, and boys for that matter, know where it is, that's all that matters.

I did what any good detective does in such a situation, I observed. There was a café situated on the corner down the block where I could get a clear view down the street all four ways. I took a seat, ordered a cup of joe, slipped the waiter a fin so he wouldn't keep pestering me but wouldn't object to my taking up table space, either. Then I sipped my joe and waited.

It didn't take long. It was a little early in the day for the trade, but with starliners coming in and departing at all hours of the day; all sorts of things go on twenty-four hours a day. I spotted a woman with badly dyed green hair wearing a too tight red skirt and a yellow top. About fifteen minutes into my vigil a guy, obviously not local, walked up to her. They haggled for a minute or so and then the woman took the guy by the hand and led him to a doorway about halfway down the block. I waited for a bit, and then flagged the waiter for another cup of joe. About thirty minutes later the guy came out looking flushed but happy. The woman reappeared a couple of minutes later. While they had been at it, several other mismatched couples had either gone in or gone out. The conclusion was obvious.

I got up, left a credit on the table and sauntered down to the doorway. The door was unmarked by any signage, and through the dirty glass I could see a narrow stairway leading upwards. When I tried the door it opened. A little mechanical bell was hooked up to ring. I thought it very quaint.

At the top of the stairs was a desk. Behind the desk was an alien; don't ask me what species because I sure as hell didn't recognize it. I knew he was an alien because he was green and maybe a hundred and fifty centimeters tall. His ears, if that was what they were, came to a double point. He was wearing a jacket with a large black and white checked pattern and no pants. Other than that he could almost have passed for human.

"No vacancy, Max." His Terran, if grammatically dubious was unaccented, at least as far as Star City went.

"My name isn't Max and I'm not looking for a room. I'm looking for information."

"This is a hotel, Max. Public library is somewhere thataway." He pointed uptown in more or less the correct direction.

I leaned over his desk in a way that let him see my shoulder holster. "I'm not looking for a book, Junior. Like I said, I'm looking for information. You give it to me straight and their might be a Crockett ten spot in it for you. Otherwise—"

"Look, Max, this is a respectable joint. I don't want no trouble. It's just that I've got to be careful, you know. We've had trouble enough lately."

"Oh? How's that?"

"Guy got himself croaked a couple of weeks ago. Cops were all over me about that."

"I thought you said this was a respectable joint."

"It is. The guy came in with one of the regulars. She swore that he was still alive when she left. He'd just stayed to comb his hair, if you know what I mean."

I didn't, but I didn't really care. "The girl he was with, was she a blueskin?"

"Nah. She's as human as you. As ugly, too." I let that slide. "Who was the guy that got himself killed?"

"Don't know. Cops didn't say, but they seemed mighty interested. I figure they know, they just didn't see the need to tell me. I didn't press them."

"If the woman he was with didn't kill him, who did?"

"Got me. The place was kind of busy. Most of the rooms were booked at the time. Could have been any one of them."

"This place have a back entrance?"

"Just the front. And I'm always at the desk. No one came up the stairs that wasn't accompanied."

"I see—" I said, sounding suspicious. I didn't really think the little guy was the killer, but he didn't have to know that.

"Hey, listen Max. I didn't do it. I had enough of that kind of talk from the police. I never left the desk."

"Sure, sure." I sensed that I'd got about as much on the subject out of the alien as I was going to. "You ever rent a room to a blueskin girl that goes by the name Lili Blue?"

"I don't ask their names, Max. And I'm colorblind. My species are normally nocturnal. Black and white vision only. As far as I can tell, you all look alike."

"What about the register?" The sex trade is legal on Star City, which isn't to say that it's unregulated.

"Check for yourself, Max."

He spun the computer terminal around so I could inspect it. I saw what he meant. There were a whole lot of Jane Smiths registered. One joker had signed as Jean Jones. Flipping back a few days it was all the same. So much for the regulations. The blueskin girl might have been any one of the Jane Smiths, but there was no way to tell. I turned to go.

"Hey, wait Max. What about my ten spot?"

"Sure." I was about to drop it into the outstretched three fingered hand when a thought struck me.

"Just one more question. Did a big muscular guy ever come here? About so high—" I held my hand about ten centimeters over my head. "Maybe wearing an expensive sort of suit."

"Now that you mention it, Max, there was a guy in here like that once. Seemed local, but never in here before or since."

"When was this?"

"I don't know. A couple of weeks ago. About the same time the guy got croaked."

"Thanks," I said and let the bill flutter into his hand.

Out on the street I started to think. Had the blueskin girl's death been tied to the murder in the hotel? I still had nothing to tie her to the place besides probabilities, but the fact that the guy Sing Lee had seen kill her matched the description of someone who might have been at the hotel at the time of the murder seemed to up the odds. There were still a lot of missing pieces, but a pattern was starting to form.

I felt the need for a drink. Fortunately it was still early enough that the Blue Moon wouldn't be too crowded.

As I entered the darkened bar, I paused while my eyes adjusted from the relative brightness of the street. The middle of the afternoon is a slow time for most drinking establishments, and that day in the Blue Moon was no exception. From force of habit my gaze ran the length of the bar. It didn't take long; there were only three patrons, each of whom had strategically positioned themselves so as to be as far from the others as possible. The drinker at the far end I recognized as a regular. He worked the four to noon shift at one of the hotels and came in most afternoons for a quick one before heading to bed. He always drank something blue, I never bothered to ask what.

The guy at the near end was a stranger to me, but that didn't mean much. It wasn't like I spent all my afternoons in the Blue Moon.

The shoulders hunched over the bar in the middle looked familiar, but it took me a moment to place them. They belonged to Latimer, which surprised me. He wasn't given much to socializing, and the Blue Moon certainly wasn't one of his regular haunts. It could just be a coincidence, but I have a suspicious nature.

I grabbed a stool a couple of places down from where he sat and waved a finger at the bartender. He knows me well enough to know what I wanted, a double of brown over ice.

I waited until he had slid the tumbler across the bartop at me before turning to Latimer and remarking, "Drinking on duty, Sergeant?"

His head turned a slightly bloodshot eye in my direction as he replied "I'm in no mood, Frank."

"Bad day?"

"Let's just say I needed to get away from Rossetti. I figured this would be the last place he'd come to."

Latimer's feelings about his partner weren't that different than mine. Rossetti was lazy, not too bright, and interested in what was best for Rossetti more than anything else.

"That's understandable."

I took it as an invitation when Latimer just grunted in response, and moved to the stool next to him. He ignored me and motioned to the bartender to bring him a refill.

Casually I asked, "Anything new on that blueskin girl that got herself killed?"

"That case is closed, Frank. Let's face it, no one cares about a dead GM prostitute." He was interrupted by the arrival of his drink. "I'll ask you one more time, why the interest? Is there something you didn't tell me?"

"Just idle curiosity. I didn't know her, but I think I might have seen her around, you know."

"Sure, Frank. If you say so. It doesn't matter. I've got bigger fish to fry, and if I don't resolve it, it's going to blow up in my face."

I ignored Latimer's mixed metaphors and queried, "Another murder?"

"Yeah. A guy got himself killed in a short term hotel over in the Souk."

A little bell went off in my head. Was there a connection with the blueskin girl? Was it even the same hotel that she had frequented? I decided to pump the sergeant. "So why the grief over it? Those kinds of things happen every day."

"Not to a guy like this. I turns out he was a nephew to Mr. Anthony."

I didn't have to ask who Mr. Anthony was. No one on Star City did. Mr. Anthony was the head of the organization that ran the Casino. There's an old adage that when organized crime becomes big enough it ceases being a criminal organization. The organization that Mr. Anthony was head of epitomized that concept. It owned a half dozen hotels, an equal number of gambling establishments and various other enterprises, all of them legitimate. That didn't mean that the organization had left behind all the attributes of its murky past. They could play rough when they had to, they just didn't have to very often, not when they could get civil servants like Latimer to do their dirty work.

"Was this death just incidental or was it—"

"Was it a hit?" Latimer finished my sentence. "That's the big question, isn't it?"

I knew what Latimer was thinking. Star City was largely peaceful because the organizations that ran it had long ago reached an agreement. Things were divvied up between them, they didn't step on each other's toes, and everybody made money hand over fist servicing the travelers that came through on the starliners. The only flaw in the arrangement was that it didn't leave much room for newcomers. Everything was in balance, but as with every balanced system, a small nudge could send it crashing down into instability. As things stood, any differences between organizations were handled peacefully through arbitration, break that covenant, and Star City could find itself in a cycle of violence that might destroy it.

"Anything to indicate that it was anything more than an altercation between two randy bucks?"

"That's just it, Frank. There's nothing to indicate anything. The guy that got killed, Mr. Anthony's nephew, he's solicited by a working girl, they go up to this hotel and get a room. They conduct their business, the girl leaves. When the guy doesn't come out after awhile, the desk clerk checks and finds a body. There wasn't any noise, and let's face it, the walls in that sort of place don't provide much in the way of sound proofing, no sign of a struggle, just a body lying in a pool of blood."

"So how was he killed."

"Knife thrust in the back. Very professional, the blade held sideways, slid in between the ribs, and right into the heart. He probably never knew what hit him."

"That doesn't sound like a fight, Latimer, that sounds like an assassination."

"Yeah, that's the problem." I could see his point. If the killing even hinted at a hit, the organizations would start to suspect each other.

"Are you sure the girl didn't do it?"

"No way. She's just a working girl, and not a very big one, at that. I can't see her having the strength let alone the skill to stick a knife in like that. Besides, we had her down to the station and biometted her while we went over her story for hours. The machines say she was telling the truth."

"And what was her story?"

"It turns out Giovanni, that's the dead guys name, had kind of a thing for her. Not passion or anything, he just liked to bonk her. He knew where she'd be working that day. He got the urge, looked her up, and they went to the hotel. After they were done, she left first. She says he was alive and well when she left. I believe her."

"Had he used the same hotel before?"

"A couple of times, according to the girl. The desk clerk says the same. According to his associates this Giovanni used working girls fairly regularly, different places, different girls. Whatever was convenient."

"So no reason to think it was a setup?" I questioned.

"Maybe, maybe not. If you were patient enough, it would be easy to stake the place out. You wait for Giovanni to come by, find a girl of your own so as not to attract attention, which wouldn't be hard in that neighborhood, go on up, finish with the girl, wait till Giovanni's girl leaves and then in and out. If you knew what you were doing, and the signs are that this guy did, it would be over in ten, fifteen seconds, tops. Then you leave, smile at the clerk and you're gone."

"What about the registry? Certainly that must give you some suspects?"

"Yeah, sure. Everybody registers just like they're supposed to. Problem is, no one uses their own ID."

I knew what Latimer meant. I had a couple of dozen phony ID's coded into my own comm.

"Surveillance?" They don't advertise it, but places like that always have a hidden camera taking video of comings and goings.

"Funny thing. The unit malfunctioned."

"Scrambler?"

"Maybe, maybe not. Could just have been bad maintenance."

"What about the desk clerk? He must have spotted something?"

"The clerk is an alien. He claims that we all look alike to him. He's probably right. Anyway, he says he didn't see anything out of the ordinary. We had him in for questioning, of course, but you can't biomet an alien like that. Who knows what normal is supposed to be with some screwy alien physiology."

"What about the other patrons?"

"What other patrons? We haven't been able to track down anybody that was in the joint at the critical time. Like I said, everybody used fake IDs and the clerk didn't recognize any of them. We did find a couple of the girls, but they claim they didn't see anything. The hell of it is, they probably didn't."

"I can see your frustration, Latimer. You have my sympathies."

"Great. That and a credit will get me a cheap beer."

"Speaking of that, do you want another?"

"No, I better go. There's no telling what mischief Rossetti has gotten up to."

"Good luck, then."

Latimer rose, dropping a couple of credits on the bar. "Seriously, Frank. If you hear anything, let me know. You'll be doing us all a favor. If this mess doesn't get cleared up soon, things could get real ugly. Besides, I'm sure Mr. Anthony would be appreciative."

I was sure he would. I'd done work for Mr. Anthony in the past. It hadn't worked out the way I would have liked, but I had gotten paid, which is something, I guess.

"I'll keep my eyes and ears open, Latimer."

The detective sergeant shuffled out of the Blue Moon as if he was carrying the weight of Star City on his shoulders, which maybe he was. Me, I signaled the bar keep for another drink.

Though I've done work for the Casino several times, mostly against my will, I didn't really have many inside contacts within the organization. My knowledge of what went on was limited, pretty much like any outsider. The organization tended to launder its dirty linen in private. What I knew about Giovanni was what I'd been told, that he was dead.

There was one man that I knew who might provide me with some insight. His name was Nico Polis. He'd worked himself up through the ranks at the Casino and had worked as a pit boss for a couple of decades before a disgruntled gambler who'd been losing heavily took issue when Nico had cut him off. Somehow, the gambler had managed to sneak a laser onto the floor of the gaming room. Nico had lived, but there had been problems with the regeneration. The organization in lieu of a pension had set Nico up as manager of a low-rent gaming parlor in the neighborhood where I'd grown up. It wasn't a bad deal for Nico, really. The work was easy, the money steady, and, as it was well known who was in back of the place, no one messed with it. As a kid, I'd run errands for Nico, and over the years I'd kept in touch.

I dropped by after grabbing a meat tube at the corner diner. Evenings were the busy time for the parlor, so I knew that would be the best time to find Nico there.

The options for betting are limited on Star City. It's not that there are laws against it, or that people don't want to risk their money. It's just that the lack of surface area rules out sports like horse or dog racing as well as many team sports played on other worlds. It's true that there is a cutthroat basketball league and some pretty competitive ping pong, but that only goes so far. No one will bet on events off of Star City; when all results arrive by starship, there's no way of telling if someone isn't betting using information that arrived on a faster ship. No one really trusts computer generated results to be truly random, either. Still, human ingenuity being what it is, some fairly strange games have developed for people to wager on. Rat racing is certainly one of them, and one of the features of Nico's parlor was the evening rat races.

I got there just as the first of the feature races was starting. A crowd had gathered to watch six rats run through identical three dimensional mazes. In the early days of the sport, they had tried to run all the rats in the same maze, but that had proven to be impractical, so instead, they ran through setups of transparent tubes and gates that were identical copies of each other. The layouts were changed for every race so that the rats couldn't learn the winning route.

There was a fresh face kid operating the show. He called out, "Last bets." For old time's sake I placed a credit on number three. The kid waited for the last few wagers to be made and then announced, "They're off," as he pressed the button releasing the rats from their cages.

These were racing rats, bred for generations for speed, curiosity, and fearlessness. They streaked through their mazes at breakneck speed. It was all over in thirty seconds. Number 2 came in first, followed by 6. Number 3 had finished a distant fifth. My torn up ticket stub joined the rest of the losers on the floor. The crowd thinned, while the winners went to collect their winnings.

I waited until they had cleared out and then headed to where Nico sat overseeing everything from a raised platform at the back of the room.

When he saw me, his eyes lit up with real joy at recognition.

"Frankie. It's been a while." Nico is one of the few people who I don't mind calling me Frankie.

"Nico. How's the wife?"

"Doing well. What about you? You married yet?"

"You know my luck with women, Nico," I replied.

"You should do something about that, Frankie. It's not good to live alone."

"You know how it is," I said, feeling like the kid that had swept up betting slips and run errands.

"Yeah," Nico said nodding. "So, you didn't just come here for some cheap excitement, did you? A big shot private dick like you don't need to bet on a bunch of rats. What is it?"

"I need a little insight Nico. About the inner politics of the organization."

"You working for Mr. Anthony?"

"Not this time. More personal curiosity."

"So what you wanna know?"

"I'm interested in a guy named Giovanni, Mr. Anthony's nephew."

"The one that got iced?"

"Yeah. That's the one."

"Why the interest? I may not work at the Casino anymore, Frankie, but I'm still on the payroll, so to speak."

"I'm not so much concerned with Giovanni as with the guy that killed him. He might be involved in a case I'm working. I figure that if I can find out why Giovanni was killed, it might lead me to him."

"What can I say? Giovanni was a punk. He liked to throw his weight around if you know what I mean. He traded on the fact that he was Mr. Anthony's sister's only son. Mr. Anthony gave him a job making collections thinking it would keep him out of trouble. It didn't."

"What kind of trouble?"

"The usual. Giovanni had a thing about whores. He liked the fact that paying for it gave him power over the women. Sometimes he'd take the rough stuff a little too far."

"Far enough that someone might want to get even?"

"Nah. Not with him being Mr. Anthony's nephew. But working girls got paid off more than once."

"Any beefs with any of the other organizations?"

"Are you kidding? Giovanni was really small time. He didn't interact with the other businesses, not so that any of them would risk starting a war. If anyone had a problem, they'd talk to Mr. Anthony direct to fix it up. If anything, the people who had a problem with him would be inside the organization."

"Oh?"

"Look, Frank. I don't really know about that stuff. I never got involved in politics; I just did my job, like I'm doing now. It's just that I've still got friends and I hear them talk sometimes. There was no love lost between Giovanni and the rest of the organization. It *is* possible that one of them might have seen Giovanni as a threat and taken action, but I doubt it. Everybody was just biding their time until Giovanni made a big mistake and Mr. Anthony took action himself."

Suddenly curious I asked, "Is that likely?"

"Who knows. I don't travel in those circles, Frankie, I never did."

I knew Nico wasn't trying to hide anything from me. He was right, he'd never been more than a low level soldier, loyal enough to be rewarded when he was injured, but not close to the real powers.

"So what about the guy that killed him? Any rumors about him?"

"Not that I've heard."

"He was pretty professional with a knife. That's an unusual skill these days. Any new talent in town?"

"Look, Frankie. I never got involved with that kind of thing, assassins and hit-men. That's stuff for the videos as far as I'm concerned. In the old days, I might have had a guy roughed up if I suspected he was cheating or he didn't pay his tab, but no killing. It's bad for business. You know the organization. They pretend to be a bunch of rough, tough gangster types, but they're really just a bunch of businessmen. It's all a front, a show. Intimidation is a lot more effective than muscle any day."

"Yeah. You're right about that," I agreed. Of course, I'd also seen the ruthless side of the organization first hand.

"So why do *you* think Giovanni was axed?"

"Me? If you ask me, he was caught with his fingers in the till," Nico said, suddenly sly.

"Care to elaborate?"

"You didn't hear it from me, Frank, but there were rumors that Giovanni was skimming his collections big time. Had been for awhile. Maybe Mr. Anthony got wise. Or decided he couldn't take it anymore."

I gave Nico a raised eyebrow, but he must have decided he'd said enough.

"It's been nice talking to you, Frankie, but the next race is about to start. If you're interested, you might drop a credit on number 5. I've always liked the looks of that rat."

I realized that I was being politely dismissed. Nico had said all that he was going to. I gave the old man a salute and wandered off. On the way out, I dropped another credit on number 5. It came in first, paying two to one. I guess that meant that I'd come out even.

As I walked back home, I mulled over in my mind what Nico had suggested. Was it possible that Mr. Anthony or someone else in the organization had been responsible for Giovanni's death? It was pretty clear by this time that *someone* was responsible. The death had been too neat for it to have been a random or spur of the moment act. Even by the standards of Star City, killing your own nephew was extreme, but then, I wasn't privy to the family politics of the organization. Maybe Giovanni's death had been meant as a warning to others. Maybe the fact was that Mr. Anthony had never really liked his nephew. I doubted that I was going to get at the truth.

The more important issue, at least for me, was did I really want to get involved with the internal workings of the organization? It was really none of my business. I hadn't owed the blueskin girl anything. I hadn't even known her name until after she'd been killed, and the name I knew probably wasn't even her real one. Crossing Mr. Anthony was never a good move. Look what had happened to Giovanni. The smart thing to do would be to let the whole matter rest.

I went home and had a drink, but even a shot of brown over ice and a dose of some jive samba on the entertainment unit didn't help me get a good night sleep.

I woke in the morning in a bad mood. I guess it's just not in my nature to walk away once I've started something. I'd set out to find who had killed the blueskin girl. It seemed I was the only one who cared, but that didn't matter. So what was I going to do about it?

I knew, or at least I thought I knew why she'd been killed. She'd seen something in that hotel, probably by accident, and she'd been snuffed to keep her quiet. The problem was, that wasn't going to be a healthy line of investigation to follow. So where did that leave me?

The killer had been a big man, good with a knife and willing to kill with his hands. How many of those could there be in a population of two million. Probably less than you'd think, even someplace like Star City. He hadn't looked familiar, but then that was to be expected. If Giovanni's death had been an internal organization matter, then it was only natural that talent would be brought in from out of town to handle it. It would be easier to keep things secret that way, secret even from other members of the organization, other people in the family.

The thing about Star City is that people come and go all the time. That's the whole reason for the city's existence. A dozen starliners arrive and depart for as many worlds every day, each one bringing in hundreds, even thousands, of passengers who wait around for hours or days or even weeks to make a connection with a ship heading to their final destination.

The killer had probably been brought in a few weeks before Giovanni was killed, long enough to get acclimated and to familiarize himself with the victim's routine. That narrowed down the window of his arrival.

A man doesn't develop skills like that just anywhere, either. Real precision with a knife is something that has to be learned, and usually learned the hard way. It's not something your average farmer on some pioneer world would know, nor someone from a settled place like Crockett. It's the kind of thing that you pick up in the military or maybe someplace where gang activity is endemic. The thing is, there aren't that many places where active warfare has occurred in the recent past. Nor are there many places where open gang warfare is common. That would limit the origins of the killer.

The passenger manifests of ships arriving and departing on Star City are open records available to anyone with a data link. There's also a less open record kept by security of biometric and biographical details of each passenger taken as they arrive. I say less open because access requires a pass code. Of course, it doesn't take much to obtain a valid pass code.

I spent the rest of the morning compiling a list of likely suspects. It wasn't that hard, just tedious. I had an approximate height for the killer, and I could make a good guess about his mass, as well.   Sing Lee hadn't been much help to fill in items like the color of his eyes or hair, but then, those can be changed easily enough, which limits their utility.   It's a lot harder to alter height and mass.   A search of the manifest of ships arriving in the three weeks prior to Giovanni's death gave me around a thousand suspects.   All but a hundred or so of those had departed before Giovanni was killed.   Of that hundred, I was able to rule out most of them for various reasons, age, occupation, planet of origin, and so on.   I had a specific profile in mind for the killer, and only four men fit the bill.

I uploaded images of the four into my comm along with the info on where they were staying.   After that, I put on a comfortable pair of shoes in preparation for the least glamorous part of being a detective, surveillance.

The first of my suspects was staying at the Rigel Royal Hotel.   I parked myself in the lobby at a spot where I could get a good view of the main entrance and the desk.   The house detective came by after a few minutes.   I explained what I was doing and he wandered off.   I'm known by most of the house dicks on Star City, and for the most part, as long as I don't disrupt things, they let me go about my business.

I actually had a bit of luck.   I only had to wait about an hour before my suspect came down to the lobby and checked something at the desk.   He was the right size, but he didn't strike me as a killer.   He looked like just what his entry declaration claimed he was; a moderately successful businessman.   The records said that he'd served a mandatory stint in the military on his home world, but instead of a warrior's tenseness, he had the relaxed athleticism of someone who enjoyed sports for the diversion.   Several minutes after he came down, he met up with a couple of other guys that also looked like businessmen.

I didn't necessarily rule suspect number one out, but my first impression was that he wasn't the killer.   I got up and headed for the second address on my list.

I never got to the third or fourth suspect. Number two was staying at the Landfal. The Landfal is a middle tier hotel favored by commercial travelers on tight expense accounts. It's also just the kind of place to stay for someone who wants to maintain a low profile. It's far enough off the beaten path to allow someone to avoid attention without actually looking like that's what they were trying to do so. The rooms are comfortable enough, and there are a couple of decent restaurants and bars within convenient walking distance.

It happens that I know the house dick, a guy named Rik Lane, reasonably well. We're not friends or anything, but he slips me the occasional tidbit of information in exchange for a Crockett sawbuck or two.

We spotted each other as I walked in. I nodded towards a secluded corner into which he followed me after a discrete interval.

"What's up, Frank?" Lane asked.

"Maybe nothing. I'm interested in someone who's staying here." I showed him the suspect's image on my comm. Lane's reaction to the image told me all I needed to know.

"You'd better watch yourself with that one, Frank. He's trouble."

"Oh," I said noncommittally. "Why do you say that?"

"I was talking to one of the maids, the one who does the rooms on his floor. She went in to change the towels not realizing that he was in the shower. His suitcase was open on the bed. She said there were a couple of laser pistols and a big knife in it. The way she tells it, it was like the case had been designed with a special compartment just to carry them."

"Interesting. Did you see them yourself?"

"No. The maid, when she heard he was in the shower just backed out and came back later. I didn't have no reason to check it out for myself. He wasn't doing anything illegal. Besides, he's not the sort of guy you want to mess with. Trust me."

"I'll take your word for it, Rik. Any chance that I'll catch a glimpse of him if I hang out in the lobby?"

"Hard to say, Frank," Lane replied. "As far as I can tell he doesn't keep a regular schedule. In and out all through the day."

"I guess I'll have to take my chances, then. Any objection to my hanging around just in case?"

"Is there going to be any trouble, Frank?"

"Nah. Nothing like that. I've just got a list of guys I need to check out in case one of them might be involved in something. Don't worry, Rik. I won't do anything that will bring the good name of the Landfal into disrepute."

"Sure, Frank. I know I can trust you."

Lane walked off like he'd just been explaining the tram system to me. He's a lousy detective, but he's good with the little details like that. At a place like the Landfal you don't have to be much more than that.

While I was waiting for the suspect to show, I read the details of his bio in the landing file. The name he was traveling under was Sigurd Sigson, a resident of Nordholm, which was believable enough that it might actually be true. His occupation was listed as farmer, which was also plausible. The economy of Nordholm was still largely agricultural. The important thing was that Nordholm was still recovering from a rather nasty civil war, the kind of conflict largely conducted by irregular troops who might be good at killing, but wouldn't necessarily consider themselves to be bound by laws or regulations. It was just the sort of environment for someone to pick up the way to handle a knife. Wars like that always leave a residue of men in their wakes, men for whom killing is second nature.

I hung around the lobby for a couple of hours, and then went out to get a cup of joe at a café across the street from the main entrance. It was while I was sipping the joe that I spotted Sigson exiting the Landfal. I tossed a couple of credits on the table and started after him.

I wasn't quite sure what I had in mind. For all I knew, Sigson was just stepping out to pick up his dry cleaning. Still, after what Lane had said, I was curious as to where he was going.

He seemed to have picked up the workings of the tram system in the short time he'd been on Star City. He waited at the stop for the down tram. I poked my nose into a news kiosk so he couldn't make me, and then waited until I spotted the tram coming before heading to the stop. I had it timed so that I arrived at the stop just as the tram took off. Sigson had gotten on one of the front seats, I got one at the back, looking casual. Two stops later, Sigson got off, looking around to see who else disembarked. I'd gotten off just as the tram stopped, walking past the front of the tram as if I was in a hurry. I turned at the first corner so as to be lost from sight and then turned back to peak around the corner to see which way Sigson was headed.

I doubled back to get in back of him and then followed Sigson from a half block behind. Sigson seemed to know his way around, better than someone who'd only been on Star City a few weeks should. Every block or so, he'd stop and look back to see if he was being followed. I kept switching sides of the street hoping he'd miss me.

He went about half a kilometer and then took a seat at a sidewalk café. There was a diner across the street. I went in and ordered a meat sandwich. I hadn't had lunch and was getting hungry. Besides, the diner had a big window that gave me a good view of the café.

Ten minutes later, Sigson was joined by someone. I thought I recognized him as one of Mr. Anthony's errand boys. He ordered a cup of joe. While the waiter was away, he took something from his pocket, an envelope and placed it on the table top. Sigson ignored it. The waiter returned and left again, and the two men sat sipping their drinks. Occasionally, one of them would make a remark, like when an attractive woman walked by. All very natural.

Finally, the other man looked at his comm, said something, got up and left. The envelope was still on the table. Sigson sat for a few minutes more, and then paid the bill. As he got up, he picked up the envelope and stuffed it in his jacket pocket.

I didn't bother to follow. There wasn't any need. From my point of view it looked like I had just witnessed a payoff. I finished my sandwich, left an extra credit as a tip and headed home.

What did I have? Not much. Sigson had accepted a payoff, but I had no proof as to why. I could go back and show Sigson's image to Sing Lee or the alien clerk in the hotel, but the chances are neither one would admit to recognizing him, even if they had. If Sigson had gotten his payoff, there was a good chance that he'd be heading out on a starliner within the next day or two.

I did the only thing I could think of. I called Latimer.

He wasn't that thrilled to hear from me.

"What is it, Frank?" he asked in a voice both tired and grouchy.

"Just that I've got a bit of information on the Giovanni killing."

"Spill it."

"You might take a look into a guy named Sigurd Sigson. He's staying at the Landfal."

"So?"

"He's the one that stuck the blade in Giovanni. He also killed that blueskin girl."

"What's with you and that girl, Frank?"

"Nothing. It's just something I picked up. I figure the girl was at the hotel when Giovanni was killed and probably saw something. That's all."

"Is this on the level, Frank?"

"Look. I've got no proof. It's just a hunch. I thought you should know. But you might want to act fast. I think Sigson might be planning on leaving soon."

"If you're wasting my time, Frank—"

"Hey, I'm just trying to be a good citizen. Don't kill the messenger."

"Ok, Ok. I'll look into it and get back to you." Latimer broke the connection.

I'd done what I could. I looked at the time and thought to myself that I could still get a drink in at the Blue Moon before the crowds started to show up.

I had that drink, and I followed it with one more. By then the Blue Moon was getting too noisy for my tastes and I went home and had a couple more. Eventually I fell asleep in my chair in the living room to the sound of jive samba from the entertainment unit.

A sound woke me. It was my comm. When I looked at the time it was 0900. My head was thick and mouth still tasted of the brown I'd drunk the night before. The entertainment unit was still playing, but sometime during the night it had turned down the volume so that it was just a soothing background sound. Makes you wonder just how intelligent those things are.

I fumbled for my comm. The display announced that it was a call from Rik Lane.

"Sladek," I said as I answered the call.

"Hi, Frank. Rik Lane. I didn't know if I should call you or not, but I knew you were interested in that guy Sigson. I just called to let you know that he's checking out. His luggage is being sent to Departure."

"Thanks, Rik. I appreciate the call."

"You want me to do anything?"

"No. That won't be necessary. I'll take care of it." I didn't know what I could do, but I didn't see any point in involving Lane.

"OK, Frank. Bye."

"Thanks again for the call." I broke off the connection.

I wasn't sure what I planned to do. I didn't have any right to stop Sigson from leaving. If I provoked a confrontation, there was a good chance I'd come out on the losing side. It didn't seem to matter. I splashed some water on my face to try to wake up the brain cells. After that, I strapped on a shoulder holster for a laser pistol and made sure my needle gun was tucked securely in the holster that fits in the small of my back.

It turns out I needn't have bothered. When I arrived at the Landfal, the place was surrounded by squad cars. A perimeter had been set up blocking off the street in front of it. It was easy to see why. There was a body lying in the middle of the street. It was Sigson's.

The uniform on the perimeter was going to keep me back, but Latimer saw my face in the crowd and waved me through.

"Kind of a change, isn't it?"

"What do you mean?" Latimer said distractedly.

"I'm usually the one standing over the body when you show up, not the other way around." Latimer just grunted. "So what happened?" I asked.

"We were going to pick him up for questioning. Turns out he had just checked out and was on his way to passenger departure. When we tried to stop him he resisted."

"Too bad."

"Yeah. He stabbed Rossetti in the process. I had to shoot him."

"Rossetti? A bit harsh, wasn't it?"

"Someday your mouth is going to be the death of you, Frank. Him." He gestured at the body on the ground.

I looked down at the body. There was a neat laser burn in the middle of Sigson's forehead. Latimer is a pretty decent shot.

"The doc says that Rossetti will survive." The way he said it, I wasn't sure that Latimer was happy at the prospect.

"You heard what I said the first time."

"Yeah," Latimer grunted, but there was a hint of smile. "The M.E. got a look at the knife Sigson used on Rossetti. Curious piece of work. It's not metal at all. It's some kind of ceramic plastic. Undetectable by X-rays or magnetometers. The M.E. says it's preliminary, but it looks like it probably will match the wound on Giovanni."

"That solves one problem for you, then," I commented.

"Yeah." Latimer wasn't happy, but we both knew how things would play out. "Sigson is an out-of-towner," by which Latimer meant he wasn't from Star City. "The way I see it, he had some private grudge with Giovanni. Sigson ran into Giovanni at that hotel and took his chance. End of story."

"I'm sure that will satisfy Mr. Anthony."

Latimer looked at me, his head tilted at an odd angle, trying to decide if I was being sarcastic or honest. I guess it was a little of both.

I didn't know if Latimer suspected Mr. Anthony of assassinating his nephew. What he did know was that by killing Sigson, he'd given Mr. Anthony a public reason to avoid conflict with the other organizations. For Latimer that was probably enough.

"Are you going to need a statement or anything from me?"

"No. As far as I'm concerned, Frank, you're out of it. Probably better that way. As it is, I've got enough to close the case."

"What about the blueskin girl?"

"What about her, Frank?"

"Sigson is probably the one that killed her."

"Drop it, Frank. That case is closed. The reality is it was never really open. You know that. That's just the way things are. Take my advice. Go home. Go get breakfast. Just get out of my hair."

I got.

Several days later I was crossing the street from my apartment to the Blue Moon. It was early afternoon. A long black car drove up the street and stopped opposite me. On Star City only the rich or the powerful have private vehicles, and it wasn't the neighborhood for either.

My sense of foreboding looked to be realizing itself when two big guys got out of the car. I recognized them from previous dealings. Their names were Guido and Bruno, though for the life of me I couldn't remember which was which. It didn't really matter, as those weren't their real names, but some obscure joke on the part of their boss, Mr. Anthony.

As they approached me, they split apart, leaving me no place to run. The one in front of me, let's call him Guido, said, "Mr. Anthony asked me to give you a message," as his hand reached inside his jacket.

This is it, I thought. I had a needle gun parked inside a rig in the small of my back, but there was no way that I'd be able to pull it out fast enough, especially with two of them. I didn't even try.

I expected to find myself staring down the front lens of a Kunstler 75. Instead, a fat white envelope materialized in Guido's ham like hand. He shoved it in my direction, and I gingerly took it.

They turned then, Guido giving Bruno a look that said, "Did you see the expression on that mug's face?" They got into the car and drove off.

I waited until they were gone before I looked at the envelope. It had my name printed on it, "Frank Sladek," in elegant block letters. The flap hadn't been sealed. I thumbed it open and found myself holding a stack of brand new, crisp Crockett two hundred dollar bills. I didn't bother to count them. I had a good idea how much was there. There would be ten grand worth. Mr. Anthony is a fan of nice round numbers.

There was a note inside, as well. It was hand written in the same elegant block letters on thick, expensive paper. I doubted that Mr. Anthony had written it himself, he probably had a calligraphist for that, but it was the thought that counted. It was short, and to the point.

Dear Mr. Sladek,
This is in appreciation for your part in the discovery of the person responsible for the death of my dear nephew Giovanni. I am sure you will agree that it would be the best thing for all involved if nothing more was said on this matter.
Yours Sincerely
Mr. Anthony

It was clear what the note meant. He was buying my silence on his role in the death of his nephew. What would happen if I didn't keep my mouth shut wasn't mentioned, but it was certainly implied. As always, in my dealings with Mr. Anthony, I didn't seem to have much choice in arrangement.

I stuffed the envelope into my inside jacket pocket.

Had I achieved justice for the blueskin girl? It didn't seem that way. Sure, her killer was dead, but in the end that had had nothing to do with her. Whatever satisfaction there was in Sigson's death, and I wasn't sure that there was any, I was pretty sure that it wasn't justice. I'm not sure there ever is justice for people like her, not the way the universe runs. Had I even gotten justice for Giovanni? Had he deserved any? From what I'd uncovered, he hadn't been a nice man. He'd been caught stealing from his own uncle. He'd known the rules of the game that he'd played and he'd chosen to break them. I didn't regret his death, and I didn't particularly care that the man who had killed him was now dead himself. Sigson had been nothing more than a weapon in the hands of someone else. He wouldn't ever kill again, but someone else would be sure to take his place.

Responsibility for Giovanni's death rested on his uncle, but I wasn't sure if I would call it guilt. Can you have justice without guilt? I didn't seem to have the answers to any of these questions.

So where did that leave me? It left me ten thousand dollars Crockett richer, that's where it left me. I continued on my way into the Blue Moon and the drink I had been looking forward to.

NIGHT ON THE TOWN

NIGHT ON THE TOWN

I woke up feeling like a star drive had exploded in my head. I laid there a moment, trying to collect my thoughts, things like where I was, what I was doing there, who I was. After a bit things started to come in to focus. One thing I was certain of, I wasn't home in bed in my apartment on the edge of New Minglewood. I knew this for a couple of reasons. One was that the painting of an alien landscape, a gift from Lucinda before she had grown tired of me, had been replaced with the kind of "art" that hotel chains buy up by the square kilometer and hang in the rooms of hotels on a dozen planets, the kind of stuff that is so abstract in its inoffensiveness as to be offensive.

The other reason was that there was a woman in bed with me. She was dead. I've been accused of a certain lack of discrimination when it comes to women, but not to the point of bringing dead ones home. I reached over to feel the pulse in her neck just to make sure, but my first impression had been right. She was dead.

The rush of adrenalin that discovery induced was driving the explosion out of my head. I tried to bring things into focus. It worked to some extent. I looked around me. I was in a hotel room alright, and judging from the furnishings, it was a second tier hotel, respectable, clean, but not luxurious, not like a room at the Casino. It was a room, not a suite. There were the typical hotel room furnishings, a king sized bed, a dresser, a table and a couple of chairs. An entertainment unit hung on the wall.

It looked like the dead woman had been alive when we'd come up to the room. She'd taken her clothes off with some care, draping what looked to be a very expensive dress over a chair so that it wouldn't wrinkle. So much for the theory of a night of unbridled passion. This seemed more businesslike, though the dead woman didn't look like a working girl.

My own clothes occupied a somewhat less tidy pile on the other chair. I noted with interest that it was my best evening suit. Who had I been trying to impress? I started to get dressed, operating on the principle that if I had to get out of there in a hurry, it would be better if I wasn't naked.

After I had my shoes on, I looked over the dead woman in the bed again. There were no marks of violence on her body, no visible cause of death that I could see. Maybe she had died of natural causes, I thought. Sure, and I was pope of the Reconstituted Catholic Church. Looking around, I noticed that there was an ice bucket with an open bottle of wine and a couple of glasses standing on the dresser. It was Champagne, the real stuff from Earth, and not the kind of thing that's given away compliments of the management in a second tier hotel.

The bottle was only half empty, and one of the glasses still had been barely touched. There was an empty shorty of brown, what passes for whiskey on Star City, sitting on the dresser, the kind they stuff minibars with. I spotted a tumbler from the bathroom on the nightstand next to the bed on the side I'd been lying on. It was pretty clear what had happened. We'd ordered a bottle of the bubbly, or it had been waiting in the room for us. I'd opened it and poured two glasses. I'm not really a fan of the stuff, though, the bubbles tickle my nose. So after the first sip, I'd grabbed the brown from the bar and poured it over ice. The woman, though, had drunk all of hers, and maybe a second glass.

I gave a sniff to the glass that still had some of the Champagne in it. That kind of stuff is a little beyond my normal price range, but I thought I detected something odd about the smell. Poison? That would explain the dead woman. Had I known about it? Poison wasn't really my style. Besides, I'd evidently drunk some of the wine. That was probably the cause of my pounding head. It looked like someone had wanted the dead woman dead and hadn't cared about any collateral damage, i.e. me. That made it personal.

The question was, what was I going to do about it? Now a good citizen would think it their duty to inform the police. The problem was that my own relationship with the local constabulary was, at best, erratic. Considering that, it might be wiser to leave the discovery of the body to someone else. Was there anything to tie me to the room? I did a quick sweep, and the only things of mine were the clothes on my back. I called up the room bill on the screen. The hotel was the Commodore. The room had been paid for by Helga Schmidt. Somehow I doubted that that was the dead woman's name, but it wasn't mine, either, so I was in the clear, there. The Champagne hadn't been charged to the room, which was interesting. Somehow, that hadn't aroused my suspicions the night before.

I gave a quick look at myself in the mirror above the dresser. The evening jacket might attract attention seeing as it was 1100, but if I draped it over an arm and left the shirt collar unbuttoned, I'd probably be taken for a harried businessman running late who'd had too much to drink the night before. It would have to do.

There was no point in trying to eliminate fingerprints or DNA. I didn't have the time or equipment to scrub the room clean enough. The sooner I was out of there, the better. I gave one last look to the dead woman and then slipped out the door into the hallway. Just to play it safe, I took the elevator up two floors, got out, and then waited for another to take me down to the lobby. I didn't meet anyone on the way. The lobby was busy, which was good. Without attracting notice I was out the front door and walking down the street towards the nearest tram stop.

I took the tram a couple of stops down Star City to where I knew there was a convenient Autodoc. I had a blood sample taken. I'd been right, the Champagne had been tainted with a very obscure neurotoxin. Helpfully, the Autodoc suggested that I avoid the substance in the future as it might prove lethal at a high enough dosage.

By this time, I'd remembered who I was, Frank Sladek, sometime private investigator. I'd recognized the dead woman, too. She was the woman whose husband had hired me to see what she was up to. That hadn't worked out quite as planned.

I'd gotten a call the previous day from a potential client asking if I could meet him in his office that afternoon. That wasn't unusual. I don't keep an office myself to cut down on the overhead. Usually I conduct business in the Blue Moon, the bar across the street from my apartment in the Aldeberon Arms, but that's not the sort of place that would impress my more respectable clients, so I try to be flexible.

The client gave his name as Samuel Winterd. Coincidentally, his office was in the Winterd Building. I didn't recognize the name, but a quick check on my comm unit revealed that he was a successful businessman with interests on a dozen planets. Like many men in his position, he maintains residency on Star City for tax purposes. Even with the bribes, kickbacks, and protection money, Star City can be a cheaper place to operate than any of the major planets. That and the fact that it's centrally located make it attractive to people in certain lines of business many of which are even legitimate.

Perhaps I should explain about Star City. It's a hollowed out asteroid circling a brown dwarf in the middle of nowhere, but by being in the middle of nowhere, it's also in the middle of everywhere, being located at a point in space where most of the spacelanes of human space intersect. This makes it a perfect transit point where interstellar travelers can make connections. The local government, what there is of it, operates with a minimum of interference and a maximum of graft, guided by the principle of keeping travelers happy while extracting as much as the traffic will bear. Which explains how people like me can make a living.

I showed up at Winterd's office on the dot wearing my most respectable suit. Anyone with a building named after him had money, and I was interested in getting my share. I cooled my heels in an outer office for five minutes, which wasn't bad. The chair was comfortable and the receptionist was easy on the eyes. Eventually she told me that I could go on through. I smiled as I passed her desk.

Samuel Wintered was a fit seventy, fit in the way that can only be achieved with an hour in a gym every morning exercising under the tutelage of a personal trainer who was named something like Hans or Gunther. He was impeccably groomed and tailored in a manner that screamed successful businessman. His office provided the perfect backdrop for him, a stage setting produced by an interior designer to say "I'm important." There were pictures of starliners and factories lining the walls along with various plaques and awards. What was missing were any personal touches. If Wintered had any hobbies or interests, they weren't on display in his office.

"Have a seat, Mr. Sladek," Winterd said, motioning me to one of a pair of seats facing the desk. "You've come recommended to me." I noted that he didn't say "highly recommended" nor did he mention by whom. I hadn't really expected him to. The people who require my services tend to want to keep that fact confidential.

"Thank you. Just what can I do for you, Mr. Winterd?"

"I assume that you've done some research on me?"

"I think we can take that as a give, Mr. Wintered," I said politely.

"Then you know I have a wife." It was a statement, not a question. In fact his bio had mentioned a wife.

"Yes. I take it then, this involves your wife?"

"My wife, Mr. Sladek, is quite a bit younger than myself and quite attractive. She also is a woman of spirit who enjoys the good life, as it were."

"I see," I said noncommittally. I thought I could see where this was going, and I wasn't sure that I liked it. But then that's business.

"Don't get me wrong, Mr. Sladek. I'm under no illusions when it comes to my wife. Ours was not a love match. A man in my position requires a wife, one who can play the part, who can entertain and be the charming hostess when required. Bunny does that quite satisfactorily. As far as what my wife gets out of the arrangement, well, to be blunt, she gets my position and the use of my wealth, or at least a portion of it, which she has been quite willing to take advantage of. For my part, I try not to interfere with her life as long as no scandal is involved."

"It sounds like a match made in heaven, Mr. Winterd. Just where do I come in?"

"Lately, I've become concerned. My wife seems to be spending more money than usual. I'd like to know why."

"Gambling? Drugs?"

"Bunny gambles, but I don't believe excessively. As to drugs, I've seen no evidence of addiction."

"Then what is it you are worried about, Mr. Winterd?"

"I'm concerned about the possibility that my wife is being blackmailed."

"Is there anything in her past that might be questionable?"

"I'm no fool, Mr. Sladek. Before we were married I had her background thoroughly investigated. The results were negative."

"Something more recent?"

"Perhaps. That's what I want you to find out for me, Mr. Sladek. You have to understand, I don't care one way or the other what my wife may have done. What I do care about is my reputation. For a man in my position, reputation is everything. As with any businessman, I have enemies, competitors, rivals, that would like nothing better than to see me embarrassed."

"So you want me to help you avoid embarrassment?"

"Exactly, Mr. Sladek."

"And how far do you want me to go to avoid this embarrassment?" I was concerned that he might want me to do something illegal. Not that I'd necessarily object, but I like to know that kind of thing up front.

"For the moment, I just want to find out who and how. Once I know those, I will decide what to do about it."

"Fair enough."

"Tonight my wife is going gambling at a place called Viktor's. She's been going there a lot lately, and I suspect it may play some part in the blackmail scheme. I want you to go there, Mr. Sladek, and observe her actions and interactions, and then report back to me. Nothing more. Is that clear?"

"I'm to be an observer."

"Yes, exactly. Do you agree?"

"It seems okay to me, Mr. Winterd."

"I'll pay twice your usual day rate, Mr. Sladek and advance you two thousand dollars Crockette to cover any expenses. There's also a memory disk with recent video of my wife." He reached into a desk drawer and pulled out an envelope and slid it across the desk. I thumbed it open to reveal a sheaf of bills, fifties and hundreds, used and non-sequential, and a disk. It seemed that I wasn't the only one interested in keeping the transaction confidential. A quick count showed that it was two thousand, just as he had said. I slipped the envelope into my inside jacket pocket.

"Tonight at Viktor's, then. Do you know what time?"

"2100. As far as I know, she will be alone."

"2100 it is. I'll let you know what I find, Mr. Winterd."

He gave me a look that said I was dismissed so I took the hint and let myself out. Passing through the outer office, I smiled at the receptionist. This time she smiled back.

There are any number of gambling joints on Star City. Entertaining travelers waiting for connections is Star City's major industry, and gambling is the most efficient means of separating them from their money. Some, like the Casino, are famous across human space, others are less so, but Viktor's has a certain notoriety that is unrivaled because it caters not only to humans, but because it makes a point of welcoming alien customers. There are some people who wouldn't be caught dead in Viktor's, but that doesn't seem to have affected the club's bottom line any. Alien money is as good as any is the motto of the house.

For all of that, Viktor's has been fashionable as of late, at least amongst those looking for a thrill. Dress is anything but casual, and unlike many gambling establishments, refreshments aren't cheap. As I put on my best and only evening suit, I was thankful that Winterd had provided me with walking around money.

I arrived at the club early to get the lay of the land. I'd been in the place a few times, but not recently. There was some muscle in a too small dinner jacket at the entry who gave me the fish eye. He let me pass, though as I walked by I caught him muttering something into his cufflink. I shrugged and headed for the bar.

I'll say this; Viktor's does the glitzy part up right. There's plenty of polished chrome and crystal, the lighting is subdued but not dim. The ceiling has a projection of what is supposed to be the exterior star field that moves as Star City rotates, but it has way too many stars to be the real sky. It also doesn't move fast enough, considering the rotation rate of the asteroid, but that's probably just as well. Inducing motion sickness isn't the intended effect.

The main bar runs along one wall of the gaming room and is raised up off the floor so that it offers a good view of the action. The bar is also famous for Glzz, the head bartender. No one is sure where he comes from. He certainly isn't from any known alien species from the stars that border that irregular volume of the galaxy known as human space. The legend is that he arrived one day, asked for employment, demonstrated his talents and was hired on the spot by Viktor himself. While it might prove to be a hindrance for a human bartender, Glzz seems incapable of human or any other speech other than uttering the occasional "glzz." On the other hand, he does appear to understand most human languages and dialects and many alien ones, at least to the point of accepting drink orders. What really sets him apart from other bartenders is the fact that he has four arms and has been known to apply all four at once in the preparation of his more complicated cocktails. If the orders are simpler, he sometimes will mix two at once, manipulating bottles, shakers, and glassware in a dizzying choreography that has to be seen to be believed. He seemed disappointed when I ordered a whiskey and soda.

When my drink arrived, I turned to check out the floor. There were all the conventional gaming tables that one would have been able to find in a human casino any time in the last thousand years; roulette, dice, blackjack. In addition, there were any number of more modern games as well as a some of alien origin. It was early, yet, but there were still plenty of players at the tables.

What you wouldn't find at the Casino, were the aliens at the tables. Most of the traffic through Star City originates and terminates on worlds settled by humans and consists predominantly of members of that species. Alien ships tend not to dock on Star City, or, for that matter, traverse human space. That doesn't mean, though, that members of alien races are completely absent. There are always a few, who for business, diplomatic, or cultural purposes find themselves on Star City for shorter or longer periods of time, and Viktor's is willing and able of part them from their money.

Some of these species are more or less human looking, by which I mean they have two arms, two legs and one head in the more or less the conventional locations. True, they may have scales or feathers, three fingers or seven, be green or red, or electric blue, but they are relatively recognizable as intelligent beings. Some, however, defy human preconceptions. One of these I noted playing roulette from inside the confines of a tank of a murky looking liquid, dispatching and collecting chips with one of several tentacles that would rise out of the water momentarily only to withdraw when the task was done.

I found the sight so amusing that I failed to notice the large form that had appeared next to me at the bar. Unlike the bouncer at the door, the dinner jacket on this person fit perfectly, so well, in fact, that I could hardly notice the bulge created by the laser pistol under his left armpit.

"What are you doing here, Sladek?" he greeted me. His tone was firm, but civil. I didn't know him personally, but I knew his type.

"I thought I'd treat myself to a night out. A couple of drinks, maybe play a few rounds of roulette—"

"Don't give me a line, Sladek. Are you working?"

"Maybe." I didn't see any point in denying it. He evidently knew who I was and what I did.

"Mr. Viktor is very particular, Sladek. He doesn't like any rough stuff and he won't tolerate any gunplay."

"I'm not packing. You can pat me down if you want." The fact is I usually don't go armed unless I think I'll need it. It hadn't seemed necessary. Besides it would spoil the lines of my jacket.

"That won't be necessary, Sladek. Just don't make any trouble and don't harass any of the customers or you might find yourself tossed out on your ear."

"Understood. As I said, I'm just out for a night on the town."

"Good. Glzz! The next one is on Mr. Viktor." Glzz winked with two of his three eyes. My benefactor worked his way down the bar, stopping to chat with some of the regulars. I went back to observing the floor.

It was shortly after that that I spotted Winterd's wife. The video hadn't done her justice. She had money and taste and knew how to use them both to her benefit. The dress she had on, a silver film sheathe looked simple but probably wasn't, fitting just right in all the important places. Her hair had been silvered in the latest metallic style to match the dress and cut asymmetrically to reach her shoulder on one side while revealing her ear on the other. Most women can't pull something like that off. She could.

She moved across the gaming floor with grace and assurance. From the way she greeted some of the staff it seemed that she was a regular. She surveyed the tables, finally settling on a blackjack game with an open seat. She handed a chit to the dealer who slid a tall stack of chips in her direction. One of the waitresses circling the floor handed her a drink, something blue in a squat glass. As a rule, I try never to drink anything blue.

From my slot at the bar I watched her play for a while. The other players at the table had the look of serious players. There was a guy I vaguely recognized as being "connected," another looked and was dressed like someone from Crockett, though on Star City that didn't necessarily mean anything. Sometimes I think half the population is pretending to be something other than what they are. Unless I missed my bet, the third player was a Terran, it's just hard to fake that blend of assurance and arrogance the home world breeds. He was short and fat and dressed in a suit that probably cost more than I made in a year.

The last player was a woman, a blue skin. Blue skins are human, but they've been genetically modified to adapt to a planet with a much high oxygen content than Earth standard. Their skin takes on a bluish cast when they are in what for them is an oxygen deficient atmosphere. They also have to breathe supplementary oxygen from a tank they always carry. For that reason, you don't see many of them off their home world. Once you got past the blue skin, she wasn't bad looking, a little thin maybe, but not bad. She had long white hair pulled back in a complicated braid and wore a white, knee length, sheath dress over white boots. Her oxygen tank was suspended from a silver chain belt. From that distance I could hardly see the thin tube that snaked up to her nostrils.

There weren't any non-humans at the table. They tend to prefer the ballistic games like craps or roulette. Maybe it's just that they don't feel comfortable dealing with the base ten arithmetic. Poker is just beyond them; too much depends on reading the expressions and body language of your opponents. I always find it interesting that the games preferred by serious players are those that have been around for over a thousand years without changing much, craps, roulette, poker, blackjack, simple mechanical games that depend on odds and chance. Maybe it's because games involving computers would be just too easy to fudge.

I watched the play for awhile. I couldn't see the cards, but from my vantage point it looked like Mrs. Winterd was a sound player, her stack of chips went up and down in increments but never strayed far from what she had started with. For that matter the other players at the table were doing the same, there were no big winners or losers.

I finished my drink and decided it was about time for me to earn my fee. Sauntering down to the floor, I grabbed a seat at a table where I had a good view of the table where she was playing. I passed a credit stick to the dealer who plugged it in and passed back a stack of chips. It was shorter and the chips were of a lower denomination than the ones Mrs. Winterd was playing with.

Blackjack is a game that, if you know the odds and play them, you can last a long time on a modest stake. I wasn't trying to break the bank, just stay in the game. I bet accordingly and did ok. The other players weren't as wise. There was a stormtrooper type from Nordholm and his blonde wife, obviously in transit. They were drinking too much and betting at all the wrong times. Fortunately, they seemed to have an unlimited budget, getting more chips from the dealer a few times while I played. There was a guy I took to be from Nostromo who wasn't drinking, but he wasn't playing any smarter. The other player at the table was an alien from a species I'd never seen before. He seemed to be holding his own. Maybe it had to do with the fact that his appendages ended in five fingers.

As I played, I kept an eye on Mrs. Winterd. She seemed engrossed by the game, but a little bored with it as well. She played for about an hour. During that time, the only persons she spoke to were the dealer and the waitress who brought another one of the blue things. Me, I'd had two drinks already, so I passed when the waitress came around to the table. Finally Mrs. Winterd had had enough. She cashed in her chips and the dealer added the sum to her credit stick. I cashed in at the same time. I was up a whole five credits. Not bad, actually.

She went up to the bar. Glzz made her a drink, this one sort of neon green. I meandered around the floor, keeping an eye on her so that she didn't skip and then finally took a seat at the end of the bar farthest from her and ordered a soda water on ice. Glzz raised what would have been an eyebrow if he'd had any but threw some cubes in a tumbler and splashed something bubbly over them.

Mrs. Winterd looked a little nervous which I thought was interesting. A drunken spacer from Novaya Magnetogorsk tried to make a pass at her, but she shut him down without blinking. Maybe Glzz pushed a button, maybe he didn't, but a few moments later Viktor Martian, the owner of the place came over to chat. The spacer took the hint and departed. Martian and Mrs. Winterd exchanged pleasantries for a minute or two, and then moved off. The two seemed friendly on a casual basis, but it didn't look like anything Mr. Winterd need be worried about.

Mrs. Winterd finished her drink and sat for a moment, apparently deep in thought, then she stood up and headed for the Women's lounge. That's always a problem when observing a female subject.

I was trying to figure out whether she had just gone to powder her nose or if I'd been spotted and she was trying to give me the slip when I sensed a form taking the seat next to me at the bar. Turning, I saw that it was Mrs. Winterd.

"Are you following me?" She asked. Her voice was smooth and unusually low for a woman, and I mean that in the best way.

"Who? Me?" I replied. "No, I'm just out for a night on the town."

"Sure, honey. I've seen you eyeing me up all night. Who hired you? My husband?"

"Do I look like the kind of guy that needs to be paid to look at a pretty woman?"

"No, probably not. But then one can never tell. Maybe that blue skin that was playing at my table is more your type?"

"No. I find the oxygen bottle gets in the way."

She laughed at that. It was an infectious laugh. I could see why Winterd had married her. I wasn't so sure what she'd seen in him. Except maybe the money.

"Can I buy you a drink?" I offered.

"I've got a better idea. I'm tired of this place. Let's go someplace else. Someplace quiet where I can figure out what your game is."

I didn't think that was quite what Winterd had had in mind when he'd hired me, but it seemed like a good way to keep tabs on his wife. OK, maybe Glzz had mixed that second drink a little strong and my inhibitions were a little uninhibited.

She took my arm and I escorted her out onto the street. There was a hotel in the next block, the Commodore. Not exactly first class, but they had a quiet bar with a decent keyboard player who could handle a jive samba if you tipped him. Mrs. Winterd didn't object, so we headed in that direction.

Once in the bar, the manager took one look at the dress and sat us at a prime table. I didn't even have to slip him a Crockett greenback. The waiter must have pegged us as good tippers as well, because he was at the table before we'd even sat down. I ordered a brown and soda on the rocks, Mrs. Winterd asked for a "Pink Fluvian." I'd never heard of that before, but then being so close to New Minglewood, the Blue Moon isn't long on fancy cocktails. It turned out to be pink and served in a conical glass with no foot or stem. There was a little doohickey sticking out that Mrs. Winterd extracted and tossed on the floor.

"Cheers."

"Loch Hime."

Mrs. Winterd tossed off about half the drink then asked, "So, who the hell are you?"

I was starting to like Mrs. Winterd. She seemed to be a woman who knew her own mind.

"My name is Frank Sladek, Mrs. Winterd. I find things." I prefer that to telling people that I'm a private dick. Sometimes they get the wrong idea.

"So you find things, Frank Sladek. That seems like a funny kind of occupation. What kind of things?"

"Oh, this and that. Anything that's missing."

"Does it pay well?"

"Not particularly."

"So why do you do it?"

"It beats working."

"You *are* a character, Mr. Frank Sladek." I could tell that the blue, green and pink things were starting to affect her. She wasn't drunk so you'd notice, but then, I was getting the feeling that she'd had lots of practice. "So how much is my husband paying you?"

"Enough."

"I knew it! Does Sam think I'm fooling around with other men? I'm not. At least not seriously. He should know better than that."

"Actually, I got the impression that he thinks you are being blackmailed. He wants to avoid embarrassment."

That seemed to pull her up short.

"What would make him think that?"

"He seems to think you were spending more money than usual. Or at least that's what he told me."

"Oh, he did, did he? Well I deserve every credit I spend. He wanted a good looking wife he could show off. Well that's what he's got. Except that he never wants to take me anywhere except stuffy business dinners. What's a girl supposed to do? I just want a little fun sometimes."

"Mrs. Winterd, this is none of my business. I'm just telling you what your husband told me."

"Stop calling me Mrs. Winterd, Frank. I can call you Frank, can't I?"

"Sure. Frank is fine. And I can call you—?"

"Don't call me Bunny. I hate that name. My name is Bonita. You can call me that. Or Bonnie. But not Bunny."

Mrs. Winterd seemed to have gotten a whole lot more drunk in the last few minutes. Maybe it was the pink thing. Which was empty, the glass rolling around on the table. She signaled the waiter for another round. He deftly snatched up the empty glass and headed for the bar. I'd barely touched my drink.

"Are you—Being blackmailed, that is, Bonnie?"

"Not exactly."

"How exactly?"

"Oh, not much. A thousand. Not even dollars Crockett, just credits." At the current exchange rate that was about five hundred dollars. Of course Crockett dollars are more convertible anywhere other than Star City.

"About what?"

"That's just it. There's nothing to blackmail me for."

"Then why have you been paying?"

"It just seemed easier. That's all."

I didn't quite follow the logic of that, but it was getting late.

"OK. Who are you paying it to?"

"Viktor."

"Viktor Martian?" I asked, naming the owner, or at least the front, of Viktor's.

"Yes."

The waiter came with the drinks. Bonnie slammed hers down before I could stop her. I finished my first one out of a feeling of desperation. Things were starting to get out of hand.

"Maybe you've had enough, Bonnie."

She stared at me for a moment as if wondering who I was, then said, "Maybe you're right, Frank. I'm starting to feel them. I can't go home in this condition. Sam would be furious."

I had a feeling she was right. Especially if he found out she'd been drinking with the man he'd hired to keep an eye on her.

"What do you suggest?"

"Frank. Could you be a dear and get me a room here at the hotel."

"Won't your husband be upset if you spend the night in a hotel?"

"Sam is used to me coming in at all hours. All I need is a few hours to sleep. I can be home by breakfast."

I was dubious, but I didn't have a better idea. I went out to the lobby and got a room using Bonnie's credit stick. The desk clerk insisted on winking when I said it was for the lady and not for me, but at least he gave me the key. I got the impression that he'd done this before.

It took a bit of persuading to get her up to the room. Usually I don't have that much trouble. Finally I got her up to the floor and into the room, shutting the door behind me.

"OK. Here we are, Bonnie."

"Oh, look. A bottle of Champagne. I just love the bubbles."

There was a bottle of Champagne and two glasses sitting on the dresser. Maybe the desk clerk had gotten the wrong impression. If so, it was quick work. It had only been a few minutes from the time I got the key until we got up to the room.

Before I could stop her, she had thumbed the stopper and opened the bottle. She poured two glasses and handed one to me.

I've never been much for sparkling wine. I took a sip and set it down. Bonnie had finished hers and poured a second glass. I said what the heck to myself and rummaging around the minibar came up with a shorty of brown. I poured it into a tumbler over a couple of hunks of ice from the bucket the wine had been in. For some reason the room seemed to be spinning around.

"Cheers."

That's the last think I remember until I woke up in bed with Bonnie's body.

After the stop at the Autodoc, I headed back to my apartment. The doc had given me something for my hangover and the poison, but my adrenalin levels were tapering off now that I was away from the hotel and I sensed that I was going to crash and soon. When I did it, I wanted it to be in my own bed, preferably alone. I barely made it.

The sound of my comm going off woke me. The display told me that it was 1600, so I'd had at least a few hours of sleep. It also told me that the caller was Samuel Winterd. I thumbed acceptance.

"What the hell happened last night, Sladek?" It wasn't exactly the friendliest of greetings.

"What do you mean?" Perhaps not the wittiest response, but then I was still waking up.

"I just got done with the police, Sladek. My wife was found dead in some cheap hotel room. I thought that I hired you to protect her."

The Commodore wasn't exactly a cheap hotel, but then I guess saying "a mid-level hotel room" wouldn't have had the same effect.

"If you remember, Mr. Winterd, you didn't hire me to be a bodyguard. You hired me to see if she was being blackmailed."

"I don't care what I hired you for. You were supposed to be watching her and now she's dead."

"Just exactly what did the police say happened, Mr. Winterd?"

"They said that she checked into the hotel late last night. The cleaning bot found her body this morning." The robot maids are programmed not to enter rooms if they are occupied, but then Mrs. Winterd hadn't actually been alive.

"Did the police give a cause of death?"

"She was poisoned, Mr. Sladek. Some sort of neurotoxin. They said that they found it in a bottle of champagne."

"Did your wife ever exhibit suicidal tendencies?" I thought it was a reasonable sort of question for someone who hadn't been in the hotel room to ask.

"No, Mr. Sladek," Winterd blustered. "The police think that she was murdered. What I want to know is how my wife ended up in that particular hotel room."

"Look, Mr. Winterd. I went to Viktor's as we discussed to observe your wife. Well, I saw her. She played blackjack for a while and then left. While I was watching her, she had quite a few drinks. Maybe a few too many. She might have gotten a room at the hotel to sleep it off. The Commodore is only a block from Viktor's. Had she ever done anything like that before? I mean spend the night away from home?"

"Yes. On several occasions," Winterd admitted grudgingly.

"What did the hotel say? Was she alone when she checked in?" I was trying to find out if the police knew that I had been the one who had gotten the room for her.

"The room was only registered in her name," he conceded. Of course the police and I both knew that hotels on Star City are notoriously discrete. I could count on the desk clerk not giving it up that I had been the one who had gotten the room, at least for a while. "They did say that there was evidence that someone else had been in the room with her. A man."

"Do they know who?"

"Not yet, Mr. Sladek. But they seemed to think that it was only a matter of time until they were able to identify him."

A hotel room isn't the easiest place for a forensics team to investigate. The normal cleaning only goes so far, and with plenty of people having come and gone in the last few weeks it would be hard to isolate who had been there last night. Unfortunately, the police had my (and everyone else's who resided on Star City) DNA on record.

"Did you tell the police that you hired me to follow your wife, Mr. Winterd?"

"The subject didn't come up. There were more important matters to discuss," Winterd answered acidly. Like who would want to kill his wife, but it was one break for me, even if only a small one.

"That's probably just as well, Mr. Winterd. For both of us. It might not look so good to the police if they discovered that you were having your wife tailed."

"Now see here, Sladek—"

"I'm not trying to imply anything, Mr. Winterd. I just happen to know how the police think. By the way, do you happen to know which detectives have been assigned to the case?"

"A Sergeant Latimer and a detective Rossetti. Is it important?"

"Probably not," I conceded. For a Star City cop, Latimer was passably honest and reasonably bright, a combination that might make him dangerous.

"Look, Mr. Winterd. Your wife came into Viktor's last night. Like I said, she played blackjack for a while and had a few drinks while she was playing. After she got bored with blackjack, she came up to the bar and had a few more. Now I happen to know from experience that they don't water their drinks down at Viktor's."

"What are you saying, Mr. Slade?"

"Nothing, except that she had had a few drinks. After sitting at the bar for a few she left. Now, the Commodore has a decent keyboard player working their lounge. After she left Viktor's, your wife might have gone there to listen to him. She probably had a few more drinks in the bar. Then she got a room rather than come home. Normally, that probably would have been a smart thing to do. Except that this time someone must have arranged to have a spiked bottle of bubbly waiting in the room for her."

"Just where is this going?"

"What I'm saying is that your wife's murder wasn't an act of drunken passion. Unless the Commodore Hotel supplies all of its guests with champagne laced with neurotoxins, it was a cold blooded killing, and one that had to have been planned in advance. Did your wife have any enemies that you know of?"

"Bunny? No. None that I can think of. But then I didn't know many of her acquaintances."

"Could someone have been trying to get at you through her?"

"That hardly seems likely."

"I see. I guess the question is, do you want me to continue the investigation?"

There was a pause, then: "There doesn't seem to be much point now, does there?"

"No, I guess not."

"You can keep the advance that I gave you, Mr. Sladek. I won't require an accounting of expenses." The comm went dead.

I put the comm down. My conversation with Samuel Winterd had left a strange taste in my mouth. Nothing exactly that I could point to, but he hadn't seemed that upset, not like someone whose wife had just been murdered. OK, maybe there hadn't been any great love between the two, which was certainly the impression I had gotten from both of them, but he had seemed a little too dispassionate. He knew something that he wasn't letting me in on, the question was what.

Suddenly, I felt the need for a drink, nothing fancy, just a good, honest shot of brown. It was too early in the day to drink alone, but one of the advantages of my apartment, besides the fact that the rent is cheap, was that there is a bar called The Blue Moon right across the street.

The Blue Moon is a quiet, old fashioned sort of place, no music, no video screens, just booze. It might get crowded and noisy at night, but in the late afternoon it is just the kind of place to go when you don't want to drink alone. Instead, I could go and drink with a bartender who had enough sense to leave me alone and where the only other patron would be a guy at the other end of the bar contemplating the vicissitudes of life while staring at a glass of something that glowed green.

Unfortunately, I never got to The Blue Moon. As I was crossing the street a black sedan pulled up. With a tram system that is both convenient and free, vehicles of any sort are rare on

Star City, being reserved mostly for commercial or official use. Black sedans tended to fall in the latter category. I thought I recognized this one, and it boded no good.

"Sladek," a voice called out from an open window. "Get in." I recognized the voice as that of Detective Sergeant Latimer. We'd had our run ins before, some friendly, some not. My guess was that this was going to be a not. There didn't seem to be any point in fighting it. I got in the back seat. There was an audible click as the locks slid into place.

"You packin', Sladek?" Rossetti, Latimer's sometime partner, asked through the laser proof glass separating the back from the front seat. I opened my jacket to show that I wasn't wearing a shoulder holster. I couldn't have hidden a weapon, in any case, as police cruisers are equipped with scanners. Rossetti was just trying to show what a tough guy he was.

"We'd like to ask you a few questions, Sladek," Latimer asked. "About last night."

"I'm always happy to assist the police, Latimer. You know that."

"Yeah, well we're not asking for assistance, Sladek. Just answers." With that, the sedan sped off towards police headquarters.

Now Star City, the main transit hub of human space, was established to cater to the needs and entertainment of those travelers waiting for connections. In addition to the hotels and casinos, it has some of the finest museums and concert halls ever constructed by man. This has resulted in some real gems of architecture. The police headquarters building isn't one of them. It is a squat, grey block of a building with a windowless façade and all the charm of a hemorrhoid. The interior, as I knew from experience, isn't any better.

Rossetti drove the police car through one of the doors at the base of the building leading to the underground garage. From there I was whisked up an elevator to an interview room somewhere on one of the upper floors. I was shoved into a chair—and left to stew. This, of course, was standard police procedure. Let the poor slob think about the fix he was in while the detectives enjoy a nice steaming cup of Joe, maybe even eat a pastry.

I'd been through it all before, of course, and should have taken it in stride, but then I'd never woken up in bed with a corpse. I knew my position was precarious. What I didn't know was how much Latimer knew and how much he'd figured out. It would be easy enough for him to make a case against me, even easier for him to hold me so that I wouldn't be able to figure out who really had killed Mrs. Winterd. Rossetti, I didn't worry about. Thinking isn't one of his strong points.

After what seemed like hours, probably because it was, Latimer and Rossetti entered the interrogation room. From the grease spot on Rossetti's shirt I deduced that they'd had dinner while I'd been waiting. That reminded me that I hadn't had anything to eat except alcohol for over twenty-four hours. My stomach started to growl.

Latimer took a seat across the table from me. Rossetti continued to stand, pacing back and forth around the tiny room. He thinks it makes him look menacing, but in reality, he just looks twitchy when he does that.

Latimer is a big guy, kind of beefy, with a pale face that turns bright red when he gets agitated. He looks pudgy, but that hides a lot of muscle and he can move surprisingly fast when he wants to. He can be pretty good with his fists, too.

"So, Frank, why'd you kill her?" The fact that Latimer used my first name told me something. Either he didn't have any idea who was responsible for Mrs. Winterd's death, or he thought he had enough evidence to have me jettisoned out one of the garbage tubes into space.

"Kill who? I haven't killed anyone lately, Sergeant."

"You know who I'm talking about. Mrs. Winterd."

"Mrs. Winterd is dead?" I said, feigning ignorance. "Why, I just saw her last night. Her husband had me running surveillance on her."

There was just a hint of surprise on Latimer's face. Either he didn't know that Winterd had hired me or he hadn't expected me to tell him first thing. Latimer and I had held intellectual sparing matches before, matches that I'd usually won.

"Why was that, Frank?"

"You know that's privileged information, Latimer."

"Can it, Frank. This is a murder investigation."

"Well, since you put it that way—I guess it doesn't matter if she's really dead. You wouldn't kid me about a thing like that, would you?"

"She's dead, Frank."

"OK. Mr. Winterd was concerned about the possibility that his wife was being blackmailed. He wanted me to find out for him. That's all."

"And was she?"

"Was she what?"

"Don't fool around, Frank. Was she being blackmailed?"

"I don't know. I just took the case yesterday. I went to Viktor's Club, that's a gambling joint, because Winterd had said his wife would be there."

"Was she?"

"Yeah. She showed up, played some blackjack for maybe an hour, had a couple of drinks. After she was done playing, she sat at the bar and drank some more. Then she left."

"Where'd she go after that?"

"I don't know."

Latimer brought his fist down hard on the table. Rossetti jumped.

"You're lying, Frank. We've got witnesses that saw you leave with Mrs. Winterd."

"They must be mistaken. I *did* leave Viktor's at the same time as Mrs. Winterd, but we weren't together."

"You didn't just happen to go to the Commodore Hotel at the same time as Mrs. Winterd, did you?"

"Maybe. I stopped for a drink. They've got a decent keyboard player there. You should check him out sometime."

"You're the one facing the music, Frank."

"If you don't mind me asking, just how did Mrs. Winterd die?"

"She was poisoned, Frank. Somebody slipped a neurotoxin into a bottle of Champagne. Seems Mrs. Winterd decided to take a room for the night at the Commodore. The Champagne was waiting in the room. The hotel, of course, denies supplying it. I tend to believe them. If they had, they would have used a cheaper bottle."

"Doesn't that strike you as odd?" I asked. Latimer looked at me with a puzzled frown. Rossetti was leaning in a corner cleaning his nails.

"What do you mean?"

"Well, how could someone know that Mrs. Winterd would take a room at the Commodore? You don't just go around carrying a bottle of doped Champagne on the off chance, do you?"

"So what's your point, Frank?"

"Look at it this way. Mrs. Winterd went to Viktor's on a pretty regular basis. She also drank a lot last night. I got the impression she did that on a regular basis, too. Now the Commodore is just down the street. I could be wrong, but I think Mrs. Winterd may have stayed there to sleep it off before going home fairly often. Often enough, that if someone wanted to kill her, they might take advantage of the fact. The trick with the Champagne was definitely something that was planned out in advance."

"An interesting theory, Frank," Latimer said with a smile. I knew from the smile that he knew more than he'd let on and was just playing me so I'd hang myself. "Thing is, I think you were there, Frank. At the Commodore, and in the room with Mrs. Winterd."

There it was. Either someone at the Commodore had seen me and talked or the lab boys had found my DNA. That would have been quick work, but not impossible.

"Why would you think that?"

"The neurotoxin that killed Mrs. Winterd was pretty obscure. It's not readily available on Star City. By coincidence, an Autodoc did a blood test on someone that same night and detected trace amounts of the same neurotoxin."

"I thought Autodoc results were supposed to be confidential," I commented.

"Yeah, sure. And the pope of the Reconstituted Church is a catholic. This is Star City, Frank, what did you expect? We know it was you at that Autodoc. So do you want to tell me what *really* happened last night?"

"Not particularly."

"It might go easier with you, Frank."

I thought it over. Latimer seemed to already have a pretty good idea of my movements. It was only a matter of time before he could prove I had been in the room. If I told him, at least I could put my spin on it.

"OK. Like I said, I was hired to watch Mrs. Winterd. Well, she spotted me in Viktor's and guessed I was working for her husband. She suggested that we go somewhere else to talk. I agreed and we ended up in the lounge at the Commodore. We talked, she drank. Finally, she asked me to get her a room for the night. She was pretty loaded by that time. I got the key to a room and escorted her up there. The Champagne was waiting on the dresser. She popped the cork before I could stop her and poured two glasses. I had a sip, but switched to a bottle of brown from the minibar. That's probably why I'm not dead. I only had a sip of the poisoned wine."

"What happened next?"

"I don't know. I must have passed out from the poison. Next thing I know it's morning and I'm in bed with Mrs. Winterd, except that she's dead and I'm not. I panicked, I guess. There wasn't anything I could do for Mrs. Winterd, so I left."

"That's it?"

"That's what I remember."

"That's some story, Frank. I bet some of it is even true. What do you think, Rossetti?"

Latimer doesn't like his partner any more than I do. Rossetti's mind must have been someplace else because he started. He wasn't used to being asked for his opinion.

"Me, I think we should book him for murder."

"You would," Latimer said in disgust. "I'm going to have to think about it, Frank. Maybe check a few of the details. Like why Winterd didn't mention that he'd hired you."

"You do that, Latimer. In the mean time, can I go? I haven't eaten in over a day."

Latimer just grunted. He stood up and walked out of the room, Rossetti trailing behind him like a whipped puppy.

They left me in the room until just before they served breakfast to prisoners in the morning, then they kicked me out on the street with an admonishment not to leave town. Like there's anywhere to go when you live inside a hollow asteroid light years from anywhere.

I stopped at the little food counter on the corner by my apartment and had a plate of scrambled yellow protein and a cup of Joe. The scramble was greasy and the Joe too bitter, but nothing had ever tasted so good. I hadn't really been able to get any sleep during the night, the chair in the interrogation room having purposely been designed to be uncomfortable, so I went up to my apartment and dove into the mattress.

It was 1600 when I woke up, and a day later. It was getting to be déjà vu all over again. I needed to do some thinking and I needed to do it fast. I also needed a drink. I headed across the street to the Blue Moon.

This time I actually made it. Somehow, once inside the cool, dark confines of the bar I felt safer, as if I was on home ground. I took a spot at the end of the bar and ordered brown on the rocks. The politer saloons might call it whiskey, but we all know where it comes from, the fermentation tanks at the ass end of Star City. A little food coloring and some artificial flavoring and you have yourself instant Scotch with none of the messiness of turf fires and sea salt, or if that doesn't suit your fancy, change the additives and you have bourbon or rye. Leave out the coloring and you've got vodka. At least that's what they tell us, and if you've never had the real thing, you don't know any better. I've had the chance to taste real Scotch. The fella that bought it for me said it came from Speyside, wherever that is. As far as I know, there's no such planet by that name. It doesn't really matter, it's all just ethanol.

At that hour of the afternoon, the bar was practically deserted. The lunch crowd had wandered off several hours ago, and the after work lot hadn't showed up. It was just me, the bartender and some geek I didn't know at the far end of the bar who was doing his best to ignore me. He was drinking something blue. I never drink anything blue and try to avoid those that do; just a bit of wisdom my uncle left me. That was about all that he left me, but it was more than the rest of my family.

The Blue Moon at that time of day is the perfect place to think, and think was what I had to do. I had to figure out who had killed Mrs. Winterd, and I had to do it soon. Latimer might not think I had done it, but that wouldn't prevent him from making a case against me if a better suspect didn't come along. By Star City standards, he was an honest cop, but if it came to a choice between setting me up as a sacrificial victim and his job, it was pretty clear what his choice was going to be. Mrs. Winterd had been a high profile person in Star City, by which I mean she had had money, or at least her husband had, and on Star City, money is power. People die every day in New Minglewood and nobody gives a fig, but when it happens to one of the elite, the powers demand a solution. They didn't necessarily care if it was the right one, just as long as they had something where they could say "We took care of it." The trick was going to be making sure that I wasn't the one that got taken care of.

I didn't really know that much about Mrs. Winterd. Before her husband had hired me, I hadn't even been aware of her existence. We'd talked for a few hours, but a lot of what had been said that night had been muddled by the neurotoxin and the alcohol. Still, my intuition told me that I had all the pieces of the puzzle rattling around in my brain. All I had to do was put them together.

So what did I have? The only two men in her life that came to mind were her husband and Viktor Martian. Mrs. Winterd had said that Viktor had been blackmailing her. She had never said over what, only that it had been easier to pay than to deal with.

Now in my experience, and in my line I've had more than my share, blackmailers don't tend to kill their victims. It's bad for the cash flow. The only reason a blackmailer kills is to avoid being exposed, and I wasn't sure that Viktor would have cared. No one thought of him as a saint. He was just some guy who ran a not quite respectable gambling establishment. Even if he had wanted Mrs. Winterd dead, it was unlikely that he would resort to something as complex as an obscure neurotoxin. There are lots of easier and cheaper ways to kill someone, especially on Star City.

So who did that leave? Samuel Winterd. Why would he want his own wife dead, though? That was the question. Winterd was a businessman. As such, he tended to view the world in terms of assets and liabilities. Maybe the late Mrs. Winterd had slipped into the liabilities column. Was it possible?

The impression that I had gotten was that it had never been a love match. He had been looking for a trophy wife, someone who could act as a hostess, someone who would look good on his arm at social events. Mrs. Winterd, well, she had been looking for a rich husband. They'd each gotten what they had been looking for. But maybe with the passing of time, Mr. Winterd had had second thoughts. His wife hadn't been content to sit at home. She'd wanted to go out, have a night on the town, and she'd been perfectly happy to do so without her husband.

In business, image is everything. Scandal is hard to come by on Star City, it takes a lot to shock its jaded residents, but maybe Mrs. Winterd had crossed the line, at least in the mind of her husband. It might also be that Winterd had been afraid that if he was seen as not being able to control his wife it would be taken as a sign of weakness by his competitors, and weakness is the kiss of death in business. A pretty archaic viewpoint, by most people's standards, but the rich aren't most people. Or maybe it just came down to the fact that he had come to see her as an underperforming asset that needed to be liquidated.

Why hadn't he just divorced her? The marriage and divorce laws of Star City are pretty byzantine, but the end results would have probably been that Mrs. Winterd would have walked away with a bundle. Far easier and cheaper just to have her killed. And where did I fit in? I was the patsy, the fall guy, the sacrificial goat. In short, I was a nobody that things could be pinned on. It hadn't been anything personal. Not on Winterd's part, anyway. I was just a pawn to be sacrificed to knock over a queen.

Of course, *I* didn't see it that way. I'm not squeamish about death. I've had to kill men, and women too, on a number of occasions, but only because they had been trying to kill me. It was bad enough about Mrs. Winterd. I'd liked Bonnie, what little I'd seen of her. She had had spirit and personality, and there had been no good reason to kill her. The real corker, though, was that Winterd had wanted me dead just as a step in his plans. That I couldn't accept.

The more that I thought about, especially after the second brown on the rocks, the more it made sense. Having his wife killed solved Winterd's problems. She wouldn't be seen hanging around in the wrong places without him, and she wouldn't be spending any more money. Me? I'd just been a stage prop.

So what was I going to do about it? I couldn't just go to Latimer with my theory. I'd be laughed all the way to the garbage tube. I'd need some proof of Winterd's involvement which wouldn't be easy to find. Winterd would have been careful not to get his hands dirty. But a plan as elaborate as the one to kill his wife would have required henchmen. Someone had put the poison in the bottle and someone had put the bottle in the hotel room at the Commodore.

The poison was the point of weakness. Maybe the idea had been that it would never be detected and Mrs. Winterd's death, and mine, would be ruled as due to natural causes. If so, the plan had been a failure, but only because I hadn't drunk much of the Champagne and I'd survived long enough to get to an autodoc before the neurotoxin had degraded into undetectability. And when the same obscure neurotoxin was discovered in Mrs. Winterd's body and the Champagne, the fact that it was murder couldn't be denied.

The neurotoxin had been a mistake. If some readily available poison had been used instead, there wouldn't be much chance of finding a trail pointing back to Winterd, but an obscure neurotoxin was something else, entirely. It wasn't something you could just pick up at the corner pharmacy. The Autodoc had said that it was the main ingredient of the venom of some reptilian creature on one of the planets colonized by the Lizardmen. It was rare and hard to come by. Sure, it could be synthesized, but only by a professional lab, and there weren't that many on Star City. More likely it had come in as contraband on one of the space freighters that docked at Star City, and there weren't that many people who dealt in smuggled biologicals. If I could find out who had brought the stuff in, I might find a link to Winterd.

It was getting late. Three more drinkers had come in and the place was getting crowded. I dropped a couple of credit disks on the bar and got out before the place was overrun with the evening rush. I grabbed a tube of "pork" in a bun at the corner diner and went in search of Two-bit Herri.

Two-bit Herri is what is known in the trade as an informant. He's also been called a snitch, a stooly, a rat, a fink, a rat-fink, a weasel, a ferret, several other kinds of rodent like animals from a number of planets—well you get the idea. You give Herri money and he gives you information.

No one knows how Two-bit got his name. A guy I know who works with computers once told me that the smallest unit of information In a computer is called a bit. Either it is or it isn't. The way I've got it figured is that when you get information from Herri, he'll tell you whether something is or isn't. That's the first bit. The second bit is whether what he's telling you is true or not. Either it is or it isn't. It's just a theory, but I haven't heard a better one.

Herri hangs out at a little dive place the other side of New Minglewood. From the Blue Moon, it would only be a short walk, maybe a kilometer, straight through. With luck, that hour of the day, you might make it at least three out of five times. When they planned Star City, New Minglewood had been intended as a park for working people. That hadn't happened. Instead it became a district of cheap housing where the crooks, con-men, and grifters live and feed off each other. I took the long way around, skirting the slum. It added a half hour to the walk, but it was a nice night, but then, when you live inside a hollowed out asteroid, every night is a nice night.

The place was called Loo's, and compared to the Blue Moon, it was a sewer. The latest atonal stun-rock was blaring and the illegal gambling machines along the back wall lit up the place with garish colors. The bar wasn't the sit down kind, nor were there any chairs at the few tables spaced around the floor. The whole idea was to pack as many people as possible into the place while still allowing room to get to the bar to consume alcohol.

The bartender knew me well enough that when I asked if he'd seen Two-bit he nodded towards the back corner. More explicit directions would have been difficult over the noise. To make ordering drinks easier in the chaos they have lists printed on the bar. You point at an item, indicate how many with your fingers or tentacles and they bring you what you want. Very efficient.

I spotted Herri leaning against one of the tables at the rear. There was a glass of something purple and frothy bubbling away on the table. Two-bit has no taste. I waved a Crockett double sawbuck in his face and he pointed toward the back door.

Out in the alley it was quiet enough to talk.

"It's been awhile, Frankie baby." Herri has an annoying manner. "I heard you'd taken up with the arty crowd in the Souk. What can I do for you?"

"I need some information."

"That's what I'm here for, Frank. What will it be?"

"I'm interested in a neurotoxin. It probably came in on a spacer from one of the Lizardmen systems." I rattled off the name the Autodoc had used.

"You want to buy, Frankie? Not your usual style."

"No. I don't want to buy some. I want to know who brought it in and who it went to."

"That will cost you more than a double saw-buck, Frank, baby. That kind of thing is privileged information."

"The Crockett twenty was just to get your attention, Two-bit. What will it cost me and how soon can I get the information?"

Herri got a blank look on his face as if he was gone somewhere inside his head, which wasn't far from the truth. The rumor was that he'd had some sort of neural interface implanted in his brain that connected him to half the computer systems on Star City, but that's just a rumor, I think.

"The price will be a hundred Crockett for the dealer's name, and where you can find him. If you want the purchaser's identity it will be five times that and might take me a couple of days."

I thought it over. I wasn't sure I had a couple of days. The direct approach would be quicker and cheaper.

"I'll go for the name and a hundred."

"You always were an impetuous one, Frank. Show me the money."

I pulled another four bills out of my pocket and fanned them so Herri could count.

"His name is Georgi. He claims to be a captain, but that's bull. He lost his certificate for using too much of his own product. You can find him at a place called the 'Spacer's Lot' down by the freight ring. Do you know it?"

"By reputation. Here's your money."

He grabbed the cash out of my hand. "For another hundred I'll forget this happened."

"I don't really care who knows, Two-bit. But if you sell the info to anyone, I want a cut of the fee."

"Always a kidder, Frankie. Those spacers can be a rough bunch. Watch your back."

"Sure, don't I always?"

Herri went back inside Loo's. Rather than risk the noise, I followed the alley out into the street.

I knew the place Two-bit had pointed me at, that is I knew it well enough to find it. I also knew its reputation well enough to know that if I was going to be asking questions, I'd better be armed. I backtracked to my apartment and opened the safe at the rear of the bedroom closet.

I don't normally go around packing a weapon. Carrying a pistol is too likely to encourage misunderstandings. I've been in this business too long, though, not to appreciate the fact that sometimes circumstances dictate otherwise. The fact that I've survived in the business as long as I have is due at least in part to knowing when to carry and being ready to use that weapon when it's needed. The safe contains a small but efficient armory. I settled on my favorite weapon, a needle gun.

A needle gun shoots small darts called flechettes. It's a finicky weapon with a limited range, but it's almost silent in operation which is why it's a favorite with professional assassins. Most people these days prefer the good old laser pistol. They're almost foolproof to use, have a range of hundreds of meters, and, depending on the size of the power pack can be fired hundreds of times. The down side is that unless you are talking about a military unit with an external power unit or weighs a couple of kilos, the rate of fire is limited to a couple of shots a minute. A typical needle gun only carries fifty or so darts, but you can shoot the whole lot off in less than a minute. I've never been in a situation where I've had to shoot more than a dozen or so shots, so the size of the magazine has never been an issue.

Unlike a laser pistol where all you have to do is point and shoot, a needle gun takes real skill to use. Hitting a vital spot at more than five meters takes practice. On Star City, there is an additional complication; you have to know what direction you're shooting. Star City is a giant hollow cylinder where everyone lives on the inner surface. The whole thing spins to provide the illusion of gravity through centrifugal force. Shoot in a direction perpendicular to the spin axis and you have to compensate for the drop by aiming high, shoot parallel to the axis and the shot will fly level, but you have to allow for the Coriolis Effect by aiming to the right if you are shooting up the axis and to the left if you're shooting down. Of course, if you're within a few meters of your target it doesn't really matter.

I slipped on the shoulder holster I had had made and slid the needler into the sheathe. With a jacket on, it was virtually undetectable, another advantage the needle gun had over most laser pistols. I locked up the safe and headed to the "Spacer's Lot."

Star City has two ends, the head or up end where the star liners dock and where the best hotels, casinos, and entertainment facilities are, and the other end, variously referred to as the down or working end. If you aren't in polite company sometimes another term is used. This is where the space freighters dock. It's mostly a district of warehouses, repair shops, and the fermentation and growth tanks that supply most of Star City's residents with their food and drink. Along with the warehouses, are a number of establishments that cater to the needs of spacers in port for a few days.

For most people, the term "spacer" conjures up a romantic image that owes more to videos and books than to reality. The truth is that most spacers are hard-working types that spend the majority of their lives confined to a tin-can staring at the same half-dozen faces day after day. When they hit port, they are as likely to go see a concert or visit a museum as go on a bender or seek a paid companion. The "Spacer's Lot" wasn't the kind of place for them. It catered to the five percent who wanted cheap booze, a sleazy bed-mate, and maybe a fight to liven things up. It also catered to those who skirted the limits of the law.

Now Star City has a pretty relaxed attitude towards things like recreational drugs, pornography, or other items that might be proscribed by some governments. Tariffs are minimal and restrictions, with the exception of heavy weaponry, are few. Smuggling to Star City is pretty limited. Smuggling *from* Star City is a different matter. There is a brisk trade in items that might be legal on one planet but not on another. The authorities turn a blind eye. After all, it's just another form of business. The Spacer's Lot was the kind of bar where arrangements were made for such items to change hands.

It is also the kind of place where when a stranger walks in the door all heads turn to look. For reasons that were obvious, I stood out like a sore thumb, which I had expected. I walked up to the bar and ordered a glass of brown on the rocks. I had no particular intention of drinking it, but I hoped it gave me the illusion of legitimacy.

As a bar went, it was a couple of rungs down from the Blue Moon, and maybe a short step below Loo's. It was dark, the floor was sticky with spilled booze, and most of the noise and light was coming from a huge screen on the back wall that was projecting some sort of sporting event I was unfamiliar with. Every so often there would be a collective groan or cheer in response to something that happened on the screen. The crowd was exclusively human, which wasn't surprising, spacers aren't a particularly tolerant lot, but a thousand years of spreading out into the galaxy had produced enough variation that it wasn't always easy to tell who was non-human.

After five minutes or so of staring at my drink I motioned to the bartender.

"Something wrong with the drink, mister?" he asked belligerently. "You don't like it you can go someplace else."

"No the drink is fine," I assured him. "The fact is, I'm looking for someone. I was told I might find him here."

"Look all you want, Mister. It's your funeral."

"His name is Georgi. Maybe calls himself Captain Georgi. Have you seen him?"

"What you want with him?"

"I want to do a little business, that's all. If you point him out to me, you can keep the change." I'd placed a Crockett ten-spot on the bar next to my glass.

The bartender looked at me, looked at the bill, and made some quick mental calculations. His hand shot out, but mine was faster.

"Table in the back corner. Guy with no hair."

I said, "Thanks," as I released my hold on the ten-spot.

I headed over to the table where Georgi was sitting with two men, one a short thin guy that looked like a weasel, the other obviously hired muscle. The weasel had a 50K Joule laser stuck in his belt. I couldn't see what the muscle was packing underneath his loose jacket, but I recognized the bulge of a holster below his armpit.

"Are you Georgi?" I said, setting my glass on the table.

"What's it to you?" the weasel replied.

"It's just that I've got a few questions for him."

"Beat it, mister. We don't deal in questions." This was from the muscle.

"Oh, I've got enough questions for now. It's the answers I'm looking for."

"Oh a smart guy," the weasel said, reaching for his pistol.

I was quicker. The needle took him in his hand, pinning it to his belt. He wouldn't die, but it would be a while before he used that hand again. The muscle started to stand, but froze halfway up when he saw the end of the needlegun pointed at his eye. Hitting someone in the eye with a flechette is a sure kill shot.

"You got a lot of nerve, mister," Georgi finally spoke.

"I've been told that a time or two," I countered.

"You think you can take on this whole place?" Someone had paused the game on the screen and everyone was looking at the action at the table.

"No, probably not. But I can take maybe a half-dozen with me. The question is, how many of these gents are willing to risk being among that half-dozen. Of course, you might be the first."

Georgi thought about that. He nodded at the muscle, who sank back into his chair. The game on the screen started playing again.

"OK, Mr. Brave Guy. What's this question you've got?"

"Sometime recently you sold a neurotoxin to someone. I want the name of the someone. That's all."

"My clients' names are my business, mister."

"Well, it's kind of my business, too, in this case. He tried to use the stuff on me. That's what I want to talk to him about."

"And if I give you the name?"

"I give you a hundred dollars Crockett and I walk out of here."

"And if I don't?"

"Then we might have to have some further discussion on the subject."

"You threaten me?"

"If I need to. I'm hoping it won't come to that."

Georgi tried to stare me down. I wasn't budging. Finally he must have decided that I had more to lose than he did.

"OK, Mr. Brave Guy. This guy came in, said he had heard I had some rare stuff. Asked about a Lizardman neurotoxin. I sold him a capsule. 50 milliliters."

"This guy have a name?"

"He said it was Jorgensen."

"Was it? I assume you checked to make sure you're customers are legit?"

"I'm no chump, mister. That wasn't his real name. His real name was John Smith. Go figure. He works as the house dick at the Commodore Hotel. We done here?"

"If what you told me is true. Here's a hundred. I'll throw in an extra twenty so weasel here can pay an Autodoc. He'd better have that hand seen to soon if he wants to keep the use of his fingers."

I dropped the cash on the table and backed out of the bar. It wasn't until I was a block away that I slid the needler back into the holster.

It seemed like there was no time like the present, so I caught an up-city tram and headed toward the Commodore Hotel.

The night clerk manning the front desk wasn't the same as the one who had been on duty the night Mrs. Winterd had been killed so he didn't recognize me, which was probably just as well. This one was wide-eyed and perhaps just a little too well groomed. I waved my P.I. license in front of him, which got his attention. The ten spot I slipped across the counter got even more attention.

"I understand that John Smith is the House Detective here. I'd like to speak to him if I may."

"I'm afraid that won't be possible, Mr. Sladek," the clerk responded prissily. He seemed to be trying to decide whether to maintain his professional reticence to divulge information or take the opportunity to break the night shift's boredom.

"Might I ask why?"

"I'm afraid Mr. Smith no longer is employed by the Commodore."

"Oh? Did he leave a forwarding address?"

"No, but that wouldn't do you much good, anyway. He's not on Star City any more. He took a starliner to Dakota or Lakota or some such planet."

Dakota was a world that had been colonized recently enough that it was still considered the frontier. It was just the kind of place where a man with enough cash could recreate himself as another person, someone untraceable.

"Kind of sudden, wasn't it? He was working here only a few days ago."

"Yes. I thought so myself. From what I heard he said that he'd come into some money recently and had decided to start a ranch or a plantation or something like that. He persuaded Dolores, one of the housekeeping staff, to go with him. It all sounded very exciting. Too exciting for me, I'm afraid."

"This Dolores, she wouldn't have happened to work nights, would she?"

"Why, yes. Now that you mention it, she did work the night shift. The upper floors where the nicer rooms are."

"That figures," I said under my breath. It was pretty clear that Smith had used the housekeeper to gain access to the room to place the poisoned Champagne. No one would ever question housekeeping entering a room no matter what time of day it was.

"Pardon?" the clerk asked puzzled.

"Oh, nothing. Just thinking out loud."

"I'm afraid a new house detective hasn't been hired to replace Mr. Smith. Is there anything else I can do for you, Mr. Sladek?"

"No. I don't believe there is. Thanks for your help." To show my appreciation I laid another ten spot on the counter. The clerk folded it neatly and placed it in his inside jacket pocket next to its twin.

I said good night and left. Outside on the sidewalk, I started to turn left towards Vik's, but thought better of it and turned right.

A quick check on my comm unit confirmed that a starliner had left for Dakota the night before while I'd been cooling my heels at police headquarters. Dakota was a good distance away, and the ship would be in translight space for the next couple of weeks and incommunicado. Even if Latimer sent a message on the next ship, Smith would have had plenty of time to disappear into the bush by the time it arrived. It probably wouldn't do much good, anyhow. Extradition between star systems was problematic at best. Latimer would want to get the case out of his hair long before Smith could be brought back, assuming that he could even be found.

Without the house dick, I'd be hard put to make any sort of case against Winterd, at least one that Latimer would act on. It might be possible to trace a payment from Winterd to Smith, but I doubted it. On Star City, there are just too many ways to conceal cash flow.

I'd have to think up something fast, or Latimer would find a way to pin the whole business on me. Winterd had set me up as a patsy real good, and it was clear that I wasn't going to get out of the mess I'd found myself in by detective work. I'd have to solve my problem by other means. I decided to walk home to give myself time to think.

There's an old saying, or maybe it isn't one but should be, "When you can't count on your friends, it's time to turn to your enemies." Viktor Martian wasn't exactly an enemy, but I certainly had run out of friends, at least for the moment. There was one thing I was pretty sure about, Viktor Martian and Samuel Winterd weren't talking to each other. It was time to play that to my advantage.

One of the quirks of Star City is that, though they may turn down the glow tubes that run down the central axis to provide an artificial day/night cycle that matches Earth, the city itself never really sleeps, particularly those businesses that cater to passengers in transit. With starliners arriving and departing at all hours of the day businesses such as restaurants and hotels operate on a twenty four hour basis to supply the needs of their passengers whether they're on Star City for a few hours or a few days. This is particularly true of the casinos, where the blackjack games never stop and the roulette wheels never stop spinning.

Despite the fact that it was 0200 by the time I got there, Viktor's was a brightly lit and busy as ever.

The bouncer on the door gave me the evil-eye when I walked in. Fortunately, I had stopped at my apartment to change. The Spacer's Lot hadn't exactly been the sort of place you wear evening dress to. Still, I wasn't exactly the sort of customer Viktor's catered to. The fact that I still had the needle gun tucked into its rig didn't allay his suspicions any.

"Just tell Viktor that Frank Sladek is here to see him."

"And he's supposed to know who that is?"

"Tell him that Bonnie Winterd sent me." This confused the bouncer. I don't know how closely someone in his profession followed the news, but the word of Mrs. Winterd's death had gotten around pretty quickly. Things like that always do. The bouncer whispered something I couldn't hear into his sleeve and then spent a few moments staring into blank space while the reply came back.

"Mr. Martian will see you. Someone will be here to escort you to his office in a moment."

It was more like five minutes, but two guys, obviously hired muscle and obviously a cut above the doorman showed up. Without even asking, one of them reached in and relieved me of my needle gun. I didn't resist. That was actually part of the plan. We headed upstairs, one of the musclemen leading the way while the other followed.

Viktor's office is about what you'd expect in a profitable but not particularly respectable casino. It was large, larger than my apartment, and decorated in a style that can best be described as cheap and flashy. There was wall to wall white carpet three centimeters thick and a row of fake windows in one wall that displayed a landscape that had never been within a hundred light years of Star City. On the opposite wall was a reproduction of a painting by Lucinda. I could tell that it was a reproduction because I own a couple of originals, but that's another story.

Viktor, himself, was sitting behind a desk that was all glass and chrome, so constructed that the top just seemed to float in mid air. I've heard the style described as mid-century modern, but I can't remember what century it's supposed to be. Viktor nodded at the hired help and they withdrew, then he motioned me to a surprisingly comfortable chair across from him.

"I know you're supposed to be some kind of private dick, Sladek, but I don't know what business you have with me."

"It's about the murder of Mrs. Winterd," I opened. "I believe she was a frequent customer here."

"So are a lot of people, Sladek. I didn't have anything to do with her death."

"Oh, I know that, Viktor. The problem is the cops don't."

"Are you trying to put the touch on me?"

"No. Or at least not in the way you mean. It's like this. I was with her that night. The poisoned bubbly was intended as much for me as it was for Mrs. Winterd, only I was just going to be an incidental casualty that could serve as a fall guy. But that isn't necessarily going to fly now, so the killer is looking for someone new to take the fall. That's someone is probably you."

"Me? Like I said, I had nothing to do with it."

"You know that and I know that, but do you think that's going to cut any ice with the cops? You know what the law is like in this town, especially if you have money."

"It sounds like you know who the killer is."

"Oh, I do. The house dick at the Commodore, him or his girl friend who worked there as a housekeeper. Not that I can prove it. Wouldn't matter anyway. They both took a powder on the first starliner to leave the docking ring. More importantly, though, I know who paid for the job. That's why I'm here."

"The suspense is killing me, Sladek. Who's behind Mrs. Winterd's death."

"Samuel Winterd." I said it quietly, matter-of-factly.

"Why would he kill his own wife? It doesn't make sense."

"It does if he wanted to get rid of her without the expense of a big divorce settlement. Even on Star City he'd have to figure that he'd be out a couple of million to his wife and probably as much to the lawyers while they fought it out in court. With her dead at the hand of some unknown schlep like me he's not out a thing other than what he paid Smith, and I doubt that that was more than 100K Crockett."

"OK. Suppose for a moment that I accept that old man Winterd killed his own wife," Viktor said. From the way he said it I could tell there wasn't much doubt in his mind that I was right. "What's it to me?"

"Like I said, the original plan was that the death was going to look like natural causes. Failing that, the blame was going to fall on me. Maybe as a murder-suicide. Maybe as a contract job by 'unknown parties.' Except I queered that pitch by remaining alive. So now Winterd is getting nervous and the best way to settle things is to give the cops someone to pin it on, someone big enough to be believable but without enough clout to counter the move. That someone is you, Viktor Martian. Let's face it, with our police, a thing doesn't have to be true, it just has to be plausible."

"Why me?"

"Like I said, it has to be something the cops can sell to the prosecutor's office. It's well known that Mrs. Winterd had been a frequent customer at your place. Maybe Winterd thought the relationship between you and his wife was too close. Or too public. There's also the fact that you've been blackmailing her."

"Who told you that?"

"Bonnie did. The night she died."

"Look, that was only small time. I knew a little something about her past. I leveraged it, but only in a small way. A few hundred here, a few hundred there. Cash flow has been tight lately. She'd lost or won more than that in a night down on the casino floor plenty of times. It was certainly nothing worth killing someone over. Bonnie and I were friends."

"Does it really matter that it was small potatoes. Blackmail provides a motive for the cops. They'll figure that maybe she was pushing back, or maybe she was threatening to expose you. If word got out that Viktor Martian was a blackmailer half your clientele might go elsewhere. It's not like there aren't other casinos on Star City. So you killed her before it got embarrassing."

"But I didn't."

"Like I said before, you know it and I know it, and the cops don't care. They just want to clear the case quickly and quietly."

"Alright. Maybe what you're saying is true. What's your angle? Why come to me?"

"Because I'm running out of friends, Viktor. Samuel Winterd planned for me to die in that hotel room. The only reason I'm not dead is that I prefer brown on the rocks over Champagne. Now, I resent it when people try to kill me. I take it personal. Especially when I was being played as a patsy. I resent that almost as much as the attempt to kill me. So anything I can do to throw a spanner in the works suits me just fine. There's nothing I can do against a man like Samuel Winterd. He's got too much money, too much power, and too many connections. You've got more of all three than I do. So I come to you and give you a friendly warning hoping that maybe you can do something before the cops have the case wrapped up and tied up with a bow."

I could see Martian thinking it over. He wasn't sweating, but he was worried. Everything I had told him was plausible because most of it was true. The rest, well the rest *could* be true, especially if I gave it a nudge.

"That's mighty green of you, Sladek. I won't forget."

"I'm just acting in my own self-interest," I said, which was the absolute truth.

"Still, I appreciate it. Look, here's a couple of hundred in chips. Try your luck downstairs. And I'll let them know that anything you want from the bar is on the house."

We shook hands and he called back the two goons that had been waiting outside the door. He whispered something to one of them who looked surprised. He reached into his jacket, pulled out my needler and handed it to me butt first. I tucked it away smiling and let myself be escorted down to the casino floor.

It only took me about fifteen minutes to run through the stack of chips, which just goes to prove that gambling is for suckers. I tossed my last chip to the dealer as a tip and headed to the bar. I'd been trying to act casual all evening, but I felt the need for a drink.

As long as it was on the house, I thought I might as well treat myself.

"What's good, Glzz?" I asked when the four-armed bartender came to take my order.

"What kind stuff you like, Sladek?" The voice was kind of buzzy and it wasn't coming from his mouth.

"Hey, I didn't think you could talk," I said in surprise.

"No talk. Synthesizer." Now that he had said it I could tell. There was a tiny keyboard attached to a belt that was strapped around his middle which he worked with whichever of his four arms wasn't busy.

"So how come I never heard you talk before?"

"Glzz not talk, people not talk back. Most people boring. What you want?"

I ordered an expensive brandy from Crockett that I'd heard about but never sampled. Glzz looked disappointed.

"Glzz hurt. Glzz best mixologist in galaxy and Sladek just want brandy. Not even ice."

"OK. Be inventive. Just nothing that's green or glows."

Glzz's arms went to work, two fetching bottles and two working a shaker. He went at it for a couple of minutes and people at the bar were starting to stare. Finally he emptied the shaker into a martini glass the size of a soup bowl. It wasn't green and it didn't glow. Instead, it was thick and cloudy. Occasional bubbles would break to the surface releasing small clouds of pearlescent vapor. I took a hesitant sip. It wasn't half bad.

Before I stumbled home, Glzz had plied me with three more of his concoctions. It was a wonder I could find my apartment.

I woke with a head that felt like it had been turned inside out. It didn't matter; half my plan had been accomplished. It was time for the second part. I brewed a pot of Joe and took a couple of magic pills. By the time I had put away a plate of egg powder scramble I could almost focus again. I got my comm unit out and called Samuel Winterd. To show you how rich the guy was, he actually had a live woman answering his comm. She tried to foist me off to an auto attendant, but I mentioned that I was calling about Mrs. Winterd. There was a moment of silence, and then I was put through.

"I don't know what you're playing at, Sladek, but our business arrangement is done. I've nothing more to say on the subject."

"But I do, Mr. Winterd," I said, trying to sound respectful and subservient.

"And just what might that be? You weren't able to protect my wife."

"Like I said, I wasn't hired to protect your wife. I was hired to protect you from embarrassment. That's what I plan to do, if you'll let me."

"Alright. Say your piece, Sladek. You've got two minutes."

"You've heard about Viktor Martian. He owns Vik's."

"I've heard of him." There was a sour note in his voice.

"Well, he was the one blackmailing your wife."

"My wife is dead, Sladek. I don't think there's anything more he can do along that line."

"No, but he might be able to blackmail you."

"Just what is that supposed to mean, Sladek?"

"It seems that Martian has dug up some information about a man by the name of John Smith. He used to be the house detective at the Commodore Hotel before he took off for parts unknown. He's the one that provided the Champagne with the neurotoxin that killed your wife and nearly did the same for me."

"Well, if you know this, why don't you go to the police?"

"The police and I aren't on the best of terms right now, Mr. Winterd. But that's neither here nor there. It also seems that Martian thinks he has information tying Smith to you, information that the police might construe as implicating you in your wife's death."

"That's a lie, Sladek."

"Maybe. But the police might not see it that way."

"Is that a threat, Sladek?"

"No. It's a warning. If the police turn their attention to you, I might be dragged in. After all, I was in that hotel room, too, and you *did* hire me. If you go out the garbage chute, I might be dragged down with you."

"I see. Well we wouldn't want that, would we?"

"No, we wouldn't."

"What do you want, Sladek?"

"It might be the best thing for both of us if I were to disappear, at least until things blow over. If the cops can't find me, they'll look for someone else to hang the crime on. Someone like Viktor Martian."

"Am I to take it that you're short of funds?"

"I didn't say that, Mr. Winterd."

"But if I were to, say, deposit five thousand credits into your account that might facilitate matters."

"It wouldn't hurt."

"Consider it done, Sladek. And it might be best if you don't call me again."

"I'll keep that in mind." The link went dead before I had finished.

They say the best way to hook a fish is to make the lure believable, though why one would want to hook a fish is something I, as a poor boy raised on Star City, wouldn't know about. By pretending that I was only interested in money I was acting in a manner that Winterd would find completely believable. Now all I had to do was wait and see if I had landed my fish.

The seeds, as they say, had been sown, but not yet brought to fruition. Not that I have any idea what all that horticultural talk means. I was born and bred on Star City where the only place food grows is in the vats at the ass end of the city. No seeds, no soil, just cells multiplying ad infinitum until scooped out and processed for consumption.

I had created an atmosphere of mutual suspicion between Winterd and Martian, but what I needed to do was bring them into contact with each other, and I needed to do it quickly before Latimer came breathing down my neck again. I figured that if I got the two of them face to face nature would take its course.

What I did next isn't strictly legal, but this being Star City, it wasn't exactly illegal, either. Very little is. Once upon a time, I had downloaded spoofing software onto my comm. I don't understand how it works, and I don't need to, but what it does is make it appear like someone else is doing the talking when I made a call. Using stored data, it replaces my image and voice with another person's. Of course it replaces the calling address as well, so the person on the other end of the link has no idea that it isn't the real thing. Sure, experts can sort things out later, but it's nothing that can be done from a regular comm.

Imitating Winterd would be no problem. I had received enough calls from him that my comm had all the stored data that it needed to create a very convincing simulacrum of the businessman. I hadn't talked with Martian over the comm, so I had to be content with what I could grab from the cloud. It probably didn't matter, though, because I didn't think that Winterd had ever met Martian, so the little nuances of his speech patterns wouldn't be needed.

I called Martian first. Without waiting to introduce myself, as soon as the link was up I opened with:

"You won't get away with it, Martian." It's a little weird hearing the echo of what you say bounce back in another person's voice, but the software seemed to get Winterd's bluster just right.

"Who is this?" Martian asked, puzzled and a little annoyed.

"This is Samuel Winterd. I know you were blackmailing my wife, but I won't let you pull the same thing on me."

"Look. I don't know where you got your information from, but you've got it all wrong. I wasn't blackmailing your wife and I have no intention of blackmailing you." Running a gambling house, Martian had had a lot of practice dealing with irate customers, and I could tell he was using those skills now, trying to placate Winterd while not saying anything he might regret later.

I, of course, was not operating under any such restraints.

"I've had my eye on you, and I know you were blackmailing my wife. For all I know, you were the one responsible for her death. I'm warning you, Martian; I'll go to the authorities if you try anything on me."

"You can't pin the murder on me, Winterd. I've got my sources, too. From what I've heard, you were the one behind her poisoning. If the bulls look into where John Smith got the cash to take a powder, they'll find it all leads back to you. I know more than you think, and I can go to the 'authorities' too."

"Are you threatening me, Martian?" The software was really working. My words in Winterd's voice were positively seething with anger.

"Take it any way you like, Winterd. I don't know what Bonnie ever saw in you. She deserved better."

Things were bubbling up nicely. Martian had dropped his cool public persona and was taking things personally. I didn't want to overplay my role, but my next words were:

"You leave my wife out of this, Martian. This is between the two of us."

"I'm warning you, Winterd, you come around threatening me, and I'll kill you."

I broke the connection. I figured that I'd gotten Martian in exactly the frame of mind I wanted. I diddled with the profile on the software and placed a call to Winterd. Winterd must have been half expecting a call, because it bypassed his receptionist based on the caller id.

"What do you want, Mr. Martian? I'm a busy man."

"So I've heard, Mr. Winterd." The software got the sarcastic tone just right as it replaced my words with Martian's voice.

"Just what is that supposed to mean?"

"I know about John Smith. I know about the poison."

"I don't know what you're talking about. What's your point?"

"I know that you paid Smith to put the poisoned Champagne in her room at the Commodore. The police don't know that yet, but I'm sure they'd be interested."

"Are you threatening me, Martian?"

"Let's just say that I'm talking about what *could* happen unless we come to an arrangement."

"Why you little weasel—"

"That's no way to talk to someone you want to do business with, Mr. Winterd."

"Who says I want to do business with you?"

"I'll deal with someone, Winterd. You or the cops. One thing is certain; I'm not going to take the fall for your wife's death. Pin it on that low-rent shamus you had working for you if you like, but don't try to pin it on me. I'll make sure it's you that they shove out the garbage chute if you try it."

I thought that calling myself a low-rent shamus was a nice touch.

"Just what do you want, Martian?"

"Now you're seeing reason. What I want is twenty-five large in dollars Crockett, and I want it tonight."

"And if I don't?"

"I hear Sergeant Latimer is the detective on the case."

"All right, Martian. I'll pay. This once. I'll send the money over."

"No. You'd better bring it yourself. I don't think either one of us wants to bring more people into this business. Tonight, my casino, 2100. I'll be expecting you."

"Alright. 2100 hundred. I'll be there. What about Sladek?"

"You hired him. He's your problem."

Well, I guess I knew where I stood with. The link broke. I didn't know if Winterd really intended to pay, but I didn't doubt that he'd be there.

After I finished the calls I looked at the clock. I had a few hours to kill. I took a long, hot shower. With Winterd's five grand in the bank I could afford the water bill. After that I made myself a steak. Not the real thing, of course. Like booze, meat on Star City comes out of a vat unless you're rich. It comes in brown or 'beef,' white or 'chicken' and pink or 'pork' flavors. There's also something called 'fish.' There's some pretty good tube meat called 'sausage,' but you don't want to ask what goes into it. I fried up some starch cubes to go with the steak. A meal like that calls for a nice red 'wine' but I thought it best to keep my head clear, and I stuck to Joe.

After dinner, I got dressed, shirt, trousers, my evening jacket, the shoulder holster that fits under it. I slipped my needle gun into the holster after checking to make sure it was charged and the magazine was full. I figured that both Winterd and Martian would be packing laser pistols. Most people do. The needle gun didn't have the range, but the cops wouldn't be able to pin any stray shots on me. I checked myself in the mirror, made sure the needler wasn't obvious, and gave my hair one last pat.

I got to Viktor's in plenty of time to get a front row seat. Of course, I was the only one who knew there was going to be a show.

I slid into a seat at the bar and turned around to make sure I had a good view of the casino floor. Satisfied, I turned back and caught Glzz's eye.

"Mr. Sladek. You becoming regular," his synthesizer buzzed. "What you want?"

"Oh, I don't know. Surprise me."

Glzz came back a few moments later and slid a glass across the bar. It was brown on the rocks. He started his routine of polishing two glasses at once using pairs of opposing arms. It's always hard to read the expression of an alien, especially when, as in the case of Glzz, you've only come across one example, but I seemed to catch a hint of excitement in the bartender's green visage.

"Why you here, Sladek? Something up?"

"Does a fellow need a reason? Maybe I'm just here for your sparkling conversation, Glzz."

"You no fool Glzz. You got look like feline consumed canary, Sladek. You got something planned."

"Not me. I'm just sitting here having a drink."

"Sure thing. Glzz be worried?"

"Nothing to concern you, Glzz."

"OK. I got customer other end of bar."

"Oh, Glzz."

"Yes?"

"If I say duck, don't hesitate. OK?"

"Sure thing." Glzz went to deal with his customer, still polishing the same pair of glasses.

I turned back to watch the casino floor. Viktor Martian was out in the middle talking to a couple of his pit bosses. Every once in a while he'd throw a greeting to one of the customers like nothing was up. I did notice that the two musclemen that had escorted me to his office earlier had taken up positions at opposite ends of the room where they could watch the floor.

There was a big clock up high on the wall, one of the old-fashioned kind with hands. The big hand was pointing straight up while the other was pointing at the nine. I did some quick arithmetic and came up with 2100.

Winterd was prompt. It must have been the businessman in him. He stopped and asked a question of the hostess at the steps leading down to the gaming floor. She pointed a hand at where Viktor was standing. Winterd thanked her and slipped a bill into her hand.

Right after Winterd entered I noticed the two newcomers that were following in his wake. They didn't look like hired muscle or bodyguards, but then the best ones never do. These two looked like a pair of fit athletes in their late twenties out for a night on the town, but they were wearing tailored evening jackets that couldn't quite conceal the lasers hidden underneath. I wondered how they had gotten past the bouncer at the door.

Winterd crossed the floor to where Viktor was talking to the pit bosses. Martian didn't so much see him as sense his approach. He waved his employees away and turned to face Winterd.

I was too far away to hear what they were saying, at least at first, but the conversation quickly got heated. Some of the gamblers in the neighborhood got nervous and started to edge away. Most of the rest of the patrons turned to see what the commotion was about.

Now most gunfights take less time to happen than it does to tell about them. This one was no different. Winterd and moved around so that his back was towards me and he was between Viktor and myself, so I didn't see exactly what happened, but suddenly Winterd appeared to shove Martian. The two were standing that close, less than an arm's length away.

From where I sat, it looked like they both went for their lasers at the same time. Neither had time to aim, but at that range it really didn't matter. There was that peculiar snap that happens when the capacitor discharges as a laser pistol fires. A spot appeared in Winterd's back right about where the heart is and a hole appeared in the shade of a light fixture over one of the craps tables. Winterd's shot must have counted, too, because Viktor's body started to slump.

The two men that had followed Winterd had their own pistols out, as did Viktor's muscle that had been watching the floor. A couple of more shots cut the air, and one of the casino men went down.

By this time the crowd had realized what was happening, and bodies were flying everywhere as people dove for cover. There was a lot of screaming going on, and it wasn't just the women.

Most of the patrons at the bar were on the floor. Me, I was sitting there with a drink in my hand trying not to look like a threat to anyone. It took a couple of seconds for the lasers to cycle and then there was another flurry of shots. One of Winterd's men went down. The other was still on his feet, but clutching the upper arm of his gun hand.

By this time, Winterd and Martian were dead, and two of the shooters were down. The wounded man got off another shot taking down the second man from the casino. A couple of the bouncers from the front door had responded and the wounded man stood up, his arms held over his head.

And then it was over.

People slowly picked themselves off the floor. A buzz of conversation started. Up until then I hadn't realized how quiet it had gotten. A couple of the women who had fainted needed attending to. Over at one of the roulette tables there was an alien who appeared to have two heads who was demanding that the next roll take place.

A couple of bystanders had been caught in the crossfire, but fortunately, neither was serious. A few people had hit their heads when they dove for cover and were bleeding from scalp wounds. It turned out there was a doctor in the house, a human one and not a machine, and he started wrapping napkins as bandages where needed.

There were a few casualties, but it could have been worse. Only Winterd and Martian were dead.

"What now, Sladek?" Glzz asked. During the shooting he hadn't moved, but he'd stopped polishing the glasses he held.

"Now. I think now it's time to call the police." I got my comm out and called Latimer's number.

It took some time for the police to show up. I guess Latimer must have been chowing down on a tube steak and a cup of Joe at some diner. When they did arrive, Latimer spotted me at the bar and made a straight line for me, Rossetti following in his wake.

"Why is it, Sladek, that every time I get called out for one of your little capers it's like you were rehearsing the last act of Hamlet with live ammunition?" Latimer makes a pretenses of some level of education. At least he can read which is more than I can say of his partner.

"That line's getting a little stale, Latimer. Seems to me I've heard you use it before. Let's just think of it as the 'Scottish Play.' No, on second thought it reminds me more of Othello."

Rossetti chose to chime in, "If you ask me, it's Much Ado About Nothing."

Latimer gave his partner a dirty look. "No one asked you, Rossetti. Why don't you go interview the witnesses while I have a talk with Frank here?"

Rossetti sulked off in a huff. Latimer waited until he was out of earshot before continuing:

"So what's the real story here, Frank?"

"It's like this, Latimer. It seems Viktor was blackmailing Mrs. Winterd in some smalltime sort of way. A few hundred here, a few there. I'm not sure what he had on her, but it was something she decided that it was cheaper to pay off than deal with."

"OK, so Martian was blackmailing her. Blackmailers don't usually croak their victims."

"No, they don't. Somehow Mr. Winterd found out, or at least suspected. That's why he hired me, and that's why I was here the night Mrs. Winterd was poisoned."

"I follow you so far, Frank. But why the dust up tonight?"

"It seems that Vik got a hold of some information about who slipped the neurotoxin in the bubbly. It turns out it was the house dick at the Commodore, a guy named John Smith if you can believe it. Don't bother tracking him down, Latimer. He skipped out on the first starliner along with one of the housekeepers at the hotel. My guess is that whoever hired him to kill Mrs. Winterd paid him enough to blow town."

"OK. So this 'John Smith' did the actual murder. What has that to do with Winterd and Martian dueling it out on the casino floor?"

"Martian got a bright idea. Maybe too bright in retrospect. He thought he could make a connection between Smith and Winterd. Maybe he could. Anyway, his plan was to shake down Winterd for all he was worth."

"And Winterd wasn't buying it?"

"No. Winterd got wind of the plan and must have come here to confront Viktor Martian. I guess the discussion didn't go so well. Both men were packing. I didn't really see who drew first, it all happened so fast. One minute the two of them are arguing over by the roulette tables and the next there's two bodies on the floor and women screaming bloody murder."

"And Frank Sladek just happened to have himself a front row seat."

"More like the balcony. You can see that it's quite a ways from here."

"You expect me to believe you didn't have anything to do with this mess? What were you doing here in the first place? This dive is a little high class for a two-bit shamus like you."

"Me? I was just having a quiet drink. You can ask Glzz here. He makes a marvelous cocktail."

Glzz, who had been idly polishing a pair of glasses in his four hands just nodded and croaked something that sounded like 'glzz.'

"I'd ask you how dumb you think I am, but you'd probably tell me," Latimer commented. "So what has all this got to do with the Winterd dame? Are you telling me that Mr. Winterd poisoned his own wife? Why would he do that?"

"I got the impression that Winterd was beginning to think that his wife was—well, shall we say inconvenient. She had gotten quite a reputation for enjoying the nightlife, and not in the company of her husband, if you get what I mean. Not that I know any of that was true. Sure she gambled and drank, but she could afford it. But people were starting to talk, important people with business dealings with Winterd. I suspect that he found it cheaper to hire someone to kill Mrs. Winterd than to go through a messy divorce and the ensuing settlement."

"You're saying that Winterd paid to have his wife killed, just to avoid a divorce settlement? The powers are going to love that one."

"Well, if you don't like that story, how about this one? Viktor Martian had been blackmailing Mrs. Winterd. She threatened go to her husband and expose him. Being outed as a blackmailer would be bad for business, so he paid Smith to poison her and make it look like her husband had footed the bill. Winterd found out, and confronted Viktor. In a fit of passion he pulls out a laser and shoots Martian, but not before the latter draws his own weapon. The results, two corpses on the floor of the casino. Will that one play any better?"

"Maybe," Latimer answered. I could see the wheels spinning in his head about his chances to sell it to his bosses. "So which story is the true one, Frank? Did Winterd or Martian kill Mrs. Winterd?"

"Tell me this, Latimer; do you really want to know? Both men are dead. They won't be telling any tales. Your chances of tracking down Smith about half as good as winning the Crockett lottery. You aren't going to get any answers in that direction. The way I see it, the real story is whichever way you decide to tell it. You don't have to worry about me revealing any contradictory details. My client is dead. That's when my loyalties end. Pick your poison, Latimer, and I'll go along. Just make sure Rossetti doesn't queer the pitch."

"Leave Rossetti to me, Sladek. He won't cause problems."

"Fine. So which is it?"

"Which is what?"

"Did Samuel Winterd kill his wife, or was it Viktor Martian?"

"What do you think, Frank. Winterd was a well respected businessman, Martian just ran a casino of dubious reputation."

"Yeah. That's what I thought. Care for a drink. Glzz here just came up with a new cocktail in honor of the occasion."

"Naw. I don't drink them fancy things. They're bad for the liver. Besides, I've got to go and ride herd on Rossetti before he mucks things up too badly. See you around, Frank."

Latimer stalked down the stairs to where Rossetti was giving the third degree to some poor four eyed alien who probably didn't speak Terran.

"Care for another, Mr. Sladek? On the house." Glzz's speech synthesizer buzzed.

"Why so generous, if you don't mind my asking?"

"Glzz feeling expansive. Glzz now owns Viktor's. Clause in contract."

"Well, in that case, sure, I'll have another. Got anything that doesn't fizz or glow?"

"Glzz got just the ting, Mr. Sladek. Real Scotch Scotch. From Terra. Fifty years old."

"Sounds fine to me, Glzz. And can the Mr. Sladek. You can call me Frank."

"Sure ting, Frank."

Glzz unlocked a cabinet door in the back bar and pulled out a bottle. It looked like the dust on it was fifty years old, too, and imported as well. He poured three fingers into a snifter and slid it across the bar towards me.

"Salute, Glzz. And congratulations."

THE BIG SCORE

THE BIG SCORE

It was the middle of the afternoon and I was in the Blue Moon staring at the ice melting in a glass of brown sitting on the bar in front of me. Brown is what passes for whiskey on Star City, at least for the low rent crowd, which, as I hadn't worked in a while, I was part of. They make it in a big fermentation vat at the down end of the hollowed out asteroid that I and two million other humans and some fifty thousand other beings call home. It comes out of the vat, gets distilled, and then various adulterants are added for flavor and color as needed. It's all very scientific and efficient. One vat produces brown which is supposed to be whiskey and clear which is meant to be vodka. They also produce "gin" and "tequila," but I've never been particularly fond of either. Now, I've had the real deal on occasion, that is Scotch made in Scotland, or at least on Crockett, from actual grown in the ground malted barley, and even I can tell that there's a difference, but both contain ethanol and both will get you drunk if you drink enough, which is really the point, isn't it?

Anyway, as I was saying, I was staring at the ice melting in my glass when I sensed a presence behind me. I turned to look and saw this short girl standing behind me looking like she was half afraid that I was going to turn around and notice her. I judged her to be twenty-six or twenty-seven, though she looked more like twenty-one, and, in the right outfit could have passed for even younger. I knew immediately that she wasn't a local product. She had the kind of complexion that you can only get from living out in the open under a G-class star; there's just no way that the glow tubes that run down the center of Star City could have produced her absence of pallor. She wasn't wearing gingham, but she looked like she should have been. Despite her small stature, there was an athletic muscularity to her that had to have come from slopping hogs and hoeing a garden or whatever it is people do to survive on agricultural worlds. Her face was that of an innocent, except for the eyes. There was a coldness to them. The only time I'd seen eyes like that had been when I looked in the bathroom mirror that morning. Maybe the coldness had come from butchering pigs, but somehow I doubted it.

"Mr. Sladek?" she said in a voice that quavered slightly.

In response I replied, "Aren't you a little young for a place like this?" I didn't say it with the intent to protect her innocence, I just wasn't sure that I wanted whatever she was selling to interfere with my drinking.

"I'm older than I look, Mr. Sladek. You are Mr. Sladek, aren't you? The man behind the bar said you were."

"That's me, Frank Sladek. There aren't any others that I'm aware of." I straightened up on the bar stool. It was dawning on me that the farm girl might be a paying client.

"You're the man that finds things." She said it as a statement, not a query.

"I've been known to do that on occasion. But only for money. As a rule I don't do charity work."

"I'm willing to pay, Mr. Sladek."

"In that case, why don't we step over to my office where we can have a little privacy." Other than the girl and me there were only two other people in the bar, the barkeep and a guy who'd been drinking something green at the far end of the bar when I came in. I glanced down at him and he was still at it. He was out of earshot and the barkeep knew me well enough not to eavesdrop, but I figured if we sat across from each other I wouldn't get a stiff neck from looking down at the girl.

I picked up my drink and motioned toward one of the booths along the far wall. As she walked across the room I could tell that she hadn't been on Star City long. Star City is a hollowed out asteroid some three kilometers in diameter. The whole thing spins around the long axis to give the illusion of gravity. Natives, such as myself, compensate for the spin automatically, and even long timers move so that you don't notice, but people who have only been on Star City for a short time tend to lean into the spin. It's particularly obvious when they change directions, from moving parallel to the axis to perpendicular to it or vice versa, and they stagger like they're a little drunk. It's a mannerism that the local comedians parody to get a cheap laugh from the locals. We need all the laughs we can get.

She took a seat sitting very straight on the edge of the bench and looking very prim and proper for a low rent bar in the middle of the afternoon on the edge of New Minglewood.

"So what is it that you want me to find, Miss—?"

"It's Penney Schotz, Mr. Sladek, and it's not a what it's a who. You do find people, too, don't you? They said you did."

I was wondering just who this "they" was that had said that, and how Miss Schotz had come to know them. Most of my business comes by word of mouth, but I didn't get the impression that Miss Schotz traveled in those circles.

"Yes, I find people too. Usually when they don't want to be found. Who is it you're looking for?"

"My brother, Mr. Sladek. That's why I came to Star City. I'm not from here, but then you knew that, didn't you?"

"Yes, I knew that, Miss Schotz."

"Do you mind my asking how?"

"Oh, it's a lot of things, Miss Schotz. The way you dress, the way you talk, the way you walk. The fact that you're in a bar like this in the middle of the afternoon. You may not be aware of this, Miss Schotz, but this isn't the best of neighborhoods. A block that way," I pointed in the direction of New Minglewood, "and things get even worse. Don't go that way on your way home, even if it is a shorter distance to a tram stop. Even I don't go that way if I can help it. Go through the Souk, it's a lot safer." The Souk is the part of Star City where most of the non-humans live. Strangely enough, it *is* a lot safer going through the Souk. The residents do a good job of policing themselves to avoid having to deal with the official police.

"I see," she said, though we both knew that she didn't.

"Now that we've established my abilities as a detective, when was the last time you saw your brother?"

"It was two years ago." I didn't ask which planet's year she was talking about. Star City nominally keeps Terran time, but separated as we were from the home planet by hundreds of light years, that's mostly meaningless. On Crockett the days are two hours longer and there are 412 of them in a year. Nifelheim is tidally locked to its sun and orbits it in thirty-two Terran days. As for other planets in other star systems, well you get the idea. What mattered was that it was probably a long time. "That's when he left for Star City."

"Just where did he leave from? Just for the record?"

"I'm from Nebraska, Mr. Sladek," she answered with a mix of pride and shame. Nebraska is an agricultural planet, still pretty raw and relatively sparsely populated. I could understand wanting to get away from a place like that; all that empty space would scare the bejezus out of me. There used to be another Nebraska once, back on Earth, but it sank under the ocean or got eaten by buffalo or something. My knowledge of Terran history has some blank spots.

"Two years is a long time, Miss Schotz," I commented. "What makes you think he's still on Star City?" From Star City there are a lot of places to move on to, that's kind of the point. Lots of people come to Star City to make their fortunes. What they find is that the locals have sewed up all the best graft long ago. Most newcomers move on to greener pastures after six months or so. The ones that don't end up dead or living in New Minglewood, which is worse.

"We kept in touch, but you know what interstellar mail is like—" There is no such thing as interstellar radio, well there is, but it travels at the speed of light so no one uses it. The fastest way to send a message is to put it on a starliner, which can take days or weeks depending on the distance and if there is a direct flight. A place like Nebraska might get a liner from Star City once or twice a month. She went on, "Sometimes it would be several months between letters, but he always wrote or sent a video. But the last one I got was six months ago. At first, I wasn't worried, but then—that's why I came here. I've been here two weeks, but I haven't been able to find him, Mr. Sladek."

She sounded like she was on the verge of tears, which was the last thing I needed.

"In these letters, how did he sound, Miss Schotz?"

"He was disappointed at first. It turned out it was a lot harder for him to get a job than he had thought. I told him he should come home, but he said he wanted to keep trying. Then in the last letter, the one six months ago, he said that he had this big opportunity, that he had a way to make lots of money. He called it a big score."

"Did he say how?"

"No, Mr. Sladek. He said that it was a secret. That he couldn't tell anyone until it was over."

I could just imagine. Star City has a whole sub-culture of con-artists and grifters who make a living fleecing innocent bumpkins fresh off a starliner of their life savings. Mostly, the victims just end up a whole lot poorer, but sometimes things go bad. I was hoping that I wasn't going to end up telling Penney Schotz bad news, but that's the racket I'm in.

"You know, Miss Schotz, maybe your brother left Star City for another planet. There are plenty of places looking for hard working settlers. Communications isn't always the most reliable on some of those places," I said trying to sound hopeful.

"I don't think Tommy would have done that. He wanted to be something more than a farmer or miner or such. He was always more interested in some big deal that would make him a lot of easy money rather than getting a good job or opening a business. That's why he came to Star City. He said this was where the opportunities were. That's why I don't think he's left. Besides, he would have left a message for me before he left, and he didn't do that. I'm sure he's still on Star City, and I want you to find him, Mr. Sladek."

"You know, Miss Schotz, I don't work for free. My daily rate is a hundred twenty credits or a hundred dollars Crockett. Plus expenses. I'll give you an itemize list of those when I'm done, but I'll need an advance before I start an investigation."

"I don't have a lot of money, Mr. Sladek. I had to buy the ticket for the starliner from Nebraska, and things are so much more expensive here than they are back home. I can pay you for five days, maybe six if I can find a job."

"Tell you what. Give me an advance for two days. If I can't find your brother in that time, we can talk about extending the investigation."

"That sounds fair, Mr. Sladek," she said as if we were haggling over the price of a horse or yak or something.

She reached into her purse and pulled out an envelope. She counted out ten Crockett double sawbucks into a nice neat stack. Like most travelers, she had been smart enough to convert her cash into dollars Crockett which are pretty much negotiable anywhere. The bills were so crisp and new that for a moment I wondered if she was trying to pass off counterfeit money in some complicated con, but then that was just the Star City in me thinking. I picked up the stack and tucked it away in my inside jacket pocket.

"I'll need his last known address. An image of him would be helpful, as well."

"I've got a good one on my comm," she said. She pulled a small hand-held from her purse and showed me the screen. There was a picture of herself and a young man. For a brother and sister they didn't look a lot alike. "Tommy" was quite a bit taller and more muscular. He was handsome, too, in a not too bright way. I pulled out my own unit and copied the image over.

"Here's his last address, Mr. Sladek, but I was already there. The manager said she couldn't help me."

"I'll try, anyway. Maybe you didn't know the right questions to ask." Or how to ask them, I thought. People on Star City don't give anything away for free. "Is there anything else that might be helpful?

"I can't think of anything, Mr. Sladek."

"Where are you staying in case I need to get in touch with you?"

She gave me the name of a cheap but mostly respectable residence hotel. It was probably the best place for her.

"I'll be in touch then, Miss Schotz. "It might be best if you leave now."

She stood, holding out one of her small hands. Gestures don't always translate well from planet to planet, but I knew enough to take it in one of my own. Then she left.

I looked down at my drink. All the ice had melted.

The address that she had given me was on the far side of New Minglewood in a district of cheap apartments and cheaper boarding houses. It wasn't surprising that Tommy Schotz had been living there. Most of the residents held jobs on the low end of the economy if they held jobs at all, restaurant and hotel workers, temporaries, that kind of thing. A lot of them were transients, lured by the glamour of Star City and then stuck with the reality of washing dishes and hauling food scraps ten hours a day just to eat, until they got sick of it and moved on to some other world where the grass is greener, or pinker or bluer as the case may be. You might think that most of those kinds of jobs would have been automated centuries ago, but the reality is as long as they can find someone willing to do the work, humans are cheaper. You don't have to tie up capital, and if times get hard you can just show the workers the door. As a kid I'd done enough of that kind of work to know the score. That's why I moved up the food chain be becoming something more respectable, like being a private dick.

I took my own advice, and gave New Minglewood a wide berth. No use tempting fate. Besides, it gave me time to contemplate my new client. It must have taken a lot of guts to leave home and climb aboard a starliner heading for a place where everything was stranger than she could have imagined and where she didn't know a soul. She hadn't said as much, but I was pretty certain that Tommy was all the family she had in the galaxy. Still, it was a long way to come when she must have known deep down that there was a good chance that her brother might not be here, or even be alive. Penney Schotz might look the innocent, but I was pretty certain she was a survivor.

The address turned out to be just what I'd expected, an older five story building divided up into lots of little rooms rented out by the day or the week, no lease and cash in advance. A sign on the door indicated that there were "furnished rooms to let." Furnished would mean a bed and maybe a chair. From the way the paper had yellowed, it had been there a long time. Given the transient nature of the area, there probably was a lot of turnover.

I glanced at my reflection in the dirty glass of the door and decided I had just the right appearance for the lie I was about to tell, respectable in kind of a shabby run-down sort of way, just what you'd expect from a guy doing someone else's legwork.

The front door was unlocked, so I walked in, immediately assaulted by the stale odors of humanity, cheap takeout and booze. It wasn't any too clean, either, but the tenants were paying for space, not hygiene. I found the door with a greasy sign proclaiming "Manager" and knocked.

I could hear the sound of slow footsteps inside, and then the sound of locks being undone. The door swung open a crack, still held by a chain and I could see a sliver of face staring out at me, a face that was somewhere between fifty and ninety and was probably female.

The eye on the face gave me the once over, running from head to feet. It spent a long time on my feet. It turns out you can tell a lot about a person from their shoes. The eye snapped back to my face and said, "Whatever you're selling, mister, I ain't buying."

"I'm not selling anything. I'm looking for some information."

"You don't look like police. You're too handsome for that, sweetie. What's your racket?" She asked the question without any negative implications; on Star City everyone has a racket.

"I'm not from the police. I work for Trans-Stellar Realty. I'm in collections." I showed her a fake I.D. card to back up the lie, the kind that are supposed to be unforgeable, but which you can pick up for five credits if you know the right people. Trans-Stellar was a medium sized property management firm specializing in low-rent apartment buildings. It was just the kind of company that would employ someone to track down deadbeats.

The face in the doorway extended a hand to take the I.D. so that the eye could give it a careful examination, though what she expected to learn I couldn't imagine. Finally, satisfied, the card was handed back.

"So just what kind of information are you looking for, Mr. Oglethorpe?"

"I'm looking for a former tenant of ours who left owing two-weeks rent and damages. His name is Tommy Schotz, and he gave this as his former address."

"Ain't no one by that name lived here. Not since I've been the manager, at least."

"And how long is that?"

"Fourteen years," the voice said with a sigh.

"This would have been more recent than that. Maybe six months ago. I've got an image of him." I showed her the picture Penney had given me.

"Oh, him. Yeah, he had a room here, but he wasn't using the name Tommy Schotz, then. Not that I blame him. He called himself Thomas Van Horn. I knew it was phony, but I didn't care. He could call himself anything he wanted. His money was good, at least at first."

"Perhaps I could come in and talk for a moment?"

"Suit yourself." The door shut, there was the rattle of the chain, and then it swung back to let me in.

It wasn't quite what I had expected. It wasn't luxurious, but the small apartment was surprisingly neat and clean. So to, when I got a look at her, was the manager. Once upon a time she might have even been almost good-looking in a plain sort of way. Now she was just an elderly woman who the years hadn't been kind to. She still tried to maintain appearances, though, including wearing a clean but somewhat threadbare dress in a style twenty years out of date.

"You'll have to excuse me, Mr. Oglethorpe. I wasn't expecting company."

"No apologies are necessary, Ms.—"

"Fenchurch, Ida Fenchurch, and it's Mrs., though Mr. Fenchurch has been dead some fifteen years now. Which is how I came to be living in this hovel."

"Mrs. Fenchurch. I gather from your remarks that Mr. Schotz, or should I say Mr. Van Horn, left owing some money."

"Yeah, he stiffed me good. Thomas could be a sweet talker when he wanted to. Talked me into letting the rent slide for a month. Said he had a big deal in the works and he'd make it up to me. I let him get away with it though it was against my better judgment and the owner's policy. Had to make it up out of my own pocket, too, when he just left one day and didn't come back."

"There wasn't any chance that something had happened to him, was there?" At that point, I figured I could get away with the question, even though it went against my cover story. By then Mrs. Fenchurch and I were no longer strangers. She probably craved human contact more than honesty.

"Oh, I checked. Notified the police. Of course, they didn't have any record of a Thomas Van Horn, but no one of his description had turned up at the hospital or morgue."

"So he just left one day? Didn't say where he was going or anything?"

"No. He used to go out during the day. Looking for work, he said, though I knew better."

"You don't know any of his associates, do you?"

"No. He never brought anyone back to the building. He was a good tenant, that way. No drinking, no loud noises, no women, or men for that matter. He was here for six months before he disappeared. Always reliable. And such nice manners, too. Not like most of the tenants. That's why I trusted him about the rent, though I know it was foolish of me."

"I don't suppose you left his room alone?"

"In a place like this? No, I had it rented within a week. Three different people have been in there since. You wouldn't have found anything, anyway. When he left I checked the room over, you know, looking for things to sell to cover the rent. It was clean as a whistle. He hadn't had that much to begin with, just his clothes, but somehow he managed to get all his stuff out without me noticing."

I got the impression that noticing would have been the kind of thing Mrs. Fenchurch would be good at.

"Yup. The only thing he left behind was a cheap suitcase. Probably realized that I'd be suspicious if he walked out with that. I've got it here, if you'd care to look, but you won't find anything."

She pulled a cheap plastic case out of a closet and set it on the table. She was right about it not telling me anything. It was the kind of thing that was mass produced on a dozen planets. It didn't even have a biometric lock keyed to a thumbprint, just a cheap mechanical one that worked with a key, though any kid with a bent wire could have opened it in seconds. I certainly didn't have any problem. There was a label on the inside from the Acme Luggage Company in New Omaha, Nebraska, but nothing else to reveal Tommy Schotz's past.

"I'm afraid there's nothing else I can tell you about Thomas, Mr. Oglethorpe."

"He never mentioned a sister back on Nebraska, did he?"

"No, he never did talk much about himself, at least about the past. It was always the big deals he was going to pull off in the future."

"No mail?"

"No. Not here, at least. The building isn't wired for net access, either, not that I'd be nosey enough to peak."

"If he was expecting anything he probably used a public info kiosk."

"Probably. That would make sense," she agreed.

"How much rent did he owe?"

"A hundred twenty-five credits. Like I said, I had to make good on that out of my own pocket."

"I'll tell you what, Mrs. Fenchurch. If I manage to track down Thomas I'll see if I can get your money out of him as well as what he owes Trans-Stellar. And if you'll let me take the suitcase, I'll pay you twenty dollars as a deposit on that."

"Oh, that would be much appreciated, Mr. Oglethorpe. I knew you were a gentleman when I first laid eyes on you. I could tell by your shoes. Good honest shoes of a man who stays on his feet all day. And a nice polish job, too."

I slipped her one of the double sawbucks Penney had given me and said my good-byes to Mrs. Fenchurch. As I walked back to my apartment I realized I had come up about as empty as the case I was carrying. The only real bit of information I'd gotten was that Penney's brother had been using an alias. In its self, that wasn't that unusual; lots of people that came to Star City tried to reinvent themselves, including giving themselves new identities, but it looked as if Tommy had done it more than once. The question was why?

When I passed a trash receptacle I dropped the case in it.

It was that time of Star City's artificial year when they started to dim the glow tubes that run down the central spar at about 1800 to produce an artificial twilight in a parody of artificial seasons. All that leg work had made me hungry, so I made a detour to the edge of the Souk where there was a place that served better food than the "meat" sandwiches at the diner by my apartment.

It really wasn't much of a place, a small nook carved out of the corner of the ground floor of an apartment building. There weren't any tables, just a counter and maybe a dozen stools. The place didn't have any windows, either, just a set of metal shutters that were lowered and locked when it wasn't open. There was a sign above the place in some alien script which might have been a name, but could just as easily been a phrase like "Earth Scum Die."

The owner, chef, and only employee wasn't human, which is why the place was in the Souk, the ghetto where most of Star City's alien population lives, as much as by choice as anything else. Not that there weren't humans there, as well. For quite a while there had been a kind of floating artist's colony in the Souk drawn from around human space by the promise of cheap rent and exotic food and drink. Most of them were no talent bums who spent their time boozing and taking recreational drugs and having sex with whoever would consent, but it had produced a few artists of real ability; Lucinda the painter and the writer Marcus Fitzroy being the most prominent examples.

The owner didn't say much, I don't think his vocal apparatus was shaped to fit human speech, which was one of the things I liked about the place. For an alien, he wasn't that different looking, not like a lizard man for instance. He could almost have passed for human except for the lack of eyebrows and a slit where a nose should be, that and the fact that he was thirty centimeters shorter than your average human and had unusually long arms that terminated in three fingers and a thumb on the wrong side. His ancestors must have been arboreal creatures, and the diner had an arrangement of bars behind the counter that he swung from to reach items on the upper shelves. It was kind of entertaining in a way.

He got his meat from the same source as most of the protein eaten on Star City, the great vats at the down end where artificial tissue is grown, but the spices that he used were, well, alien. There was no menu, just a set of big pictures plastered against the wall behind the counter. To order you pointed at an item and held up the appropriate number of fingers or tentacles or whatever to indicate how many. The chef would make a noise like a dying bird and set to work with his knives and pans and whatever. A lot of what he served was stews or soups or casseroles that just needed to be spooned into a bowl from big pots simmering behind the counter.

I pointed at a picture that hadn't disappointed me the last time I'd eaten there and held up one finger. The chef made a face that may have been meant for a grin and ladled a healthy portion of one of the entrees into a bowl. Some more pointing got me a cup of joe to wash it down. What I had ordered was a kind of stew, little cubes of the stuff that pretends to be beef and bigger chunks of what I assumed were some sorts of vegetables. I'd learned long ago not to ask too many questions. It was spicy and maybe a bit greasy, but good in its own way and quite filling. There was also a plate with some little squares of something that wasn't quite bread that you used to wipe the bowl clean when you were done.

For the moment I ignored the problem posed by Penney and Tommy Schotz and concentrated on the food in front of me. It was that time of the evening when there was a lot of foot traffic out, people heading home from work or out looking for dinner. Maybe a third of them were aliens or at least not quite humans like blue-skins. From somewhere down the block came the faint rhythms of a weird alien music that seemed to catch the beat of the passing crowd. It was one of those moments that made me realize I couldn't even imagine living anyplace other than Star City.

As I was mopping up the last bit of stew the owner brought his pad over with the bill on the display. I pressed a credit stick against the induction point and a not unreasonable number of credits were transferred. There were no provisions for a tip, which was another of the things I liked about the place. I headed home.

Back at my apartment, I got down to work. I asked the entertainment unit to play some jive samba, poured myself a tumbler of brown over ice, sat down in my favorite chair and began to work my comm unit.

The boarding house had been a bust. If I was going to find Tommy Schotz, I figured I'd have to start from the other end. The passenger manifests of starliners docking at Star City are all a matter of public record. I didn't think that there would have been many liners from Nebraska during the time in question, and it turned out I was right. Only three ships had arrived during what could reasonably be considered two years ago, and one of them listed a Tommy Schotz as a passenger 4th class, which means that he had shared a compartment with seven other people and a communal dining hall where you ate what they served you. Meanwhile, four decks above, first class passengers dined in elegance to the music of a live orchestra before retiring to their spacious private cabins.

Upon arriving at Star City, Tommy had applied for and been granted a work permit. That was not surprising. The primary requirement for getting a work permit was payment of the fee.

Background checks were optional and almost never undertaken unless the applicant was stupid enough to give the wrong answer to one of the questions on the application form.

A few days later, he had taken a job as a waiter at the Rigel Royal Hotel. With his good looks and charming manner, Tommy Schotz should have made a successful waiter. The Rigel isn't quite the Casino, but it is the type of establishment that caters to well off tourists and business travelers with expense accounts. Tommy would have made a decent living on just the tips, but something had happened and his employment had been terminated after three months.

The reason why wasn't part of the public record, but that didn't stop me. I placed a call to the house detective at the Rigel. We've owed each other favors over the years, and he was more than willing to pass on what he knew about Tommy Schotz. It seems Tommy had been a good waiter, maybe too good a waiter. He'd been popular with diners. One, a fifty-year old widow on a five day layover waiting for a starliner to Dagnabit where her daughter was about to give birth to her first child, had taken a shine to the handsome young man. Tommy had appeared to return the favor to the point of sharing her bed nights after the restaurant closed. She had woken on the morning of her departure to find the handsome waiter gone along with seven hundred dollars in Crockett hundreds and fifties and some fairly expensive jewelry. She had complained to the hotel management, but by that time Tommy Schotz had disappeared for good. I thanked my friend at the Rigel and promised to buy him a drink the next time I was in the neighborhood.

Now a hotel such as the Rigel Royal depends on its reputation. They had made a good faith effort to find Tommy and recover the stolen items. They'd even filed a complaint with the police, who may be lax in some areas but who do take a dim view of those who steal from or defraud wealthy travelers. The fact that Tommy hadn't been apprehended indicated that he wasn't as dumb as he'd looked. Disappearing on Star City isn't easy. After all, there isn't anywhere to go that doesn't involve getting onto a spaceship. It either takes lots of money, far more than the seven hundred dollars he'd stolen and whatever Tommy had gotten fencing the jewelry, or contacts, which he probably hadn't had time to make.

There was, of course, a third option, that Tommy had disappeared into the bowels of New Minglewood, where seven hundred dollars could go a long way, but that hadn't seemed to be Tommy's style. New Minglewood didn't offer much in the way of creature comforts, but it did offer plenty of risk, especially for a young man carrying a large amount of untraceable cash. So what had happened to Tommy Schotz?

Now it's easy enough for someone to change names. A few hundred credits in the right quarters will get an ID and a work permit backed up with the matching entries in the appropriate data bases. They won't necessarily pass a deep investigation, but they would probably be good enough to allow the holder to rent a room or get a job. It was pretty clear that after the incident at the Rigel that Tommy Schotz hadn't been Tommy Schotz any longer. The question was, who was he?

As I said, you can change names for a few hundred credits. You can even change your appearance quite a bit by getting a haircut or changing hair color or growing a moustache or wearing tinted contact lenses. What you can't change, at least not without expensive surgery, is your basic biometric profile, things like height, skull shape, distance between the eyes, the difference in lengths between the first and second finger, those sort of things.

Now it's not widely known, and intentionally so, that all these parameters are recorded upon entry to Star City. They don't show up on ID cards or landing passes, but they are saved in a computer buried somewhere deep in the rock that makes up the shell of the city. Access to this data base is restricted, of course, and civilians like me aren't supposed to be able to make inquiries, but a couple of nice dinners and a few drinks with a woman in the records section had gotten me a valid password. The expense had been well worth it.

Tommy Schotz was tall, but not exceptionally so. His other parameters weren't that unusual, either. When I looked for matches to his profile I came up with a few dozen individuals that fit within the usual margin of error. By eliminating all of those that had a recorded existence before Tommy first arrived, I narrowed that number to just under a dozen. Thomas Van Horn was on the list, of course, but there were others. Of these, one, Eric Miller, had made his first appearance a couple of weeks after Tommy pulled his vanishing act. Interestingly, Eric soon found employment as a bartender at the Cosmos, another top tier hotel. His tenure there had been fairly brief, a mere six weeks, after which Eric Miller disappeared never to be seen again. I didn't have a contact at the Cosmos like I did at the Rigel, but I was beginning to sense a pattern.

Sure enough, a week after Eric vanished, a Howard Silver showed up in the record with a profile that matched Tommy's. He got a job as a bartender at the Far Planets, where he lasted four weeks. After that, I was able to trace three more identities in sequence, all employed at occupations where they would come in contact with wealthy travelers. I knew someone at one of the places of employment and a quick call confirmed that there had been an "incident" where a wealthy woman of a certain age had complained of being robbed of a considerable sum in currency and jewelry by a handsome member of the staff.

This all went on for over a year, and then it stopped as suddenly as it had begun. There seemed to be no one matching Tommy's profile walking the streets of Star City. I did some quick math in my head, taking the average amount that Tommy had lifted from each of his marks, deducting the cut the fence would have taken for pawning the jewelry, living expenses and so forth, adding wages and tips, and the cost of changing ID's after each departure. It was quite possible that Tommy Schotz had built himself up quite a stake during that year. He could have done the smart thing and used it to buy a ticket on a starliner and head for a change of scenery and a fresh set of marks. But he hadn't. Instead, he'd ended up in a cheap rooming house as Thomas Van Horn. He'd lived there for a while, sweet talking the landlady, and then he'd disappeared again. So what was the deal?

I was getting a headache thinking about it, and it was late. I went to bed.

I got up the next morning. Actually, it was almost noon, but close enough. Regular hours have never been a part of my profession. I'd gone about as far as I could electronically. If I was going to locate Tommy, I'd have to apply some good old fashioned leg work. After a quick breakfast of scrambled protein powder and a stiff cup of joe, I was on my way.

I made the rounds of all the hotels where I was on good terms with the house detectives or managers. At one time or another, I'd done work with a number of them, so most were willing to give me some time. Not that it did much good. A few vaguely admitted to the possibility that they might have seen someone who may have looked a little like the image that I showed them, but no one knew his current whereabouts. No one seemed to have seen him for the last half year or so, either. It was all pretty vague and unsatisfying.

After a quick lunch grabbed from a food cart I tried a different approach. I knew that Tommy had been taking jewelry as well as cash from his victims. He'd have had to dispose of the baubles somehow. Star City has plenty of legitimate jewelers, shopping being one of the prime distractions for travelers stuck with a layover, but there are far fewer establishments that deal in merchandise of questionable provenance. Unfortunately, unlike the hotels which are mostly located close to the head end of Star City, these pawn brokers are scattered amongst the poorer neighborhoods that wrap around the middle of the city. Over the span of four hours I must have traveled three times around the circumference of the city visiting them.

The gentlemen that run such establishments tend to be a close mouthed lot. They tend to clam up at the sight of a detective, private or not. Even the handing out a few Crockett sawbucks didn't produce much. The few that knew me personally weren't much better. Again, a few thought such a man might have been in their shop sometime in the past, but of course, they had never bought anything from the man whose picture I showed them.

It was always possible that Tommy had used an intermediary to dispose of the stolen property, though so far I hadn't turned up any evidence of any associate. It was also possible that he'd used a fence in New Minglewood. You could sell anything there, though chances were you'd only get a few cents on the dollar for your trouble. Tommy didn't strike me as the kind that would settle for that if he had options. It was also possible that he had sold off the merchandise to spacers down by the docking ring for freighters at the down end of Star City. That wouldn't have been any riskier than New Minglewood, and the return would have been better. If he had, though, there wouldn't be much chance of tracing the deals; the spacers would be long gone.

After that I tried a few of the upscale bars and lounges up by the hotels where there was a lot of tourist traffic. If Tommy had worked at any of them, he wasn't remembered, but then those kinds of places always have a high turnover in staff. I finally gave it up as pointless and settled for a drink. At the last establishment I'd tried.

The place was a typical lounge, lot's of shiny metal, dancing strings of lights, and syntho-punk playing in the background, in short, everything I hate about that kind of bar. Fortunately, it was too early for the tourists to come looking for a drink. I was the only one at the bar, though there were a couple of guys that looked like salesmen sitting at a table playing with their comp tablets over a pair of glowing drinks the color of lemonade. The bartender looked bored as he inspected his glassware for the third time.

When I ordered a brown over ice he must have recognized me as a local, because after he served me my drink he said:

"Let me see that picture again."

I'd showed him the image of Tommy and Penney earlier, but he'd just glanced at it before saying he'd never seen either one of them before. This time he really looked at the image, studying it as if something puzzled him.

"There was a guy worked here for awhile, maybe six months back, might have been the guy in the picture. But he looked different, like he'd changed his hair color maybe. Still, he might be the same guy. What did you say his name was—the one in the picture?"

"He went by Tommy Schotz back then, but he's used different labels since."

"The guy worked here called himself George Timmson."

"Any idea where I might find the Timmson?"

"Nah. He didn't leave any forwarding address. Just didn't show up for his shift one day. Funny about that, he didn't even collect his last pay voucher."

"Yeah, that is odd. Not many people in your profession can afford to pass up cash like that."

"That's what I thought. That's why it stuck in my mind, like."

"What kind of guy was this Timmson? Was he good with the customers?"

"Oh, he was a real good bartender. Real people skills, especially with the ladies. He had some of the older dames we get in here eating out of his hand. Made a lot in tips."

"That sounds like the guy I'm interested in."

"Say, why are you looking for him, anyway? Is he in some kind of trouble?" the bartender asked, suddenly a little suspicious.

"Nothing like that. His sister is trying to find him. She hasn't heard from him in awhile, and she's worried." Even as I said it, it sounded a little phony to me.

"He never mentioned any sister, but then he didn't talk much about himself. I got the impression he was from one of those backwards sorts of places."

"Why'd you think he might be in some sort of trouble?"

"It's just that a few days after he disappeared a couple of guys came in asking for him. They didn't say why, but there was something about the way they asked it. I got the feeling they might be working for someone. Like hired muscle, you know. I'm pretty sure one of them was carrying a pistol under his coat."

"Are you sure they weren't security?"

"They didn't look like cops to me. Didn't act like it either."

"Did they say who they worked for?"

"They didn't say anything except they were looking for Timmson."

That was interesting. Some of the casinos do run to private enforcement on occasion, but they're usually only too eager to have you know who they are. I was wondering who this pair were. The bartender's description didn't help much, mostly consisting of "big" and "scary." Of course, they probably were. I was also wondering just what Tommy had gotten himself into.

"And they didn't say why they wanted to find him?"

"I didn't ask. Frankly, I just wanted them out of the place."

"I don't blame you."

"Care for another?" the bartender said, returning to business.

"No, I've got to get going." I slipped a Crockett sawbuck across the bar top. "Keep the change." I was happy. I'd gotten more out of him over that drink than I'd gotten the whole day.

"Thanks, mister," the bartender said appreciatively. I nodded and left.

About 1900 I gave it up. It hadn't been a particularly productive day. My feet were sore, I'd spent a good chunk of the expense money I had gotten from Penney Schotz trying to pry non-existent information from various informants, and I was hungry. I didn't feel like cooking, so I grabbed a seat at the counter of the diner on the corner and ordered a slab of grilled "meat" on a bun.

There are two reasons why I eat at that diner. One is that it's convenient to my apartment. The other is that it's consistent. Not good, just consistent. With my expectations low, they never manage to disappoint me. The meat was greasy, the bun that it was sandwiched between was doughy, and the deep fried starch stix were neither soggy or crisp. It was what I had expected and it was what they delivered. I slathered some red sauce on the meat and tried to forget for the moment Tommy Schotz.

I was staring down at my plate so I sensed more than saw that someone large had taken the stool next to me. It was dinner time at a lunch counter, what did I expect. I didn't look around to see who it was, but glancing at the stainless steel of the machine they use to make joe I thought I recognized the reflection.

"What do you want, Latimer?"

Latimer is a detective sergeant on the Homicide Squad. To say that we have a complex relationship would be one way of putting it. Another would be to say that we are a pain in each other's butts. Still, we've managed a fragile kind of detente over the years. At least most of the time.

"I'd like a nice steak with some real vegetables. Maybe a glass of red wine."

"Sorry to disappoint you, but you're not going to get that here."

There was a loud sigh. "No, I suppose not." The counterman came over and Latimer gave his order, a boiled tube of meat and a cup of joe. A wise choice, the tubular meat was particularly inoffensive, almost a specialty of the house.

After the counterman had gone I said, "You don't usually come slumming unless something's on your mind. What is it?"

"Tommy Schotz."

"What about him?" I said, trying to sound incurious.

"I hear that you've been asking around for him."

"That's a matter between me and my client, Latimer. What makes you think I'm looking for this Tommy Schotz, anyway?"

"Come off it, Frank. You think we don't keep track of that bootleg password you use to get into the security data base?"

There went another of my illusions, shattered just like all the rest.

"OK. So maybe I've been trying to find Tommy Schotz. What's it to you? From what I've uncovered, he's a pretty small fish. Makes his graft getting middle aged women to ask him up to their rooms and then raiding their purses before skipping out. Not in your usual league, Latimer."

"Yeah. That's the way he started out. But, with time, he's gotten bolder. He tried to get one of his old ladies to withdraw money for him. His charm wasn't enough, so he got rough. She was hurt pretty bad. That's bad for business, and what's bad for business is bad for Star City."

I knew where Latimer was coming from. Star City's reputation was pretty much all she had. The hotels, casinos and starliner companies were concerned that the passengers that they depended on for their livelihood enjoyed a safe and comfortable experience during their layovers, or at least the wealthy ones. Without those passengers, there wasn't any reason for Star City to exist. There was too much invested and too much money to be made to let that happen.

"I've never met him, but Tommy Schotz doesn't strike me as the violent type."

"Think again, Sladek. The last old lady he took advantage of ended up dead. Her body was found in an alley about five months ago. I've been looking for Schotz ever since."

I didn't say anything, but suddenly it was all starting to make sense. Tommy had grown tired of taking a few credits off of the women that he'd meet working in the hotels. He tried to get more, but he'd gotten careless or callous and it had ended up badly. Either that or he'd gotten desperate. Maybe that had something to do with the muscle that had come looking for him.

"What's your interest in Schotz, anyway, Frank?" Latimer asked between mouthfuls of his tube steak.

"His sister, Penney Schotz, came here from Nebraska looking for him. She hired me to find him."

"Tommy Schotz doesn't have a sister, Frank. When we figured out which name he had entered on we checked into him. The authorities on Nebraska sent us his complete file. Tommy Schotz was an orphan. He didn't have any family. The only relation he had was a wife, and he abandoned her."

I stopped with my sandwich halfway to my mouth. I put the bun down.

"What's this wife like? Was it in the record?"

"Yeah. She's a small woman. Be about twenty-seven in Terran years. That match your client?"

"Yeah. Looks like I've been played for a sap, Latimer."

"Wouldn't be the first time, Frank."

"No, I guess not. What do want from me, Latimer. I don't know where Tommy is. I spent the last two days trying to pick up a cold trail."

"It'll get colder if I find him," Latimer said. We both knew what he meant. Star City takes a dim view of those who kill paying customers.

"You've haven't heard of this Tommy being in any other sort of trouble have you?"

"Like what?"

"Oh, I don't know. It's just that something someone I talked to today leads me to think we aren't the only one after him."

"That's news to me, Frank."

"It's probably nothing, anyway."

"What I want, Frank, is Tommy Schotz. You hear about him, you find him, you let me know. Got it. And don't get any crazy idea about helping him or this woman get off of Star City. I'll charge you as an accessory to murder if you do."

"I'll keep that in mind."

"You do that, Frank."

The beefy detective got up off his stool, drained the last of his Joe and walked away. I noticed that he hadn't left any money to cover his meal.

I debated whether or not to hit the Blue Moon for a quick drink, but it was getting to be that part of the day when the place filled up with the after work crowd. In general I prefer my drinking quiet and solitary. Instead I headed to home sweet home, my apartment in the Aldeberon Arms.

When it had been built, the Aldeberon Arms had been a classy joint, intended to trade on its proximity to the park that was going to be built a block over. The park was to be called New Minglewood, but it was never even started. Instead, faced with the limited surface area on the inside of the cylinder that is Star City, the park had ended up as the city's worst slum, a district of cheap boarding houses for the jobless refuse of Star City. Needless to say, the property values in the surrounding neighborhoods suffered. Over the years the Aldeberon Arms had lost some of its sparkle, but it still maintained a certain elegance, in the manner of an aging call girl. Also, the rents were cheap, which is why I lived in a fourth floor apartment facing the Blue Moon. The lock on the front door wasn't working, which wasn't unusual. Maintenance tended to be spotty. The elevator wasn't working, either, also a common occurrence. I headed up the stairs. They almost always were functional.

I'd reached the second floor landing and had turned to start up the next flight of stairs when I was jumped. He must have come out of the shadows, but I never saw him. Just an explosion of pain on the back of my head, a flash of light just behind my nose, and then darkness.

When I came to I was staring into the beefy red face of Latimer. For a moment I thought I'd been having a nightmare, but then I realized that I was lying in the second floor hallway feeling like an army of dwarfs was starting a mine in the back of my skull. Irrelevantly, it occurred to me that the reason Latimer's face was redder than usual is because he had had to climb up the stairs.

I asked "What happened?" OK, maybe not the most original thing to say, but it seemed appropriate at the time.

"Tommy Schotz cold cocked you with a sandbag," Latimer said in the same flat tone that he would have used to comment on Star City's weather of which there is none. "If we hadn't been close by, you'd be a dead man, Frank."

"Thanks, I guess." With the pain in my head, I wasn't sure that being alive was such a bargain. "Just out of curiosity, why were you so close, Latimer?"

"I had a hunch. Your efforts to locate Schotz weren't any big secret. You've canvassed half of the hotels on Star City. Most of the fences, too. I thought it possible that word might have gotten back to Schotz and he'd come looking for you."

"Looks like you were right. Where is he?"

"Rossetti is chasing him down. I stopped to see if you were seriously hurt, but it's only your head. You can always grow another."

"Funny, Latimer. So you trust Rossetti to run down Schotz? He never struck me as much of a track star."

As if on cue, Rossetti came huffing up the stairs, his face redder than Latimer's, which considering his dark complexion, was saying something.

"I lost him," Rossetti gasped the obvious.

Latimer looked upward as if in supplication to the gods. "You let him get away?"

"He had a head start."

"You had a laser, didn't you?"

"I got off a shot, but it missed. While it was recycling, he ducked around a corner. When I got there, he was gone. Must have ducked into an alley."

"Must have ducked into an alley," Latimer parroted. "You see what I've got to work with, Frank?"

"Yeah. My condolences." Rossetti and I have never gotten along. He's a lot dumber than Latimer and not nearly as honest, but then that's a pretty fair description of most of the police force.

"Well, there's nothing to be done about it. We'd better get you to an autodoc and make sure there's nothing seriously wrong with you. Give me a hand getting Frank to his feet, will you Rossetti?"

"There's an autodoc a couple of blocks that way," I said helpfully.

"I know, Frank," Latimer responded as if talking to a not so bright child.

They stuffed me into the back seat of the police cruiser that was waiting out front. The familiarity of the worn plastic seat was almost reassuring. I'd sat there enough times as Latimer's unwilling guest.

It was a short drive to the autodoc. Latimer told Rossetti to stay with the car while he helped me inside the booth. He had to stay outside on the street, of course, or his presence would have confused the autodoc's diagnostic instruments.

The autodoc's diagnosis was reassuring. My skull wasn't fractured; though it was probable I had a concussion. I'd been lucky. Maybe Latimer's presence had spoiled Schotz's aim with the sandbag. Whatever the case, it had been a glancing blow. The doc demanded forty credits. I stuffed a bill into the payment slot, and was rewarded by a small vial containing some white pills.

"Take two every eight hours for the next three days. If you experience problems with your vision or ringing in the ears seek emergency help."

At least someone cared about me. I exited the autodoc booth to find Latimer waiting on the sidewalk.

"What did the doc say?"

"That I'll live. What was the idea of using me as bait without telling me?"

"I thought it would work better that way."

"Well, that worked out well, didn't it?"

"Schotz might have been spooked if he thought you were on your guard. After all, he's mostly used to beating up old ladies."

"So now he's added naïve private dicks to his repertoire. What next?"

"I've got an alert out for Schotz. We'll get him sooner or later, Frank, don't worry."

"What, me? Worry? It's my skull that's been taking the pounding."

"Look, Frank," Latimer said sounding almost fatherly. "Don't try to take on Schotz by yourself. If you hear anything, let me know."

"Yeah, sure," I answered, though we both knew I didn't mean it. "What about the girl?"

"What girl?"

"Penney Schotz. My client."

"Why? Do you think she's working with Tommy?"

"No. I'm thinking she might be in danger, Latimer."

"You might be right. I'll put a man on to watch her."

I noticed that he didn't ask for her address.

"Do you need a lift back to your apartment, Frank?"

"No. It's only a couple of blocks. I can make it. That way Rossetti and I don't have to breathe the same air."

"Have it your own way, Frank," the police detective said with a shrug. He got into the passenger side of the squad and drove off.

I was feeling a little shaky, but I managed the two blocks back to the Aldeberon. The stairs were another matter, but finally I made it up to my apartment. I poured some brown over a couple of ice cubes, washed down a couple of the autodoc's pills with it and fell into bed. A moment later I was sleeping the sleep of the innocent.

I woke with a pounding head and ringing in my ears. It took me a few seconds to realize that the ringing was my comm. The pounding, though, was coming from inside my head, a residual effect of Tommy's love tap the night before. As I picked up the comm I glanced at the time. It was 1200. I'd slept half a day, which was probably for the best.

The ID of the caller announced that it was Penney Schotz. I debated whether to ignore the call, but decided that technically I was still working on her dime.

"Sladek here."

"It's been two days, Mr. Sladek," she replied with no small talk.

"Yes, it has been," I replied. I admit that I may have sounded a bit cranky, but then being conked on the noggin will do that to a man.

"It's been two days and I haven't heard from you, Mr. Sladek. I want to know if you've found Tommy."

"I have, in a manner of speaking."

"What's that supposed to mean, Mr. Sladek?"

"Tommy found me. Last night. He tried to bash in my skull with a sandbag."

"Were you hurt?" The way she asked the question made it sound that she was more concerned with whether my incapacitation would hamper the search for Tommy than with my health.

"If you're asking whether I will survive, the answer is yes. Though if a flat-foot by the name of Latimer hadn't showed up I'm not sure we'd be having this conversation, Ms. Schotz."

"I'm sorry if I sounded callous, Mr. Sladek. Of course I'm glad you weren't seriously injured. It's just that I'm so desperate to find my brother."

"About that, Ms. Schotz—" I interrupted. "But perhaps it would be best if we discussed the matter face to face. Could you meet me in the Blue Moon later this afternoon, say about 1500?"

"Yes, Mr. Sladek. I can do that. If you think it's best." There had been a hesitation in her answer. Perhaps she had sensed something in my tone of voice.

"I do, Ms. Schotz. I really think that it would be best."

"At 1500, then."

"'Till then." I broke the connection.

It took me fifteen minutes to shower, dress, and pop a few more of the autodoc's pills. As I hit the pavement outside my apartment I was trying to decide which I needed more, a drink or something to eat. That's when they grabbed me.

I have to admit, they were very professional about it. I could tell they'd had practice. One of them stepped in front of me to block my progress; the other grabbed me from behind pinioning my arms so that I couldn't move. The first one reached a ham sized fist under my jacket and came out with the laser I'd been carrying in a shoulder holster. He dropped the pistol into his pocket and said, "There's someone wants to see you."

Now you are going to say that then is when I should have pulled some ancient oriental martial art trick to turn the tables on my attackers. The problem is that I'm not an ancient oriental and these guys both had about ten centimeters and twenty kilos on me. And there were two of them. Also, they'd not really resorted to violence, just muscle. I decided to let things ride and see where they ended up. It was bound to be interesting.

I asked, "Who wants to see me?" Not the most original line, perhaps, but it showed I was willing to think about cooperating.

"You'll find out when we get there," the goon that had grabbed my pistol said.

In video dramas this is where I would have been bundled into a long black limousine and whisked away to the villain's lair. The problem with that is that on Star City most people use public transport; the trams are convenient, frequent and free. Vehicles are mostly reserved for the rich and the government. So instead of being whisked away, we hiked to the nearest tram stop, caught a down city car and rode it about a kilometer before getting off.

So you're going to ask why I didn't try to break free and call for assistance on the tram. The reason was that the only other passenger was a guy about twice my age, ten centimeters shorter than me and twenty kilos lighter. I didn't think he'd be much help, and I saw no advantage in getting him injured. As far as he could tell, we were just three chums heading for lunch.

The stop we got off at wasn't in the best part of town, but it wasn't New Minglewood, either. The farther one gets from the head end of Star City, the lower the rents get. We were in a district that mostly housed laborers that worked on the freight docking ring or the vat farms.

My companions seemed to know their way around. We walked a few blocks, turned and walked another block. All the while one of them was close on my right side while the other was just a step back on my left in the perfect position to stop me if I tried to make a break for it, but not obvious enough to attract attention.

Our destination turned out to be what is called a pachinko parlor for reasons lost in history. What it really was, was an arcade with various electronic games. The only difference from a pin-ball place, another obscure term from the past, was that these games, occasionally, very occasionally, paid out cash to the players. Now Star City has plenty of casinos and other gambling establishments, but those are targeted at the tourists and travelers on layovers and are a bit upscale for your average working stiff. This place and others like it were definitely not high rent, offering a play for a half credit with the promise of a five credit payout on long odds. They weren't really legit, but as long as they didn't cut into the profits of the powers that be they were mostly left alone, viewed as cheap entertainment for the masses. At that hour, there weren't many players. My companions hustled me through the machines to a door marked "OFFICE" at the back. That's when I met the boss.

The only person in the office was a man with thinning oily hair sitting behind a battered desk. I hadn't recognized the muscle that had grabbed me, but this guy I knew by sight. His name was Tory Vincent, also known as "Mr. Vincent" or "Vinnie the Shark" depending on one's position in society. He ran an operation that made small loans at exorbitant interest to working types down on their luck. It wasn't legal, but as all transactions were carried out in small denomination unmarked bills, the authorities had never been able to close it down. The collection of monies owed was enforced rigorously by goons like the two that had picked me up.

"Have a seat, Sladek."

"What can I do for you, Vinnie?" I said, just to show I wasn't cowed by his two goons.

"The word is out that you've been looking for a Tommy Schotz. Is that right?"

"I haven't been making any secret of the fact."

"What's your interest?"

"His sister is worried about him. What's your interest?"

"Right to the point, boys," Vincent said to the goons standing behind me. "I like that Sladek."

"You haven't answered my question." We were both playing games, posturing to show what tough guys we were. Of course, Vincent had more players on his side.

"You've got a reputation for finding things, Sladek. That true?"

"Sometimes. Are you missing something?"

"See," Vincent continued his monologue with his muscle. "No beating around the bush."

Turning back to me he said, "As a matter of fact, I am missing something."

"Let me guess. You think Tommy Schotz took it."

"Right on target."

"Care to enlighten me as to what it is? That's the whole point of this meeting, isn't it?"

"It is. About six months ago one of my collection agents was mugged, hit from behind with a sandbag. When he woke up he realized that his collections were gone."

"I can sympathize with him. I had an unfortunate encounter with a sandbag myself quite recently. Perhaps wielded by the same person. How much are you out?"

"Thirty K, mostly in Crockett tens and twenties."

Crockett, being the conservative planet it is, still relied on printed money rather than credit sticks. Crockett dollars were also rock stable and the defacto medium of exchange between planets, good almost anywhere in human space. This made them the preferred medium for transactions legal or not. Thirty thousand dollars Crockett wasn't a huge sum in the overall scheme of things, but it was substantial. It looked like Tommy, if he had been the one to knock over the bagman, had finally made his big score.

"What exactly do you want me to do about it, Vinnie?"

"You're looking for Tommy Schotz. When you find him, I want you to let me know."

"I'm not sure I can do that, Vinnie. I'm already working for someone else."

I could feel the two goons tensing up behind my chair. Vincent waved them off.

"Sladek, this doesn't have to be a conflict. All I want is my money back. You can still tell your client that you've found him. You just tell me first."

"And if I do?"

"You get a ten percent finder's fee of whatever you recover."

"And what about Tommy? What happens to him?"

"That's not really your concern, is it Sladek?"

I had to admit he had a point. From what I knew of Tommy Schotz, I had no reason to like him. As for Penney, well she might be better off with him out of her life.

"OK. Say I find Tommy. Six months is a long time to be on the lam. He's probably spent some of the 30 K."

Vincent sighed. "I'm a realist, Sladek. That's why I'm offering you ten percent of what you recover. I figure that will keep you honest."

"Fair enough. I'll take your offer under consideration, Vinnie. But remember, I haven't had much luck tracking Tommy down so far. There's no guarantee I'll find him."

"As I said, Sladek, I'm a realist," Vincent replied with a shrug. "Here's a card with my comm number. You find the money, you give me a call. I'll send someone to pick it up."

I pocketed the card and asked, "Are we done?"

"We're done. For the moment."

"Can I have my gun back?"

Vincent nodded to the goon that had taken it. He reached into his pocket and pulled it out. It looked pathetically small in his big paw. I grabbed it and slid it back into my holster. As I walked out the door, I realized I'd never revealed the fact that I had had a needle gun tucked into the small of my back the whole time. It was probably better that way.

It was nearly 1450 when I reached the Blue Moon. That gave me ten minutes to finish off a glass of brown on the rocks and order another before Penney Schotz walked in the door.

When she came in, I motioned to a booth, the same one we had sat in on our first occasion. I didn't ask if she wanted a drink. She didn't strike me as the drinking type, but the fact was, I didn't care. I wasn't in a particularly good mood.

"Do you know where Tommy is, Mr. Sladek?" she asked without preamble.

"No, not at this moment. Though I expect I'll be able to find him easily enough. That is if someone else doesn't find him first."

"I'm not sure that I understand what you're saying, Mr. Sladek."

"You haven't been entirely honest with me, Ms. Schotz, or should I say Mrs. Schotz?"

"I don't understand what you're saying, Mr. Sladek." She was trying to play the farm girl, all young and innocent. She had the face and body for it, but there was something in her eyes that spoiled the effect.

"What I'm saying is that Tommy Schotz isn't your brother, no more than I am. Tommy is your husband. Isn't that correct?"

"What makes you think—that, Mr. Sladek?"

"A conversation I had last night with a detective sergeant by the name of Latimer. Now Latimer may be a number of things, but one thing he isn't, is a liar. It seems that the police have been trying to find Tommy for some time. Long enough to get the file on him sent from Nebraska. The one where he's listed as having a wife named Penney. Now, maybe Penney is a pretty common name on Nebraska, but somehow I doubt it."

"I don't know what to say, Mr. Sladek."

"You've been playing me as a patsy from the beginning, Mrs. Schotz, coming in here with your farm girl innocence and handing me a sob story about trying to find your brother because you were worried because he had stopped writing to you. But that's not the case, is it? Tommy isn't your brother, he's your husband, and you're looking for him because he ran off and left you. That's the truth, isn't it?"

She tried to cry then, bring tears to her eyes, but they wouldn't come. I got the feeling those eyes would never produce tears.

"You're right. Tommy is my husband, and he did run off and leave me. Are you satisfied, Mr. Sladek?"

"Why the lie? It wouldn't have been the first time I've been hired to find a missing spouse."

"I thought that if I appealed to your—sense of chivalry— you'd work harder. I've learned, Mr. Sladek, not to trust men. I couldn't afford to take the chance that you might view Tommy's situation with sympathy. My resources are quite limited. When I told you it took nearly all I had saved to get here I was telling you the truth, Mr. Sladek."

"I always sympathize with the one who's paying my bills, Mrs. Schotz. In this case, though, I think you've wasted your money.

You'd have been better off if you'd stayed on Nebraska and opened up a café or a horse shoeing parlor or whatever you do out there. I don't know what you hoped to accomplish by finding Tommy, but I'm afraid you're going to be disappointed."

"What do you mean?"

"I don't know what Tommy was like back on the farm, but since he's come to Star City he hasn't exactly been a model citizen. He's taken to seducing middle aged tourists and then robbing them of their cash and jewelry."

I watched her expression, but if she was surprised by my news she wasn't showing it.

"He's wanted by the police. He got rough with the last couple of old dames he took up with. One of them ended up dead. The police have been after him for some time, and when they find him they're going to kick your husband off of Star City."

"Oh, I see." There was disappointment in her voice, but I wasn't sure at what.

"I'm not sure you do. When I said they'd kick him off Star City, I meant that literally. They won't wait for the next convenient starliner. Tommy is going to end up with a one way ticket down one of the garbage chutes. The authorities take the health and welfare of traveler's seriously, the wealthy ones, that is. Tommy picked the wrong kind of graft to work. He would have been better off just seducing the old bags and settling for whatever they chose to give him. No one on Star City would have minded that. But croaking little old ladies? That's another story."

"I wouldn't know anything about that, Mr. Sladek. Tommy was never a saint, but he was never rough. It would be too much like work."

"Well, your Tommy has changed. He's not such a charming guy anymore. And that's not all. The police may be the least of his troubles. Tommy has pissed off some dangerous people. I don't know all the details, but it wasn't for knocking off some old lady. He took something from someone he should have left alone."

"That sounds like Tommy," Penney said, shaking her head. "He was always looking for the big score rather than working for it."

"I don't know what you were hoping to get from Tommy when you found him, but the reality is that he probably doesn't have a credit left to his name, and if he does, the police will confiscate it before they chuck him out into space. That is if someone else doesn't get to him first and save them the trouble."

"It was never about money, Mr. Sladek."

"Then what was it about?"

"Retribution." The farm girl façade was gone. The way she said that one word was colder than I've ever heard a woman say anything.

"You aren't likely to even get that, except vicariously. The police are hot on his trail. You might as well just pack up and go home, Ms. Schotz. You do have enough money to buy a ticket off this rock, don't you?"

"I bought a round trip ticket, Mr. Sladek. There's a liner heading for Nebraska in three days. It looks like I'll be on it."

"Buying a round trip ticket was probably the smartest thing you ever did, Ms. Schotz. Look, you paid me for two days work. That's what I've done. Let's call it even."

"But I still want to find Tommy, Mr. Sladek."

"What for? Don't you understand? It's over. Go home to the cows and pigs or whatever it is you raise on Nebraska. They've got to be better for you than whatever you'll find on Star City."

"You're quitting, Mr. Sladek?"

"It's over. I'm going home, pour myself a drink or two and nurse an aching head. You'd be smart to do the same."

She looked at me. There was something in her eyes. I didn't know if it was pity or pleading.

"You don't like women very much, do you, Mr. Sladek?"

"Oh, I like them fine," I answered with a wry grin. "The problem is they don't seem to like me much once they get to know me."

"I can understand that, Mr. Sladek. I'll be going now."

She stood up, all one hundred and fifty-five centimeters of her and walked out of the bar.   Me, I sat in the booth until I had finished my drink and then went back across the street to my apartment to drown my sorrows in ersatz whiskey and jive samba.

I had thought that would be the end of it, but of course it wasn't. Three days later I got a call. It was from Tommy Schotz. He said he was in trouble, which we both knew. He said he needed help and that he could make it worth my while. I think we both knew that was a lie, but I let it slide. He wanted to meet.

The smart thing to do would have been to get the address, pass it on to Latimer, and then go back to bed. I guess I've never been one for the smart thing. Maybe I wanted to get payback for the bump on the back of my skull that still hurt every time I moved quickly.   Maybe I wanted to get some modicum of revenge for Penney's sake. Maybe I just can't let go of something until it's ended. Whatever the reason, I agreed to the meeting.

I had expected Tommy to be holed up in some flea infested room in New Minglewood. Instead, he'd taken a room at the Landfal, a mid-grade hotel used by commercial travelers with not overly generous expense accounts. It's a perfectly respectable sort of establishment which might have explained why the police hadn't spotted him. He was in room 731 under the name William Thomas. He wanted to meet in half an hour.

I strapped on a shoulder holster for my laser pistol. It's a little item a guy I know whipped up for me; a standard low power 25 kilojoule laser pistol grafted onto the power-pack of a 75 kJ weapon. It doesn't have a lot of stopping power, but the recycle time is surprisingly short. You could ask the guys that have been surprised, but they're mostly dead. For good measure, I tucked a needle gun in the small of my back. This might have been overkill, but as I said, the bump on the back of my skull was still making me cranky.

When I walked into the lobby of the Landfal I caught the eye of the house dick, a guy named Rik Lane. I headed to one of the seating groups in a discrete corner and a moment later Lane followed. Lane owed me a favor and I figured that this was as good a time as any to cash in.

"What's up, Frank? Not trouble I hope."

"Me too, Rik. It's like this. I'm meeting a guy in room 731. His name is William Thomas, or at least that's the one he gave me. He says he has some information I'm looking for." I didn't see any reason to clue Lane in as to what the meeting was really about. He didn't need to know, and I didn't want him messing things up.

"But you think it might be a setup?"

"Maybe, maybe not," I answered non-committally.

"Do you want me to back you up?" Lane asked. I could see he was nervous in case I accepted his offer. Lane knew my reputation just like I knew his. He was a low wage house detective in a hotel where he usually never had to deal with anything worse than drunken salesmen or the occasional con-artist trying to shake down the guests. Me, well I was a guy carrying two guns who knew how to use them.

"No, nothing like that. I'm not really expecting trouble. It's just that if I don't get back to you within, oh let's say an hour, you get word to Latimer that I'm in room 731."

"That's all?" Lane asked, sounding relieved.

"That's it. Now if you'll excuse me, I have an appointment."

I took the elevator up to the seventh floor. I knew the general layout of the Landfal, having been there before. Room 731 was to the left as you got off the elevator.

I knocked on the door and was greeted by the face in the image that Penney had given me. He'd dyed his hair so that it was a little darker and his skin tone had lost the outdoor tan that it had in the image, but there was no doubt that it was the same face. It was a handsome face if you like that sort of thing, the kind that would be viewed sympathetically by women of a certain age, but there was something about it that I didn't trust. I'm usually pretty good with first impressions.

All the same, I inquired, "William Thomas?"

"Yes. Thanks for coming Mr. Sladek." His voice had that warm personable tone that you get in bartenders and con-men, but there was an edge to it. He let me in, shutting the door behind me. I noticed that he didn't bother to lock it.

"Just what is it you want, Mr. Thomas, or should I just call you Tommy?"

"Either will do. I've had so many names the last two years that it doesn't really matter."

"You still haven't answered my question."

"I have to get away from here. Star City, I mean."

"There's plenty of starliners. One leaves nearly every hour." I had no intention of making this easy for Tommy. The fact was that I was kind of enjoying making him squirm.

"The thing is, I'm in a little bit of trouble. The police want me. For questioning. I don't think I'd be able to leave in the normal fashion."

"The truth is, the police are the least of your worries, Tommy. I had a talk with Vincent."

"So you know about that, do you? Well, then you know that I've got the money to pay you."

"So why come to me, Tommy. I'm not a travel agent."

"I've heard, well, I've heard that you know people that could get me off of Star City without going through exit control."

The truth was that I did know people, some of whom could arrange to get a person off Star City without going through the formalities. I'd made such arrangements in the past for friends that needed to get away for the right reasons. But then, Tommy wasn't a friend, and I didn't think he had the right reason.

"Even if I did know such people, the deal is they aren't cheap. Can you pay? How much of Vincent's cash is left?"

"About twenty thou. I've burned through the rest trying to hide. But get me off this god-forsaken rock and you can have half of it."

"I don't know what you've heard about me, Tommy, but one thing is that I'm not easily bought. I'm not sure I'd want to touch Vincent's money, anyhow. Besides, ethically I'm not sure I should help you. After all, your wife paid me good money to find you."

"Penney? Penney's here on Star City?" Somehow that seemed to worry him more than the police.

"Yes. She's here. Though she gave me some story about being your sister. Which is it, Tommy? I don't know how they do things on Nebraska, but usually it's one or the other." I have to admit that I was giving him the needle just to watch him squirm. I didn't like him. I didn't like that he'd bashed me in the head and nearly killed me. I didn't like that he'd done the same to some perfectly nice middle aged women. I wasn't sure what I thought about what he'd done to Penney, but I was sure I didn't like him.

Tommy seemed to sense that turn the conversation had taken. "Penney was my wife, Mr. Sladek. Nothing more."

"Whom you seem to have abandoned back on Nebraska."

"Yes. I admit that. Maybe that was wrong of me. But I had to get away. I wasn't cut out to be a farmer. I wanted to make more of my life. That's why I robbed Vincent's courier. I don't suppose you can imagine what it's like. Have you ever been to Nebraska, Mr. Sladek?"

"Me? I've never been anywhere. I kind of like it that way."

"I'm desperate, Mr. Sladek. If Vincent or the police find me I'm dead. You've got to help me." The edge to his voice was verging on panic.

"No, Tommy, I don't think I do. I don't owe you a thing except maybe a thump on the head. The business between you and your wife, well that's something for you to work out between the two of you. You tried to kill me and she lied to me. I did my two days work for her and got paid for it. Now I'm done. I could say I wished you luck, Tommy, but that would be a lie."

I was about to leave when the door opened. It was Penney, and she was holding a laser pistol in her hand. It was a Kunstler, 65 kilojoule, a big enough weapon, but it looked enormous grasped in her slender fingers. For a moment I thought she meant it for me, but then I noticed that it was aimed dead center at Tommy's chest. The way she held it left no doubt that she knew how to use it.

She pushed the door shut behind her, pressing the button that worked the lock.

"If you don't mind, I'll leave you two alone to work things out."

"No. I'd rather you stayed, Mr. Sladek. As a witness. Don't worry; I have no intention of killing you, Mr. Sladek. Unless you try to stop me."

"I wouldn't dream of interfering."

"Good. Out of curiosity, just what did he tell you, Mr. Sladek?"

"Well, he did give me some line about not being cut out to be a farm boy."

"At least he was honest about that. I was a fool to marry him. But Tommy can be very charming when he wants to be. Do you want to know what really happened, Mr. Sladek?"

"Sure, why not. I've got the time." I was starting to wonder if Rik Lane would keep his word when I didn't come down, and call Latimer. That, and what might happen if Latimer came busting in through the door.

"Nebraska isn't much of a planet, Mr. Sladek. Most of it is still undeveloped prairie. Tommy and I grew up in a little village. Only a couple of hundred people. We got married right out of school. I was seventeen. It seemed like a good idea at the time.

"On Nebraska they've got this thing called homesteading. You go out and find an unclaimed chunk of land. If you develop it, build a house or a barn, plant some crops or raise some animals, after five years it's yours. That's what Tommy and I did. We found a nice place thirty kilometers from anywhere. Built a house and barn with our own two hands, though I seemed to have done most of the work. We were doing alright, too, Mr. Sladek. Not rich, but we had saved up a little bit of money. We could have put that back into the farm and done well, at least by Nebraska standards. But Tommy wanted more. He wanted the stars, the bright lights of the city, fancy clothes, things like that."

"I wouldn't have minded so much if he'd just left. With a working farm, I could have found someone else easily enough. But that's not what he did. Do you want to know what Tommy did, Mr. Sladek?"

"It seems you want to tell it, so go ahead."

"It gets cold in winter on the plains of Nebraska, Mr. Sladek. Sometimes twenty, thirty degrees below freezing. That's when Tommy decided he'd had enough and took off. Only he didn't just leave. He took the only vehicle we had. He took the power unit for the farm with it. Do you know what that means, Mr. Sladek?"

"It's obvious I don't, Penney."

"There I was, thirty kilometers from the nearest neighbor, no power, no heat, no communications. He left me with nothing. He took the truck and the power unit to the nearest decent sized town and sold them. Took all the money we'd saved in the bank and bought a ticket to Star City. And he left me to freeze to death in the middle of nowhere, Mr. Sladek. Does that seem right?"

"No, I guess it doesn't."

"It was too far and the weather too bad to try to walk out of there. I only survived by taking the siding off the barn and burning it. Of course that meant the animals mostly died, but Tommy was nice and warm on some starliner dining on fancy food and drinking wine."

She paused a moment, as if the image of Tommy drinking wine while she froze was the greatest injustice of the situation.

"I'd have died there if a neighbor hadn't come by looking for some stray stock. Tommy left me to die, Mr. Sladek, and he took everything that we had worked all those years for with him. He would have sold the farm, too, if it had been worth anything. Do you understand now, Mr. Sladek? I had to work my ass off for two years to scrape enough money together to come after him, but now here I am."

"And what are you going to do now, Penney? You're crazy if you think I'm going back to Nebraska with you."

"No, I didn't come here to Star City to take you back, Tommy. I came here to kill you."

"What are you going to do, Penney, shoot me?"

"Yes."

And she did. She was a good shot, too, not that she needed to be at that range. Tommy was dead before he hit the floor though the last spark looked out of his eyes in disbelief.

"What now, Penney?" I asked.

"I guess that depends on you, Mr. Sladek." She'd let her arm drop so that the Kunstler was pointing at the floor.

I thought about it for a moment. I didn't owe Penney anything. She'd paid me for the work that I'd done and nothing more. I owed even Tommy less. He'd been a doomed man, anyway. He'd never have gotten off of Star City until they stuffed him into a refuse chute and shot him out into space. I didn't really owe Latimer anything, either.

"Do you still have that return ticket?"

"Yes. The liner leaves in just over an hour."

"Then I suggest you get on it. I can stall the cops long enough for you to get clear. Once you're off Star City, well, I doubt if they'll bother to try and extradite you from Nebraska. Once you're gone, I doubt if they'll care."

"Thank you, Mr. Sladek."

"Just one thing. Leave that cannon here. I wouldn't want there to be any accidents to happen between here and the docking ring."

She let the Kunstler slip from her fingers to fall on the carpet. I didn't bother to pick it up.

"One last thing." I opened the case lying on the bed. There was a wad of cash, mostly Crockett tens and twenties. I didn't bother to count it, but it looked like about twenty thousand in all. I counted out a thousand in twenties and handed it to Penney.

"Here, take this and don't look back. Ever."

She stuffed it into her purse. There was plenty of room without the Kunstler. "Thank you, Mr. Sladek." For once the hardness in her eyes seemed to soften.

"You'd better hurry," I said.

She unlocked the door and left. After she was gone I counted out another thousand and stuffed it in my pocket.

I waited until she had time to get clear of the building and then called Rik Lane down in the lobby and told him not to worry. Then I called the number Vincent had given me.

"I've got your money, or at least some of it. There was only twenty K left. Schotz must have spent the rest of it. You can have someone pick it up at the Landfal Hotel room 731, but you'd better make it quick before the police get here.

"What about Schotz?"

"He's dead. His wife shot him."

"Ironic, isn't it?"

"Yeah, sure. Like I said, I can't hold off the police for long."

Ten minutes later one of Vincent's goons showed up. I handed him the suitcase with the cash.

"I've already deducted two thousand for my fee."

"I don't know if Mr. Vincent will like that."

"I don't really care. Now take the money and get out of here."

He left.

I waited another hour after that to call Latimer.

"I've found Tommy Schotz for you, Latimer," I said when he answered.

"Where is he?"

"Room 731 of the Landfal Hotel. There's no need to hurry. He's dead."

"Dead? Did you kill him, Frank?" He didn't sound particularly upset by the news.

"No. It seems you and I weren't the only ones looking for him. He was dead when I got here. The killer left the laser that did it lying on the floor."

"Any idea who it was?"

"My guess is that it was his wife. She was my client for a couple of days. She's the only one I know that was looking for him besides you and me. I saw her in the lobby leaving as I came in."

I didn't figure that Latimer needed to know all the details. I don't think he really cared. Tommy Schotz was a closed case. I'd saved Star City the expense of a trial and an execution. Everyone came out ahead by Penney killing him, except of course, Tommy. But then nobody had cared what happened to him.

Latimer showed up in his own good time to take a statement and watch as the M.E. bagged and tagged the body. One way or another, Tommy had been destined to leave Star City via the garbage chute. After the body had been taken away, Latimer and I went down to the hotel bar and had a shot of brown before calling it a day.

As far as I know, nothing happened to Penney Schotz. Once the starliner had pulled away from the docking ring, she was out of Latimer's jurisdiction. He filed a report and that was that. I don't know if she made it back to Nebraska, and in the end I don't care.

Vincent wrote off what money hadn't been recovered as a business loss. With Tommy dead, it had all reverted to a commercial transaction. It seemed only fair.

LIES
THAT ARE TOLD

LIES THAT ARE TOLD

You wouldn't think blackmail would be much of a racket on Star City. Pretty much anything goes unless it cuts into the profit margins of those that run the place. Gambling, sex, recreational pharmaceuticals within reason are all seen as legitimate profit centers by the businesses that provide entertainment for travelers on a layover waiting for a starliner that will take them wherever it is they want to go. That, after all, is the whole purpose of Star City, a waystation stuck in the middle of nowhere that serves as the main transfer point for that irregular chunk of the galaxy known as the sphere of human influence; to provide accommodations and entertainment for people making connections and to relieve them of as much cash in the process as the market will bear. Star City, though, in addition to the hotels, bars, and casinos, has people with secrets, and whenever you have people with secrets there will be other people offering not to reveal those secrets—for a price. That's where I come in, not as a blackmailer, but as a go between, an arranger, a fixer. My name is Frank Sladek. I've got a license of sorts that says I'm a private investigator. I've also got a reputation as someone who can find things—and people, if the price is right. But I also help out people with trouble, and blackmail is trouble.

It was the middle of the afternoon and I was drinking a glass of brown over ice in a saloon called the Blue Moon. I was there because at that time of day it's dark, quiet, and nearly empty, all qualities that I prefer. Mostly, though, I go there because it's convenient. I live in an apartment just across the street in a building that's seen better days known somewhat grandiloquently as the Aldeberon Arms, and yes, the name is misspelled, always has been. Being so convenient, it does mean that I spend too much time there drinking, but it beats drinking alone—sometimes.

There was a song playing in the background, a jive samba vocal. Normally, I'm not that fond of vocals, but maybe I should have taken the words as a premonition:

Love conquers all, so I've been told
But that's a story that's getting old
Just one of those lies that are told
About love, about love.

I was staring at the ice dissolving in the tumbler of brown liquid that passes for whiskey on Star City. I was between clients, but that wasn't worrying me because for once I had credits in my bank account—and a stash of Crockett dollars in the safe in the back of my bedroom closet. Life was good if temporarily boring. That's when she walked in.

I didn't notice her at first, not until the bartender caught my eye and nodded towards the door which had just opened. It was bright outside, or as bright as the glow tubes that run down the central axis of Star City can make it, and there was a figure silhouetted in the open door. My eyes were temporarily dazzled by the light, but I could tell that the person in the door was human and female. She hesitated a moment on the threshold and then entered, letting the door swing shut behind her.

That let me get a good look at her. She was tall, maybe a hundred seventy five centimeters, a dressed in a sleeveless white dress that accentuated a figure that didn't need it, and set off the light tan of her lean, smooth arms. Hair the color they call ash blonde fell in a soft curl to just below her shoulders. If it wasn't natural, her hairdresser had earned his fee. A pair of knee-length high heeled boots sheathed her legs. I have to admit I've always been a sucker for a woman in boots. Maybe that explains why things happened the way they did.

She took in the layout of the place and then stepped over to the bar. I could tell from the way she walked that she hadn't been born on Star City, but that she'd lived here long enough to automatically compensate for the spin that provides the centrifugal force that substitutes for gravity. She held a short conversation with the bartender who nodded in my direction. She looked my way, giving me an examination as thorough as I had given her, and, after dropping a Crockett silver dollar on the bar, came over.

"Mr. Sladek?" she asked uncertainly.

"If you've talked to the bartender, you already know that, Miss—?"

"Phillips, Margaret Phillips," she replied in a voice that would have melted the ice in my drink if any had remained.

"Do your friends call you Maggy?"

"Not if they want to remain my friends." She had said it in a way that made me think it was an old line with her, but there had been just the hint of a smile to her crimson lips when she said it.

"Miss Phillips, then."

"Mrs. Phillips to be accurate."

"I'm all in favor of accuracy. Just what can I do for you Mrs. Phillips? I assume that you've sought me out for something other than my rugged good looks and charming personality."

There was that hint of a smile again. "I think that's a fair assumption, Mr. Sladek." I've always liked a woman who can hold her own in a conversation, but I had the feeling Mrs. Phillips could beat me hands down in the banter department.

"Could we speak someplace a little more private?"

"One of the booths should do. They're not bugged. I've checked. The bartender is hard of hearing when he needs to be, and the old guy at the end of the bar drinking something blue has been doing so since before noon, so I don't think we need worry about him. Can I get you something to drink?" I asked mostly because my own glass was empty.

"Yes, I could use a drink. A Scotch and soda, please."

She said that like it was something she drank everyday, which she probably did. Us poor locals mostly drink brown or clear depending on our preference, alcohol produced in a vat at the down end of Star City and adulterated with flavorings and colorings until it bears a vague resemblance to the whiskey or vodka it is an imitation of. Real Scotch costs about ten times what brown does, and that's for the cheap stuff, but given the freight rates to bring it in, no one imports cheap Scotch.

The bartender came over and I told him, "two Scotch and sodas."

He raised an eyebrow at my order and asked, "You want the real stuff?"

"Anything from Crockett will do," Mrs. Phillips said. Crockett is closer than Earth, and the best whisky from there is probably as good as the original if less expensive. "And don't worry. Mr. Sladek. I'm buying."

The bartender reached for a bottle on an upper shelf, and briefly flashed the label in our direction to show he was being honest before splashing a healthy pour over the ice in two glasses. He added the soda from a bottle he pulled from the cooler rather than the normal dispenser. Not all the Blue Moon's clientele are as low rent as the location would indicate.

I picked up the glasses and escorted Mrs. Phillips over to the booth along the far wall that served as my office.

We sat down, and I took a sip of my drink. "Now just what is this about, Mrs. Phillips?"

"I'm being blackmailed, Mr. Sladek. I want you to put a stop to it."

There it was. No nonsense, no crying, no forcing me to wheedle it from her. She'd stated her position in much the same way she might have said, "Pick up my dry cleaning," or "take out the garbage."

"I see. When you say you want it stopped, I take it you asking me to do more than just act as a go between or handle a payoff?"

"You are correct, Mr. Sladek. I've tried paying. It doesn't work. I want it to end once and for all."

"That may take some doing, Mrs. Phillips. Just so you understand, my fee will be based on just how difficult the job is."

"I understand, Mr. Sladek. I'm willing to pay—within reason. Whatever you charge, I expect it will be less than what it has cost me so far."

"As long as that's understood. Now down to particulars, do you know who's blackmailing you?"

"Oh, yes. I've known from the beginning. It's a man named Hari Fiskin. He's owns a shop that sells art."

"That makes it easier. Do you care to tell me what he's holding over you?"

"Is that necessary?"

"No, it's not. It might make my job easier, but I can work without it—if you're willing to pay."

"I can tell you this, Mr. Sladek. Fiskin has a recording that could prove extremely embarrassing to me if it got out—or was given to my husband. You can understand that, can't you?"

"Oh, I can understand that. I'm an old hand at this kind of business, Mrs. Phillips. I expect that's one of the reasons you came to me. I take it that this recording is of you?"

"Amongst others. I'm not proud of it, but—Well, I was young and foolish. Were you ever young and foolish, Mr. Sladek?"

"Oh, I was young, once, and I've certainly been foolish. I'm not sure that I was ever both at the same time. I wouldn't have survived to be the man I am now if I had been. But I can certainly sympathize with your situation. Mrs. Phillips."

She gave me a long hard look in the eyes. Not many women will do that. Men either, for that matter. "Yes, I believe that you can, Mr. Sladek." She took a sip of her drink.

"Now this recording, I imagine it's on a memory stick or something—"

"Yes."

"If I were to get this recording or destroy it, then this Fiskin wouldn't have a hold on you. Is that right?"

"Yes, Mr. Sladek. If I knew that the recording had been destroyed, then I could laugh in Hari's face. I'd enjoy that." I got the feeling she would.

"And there aren't any duplicates? Any copies?"

"No. I don't think Hari would risk a copy falling into someone else's hands. That would cause difficulties for him, as well as for some others. I'm pretty sure that there is just the one instance of the recording."

"Good. That's a point in our favor. Tell me, Mrs. Phillips, just how far are you prepared to go to retrieve this item?"

"Just what do you mean, Mr. Sladek?"

"What I'm asking—what I mean—is that some of my methods might not be, strictly speaking, legal. Are you OK with that?"

"Mr. Sladek, I came here today with a full understanding of your reputation. And your discretion. There are some people that think quite highly of your abilities."

"And there are some that don't. I'm just telling you that in any operation like this there are always some risks. Of course, I'll do my best to keep you out of it, but I can't make any guarantees."

"I understand that, Mr. Sladek. Believe me; I'm willing to risk anything to put an end to this matter."

"That's settled, then. One more thing. Is there any urgency in this? Is there a time limit?"

"Fiskin has made a demand of me. Something I'm not prepared to do. He's given me a deadline of ten days. If I don't satisfy him within that time he's threatened to go public."

"That should be workable. Ten days isn't a lot of time for something like this, but if I work fast, it shouldn't be a problem. Give me a couple of days to do some research and I'll get back to you."

"That's it?" she said skeptically.

"There is one more thing. My usual fee is a hundred and twenty dollars Crockett a day plus expenses. I won't know just what the expenses will entail until I've had a chance to check things out, but five hundred should do for now."

"That seems fair, Mr. Sladek."

She reached into her purse and pulled out an envelope. She counted out five Crockett century notes that were so crisp and new that if I hadn't known better I'd have suspected they were counterfeits. The envelope held a lot more than just the five notes. She put it back in her purse.

"I'll be in touch, Mrs. Phillips."

"Thank you, Mr. Sladek."

"Thank me when it's over."

She rose, then, and left. I watched her as she walked out of the Blue Moon. It was quite a sight. From the look on the bartender's face, he thought so, too. The old guy at the end of the bar drinking blue didn't look up. It was his loss.

After she'd gone, I noticed that she'd left her drink half unfinished. It seemed a shame to waste good Scotch. So I didn't.

Mrs. Phillips hadn't given me much to go on, just a couple of names, hers and Hari Fiskin's. The name Phillips was vaguely familiar to me, but Fiskin didn't make a connection. Obviously, it was time for a little research, and the Blue Moon wasn't the place for that. Besides it was late afternoon and soon the after work gang would come streaming in making the place noisy and crowded. I got up, paid my bar tab and left.

After a short detour to grab some takeaway from a food cart in the Souk, I headed back to my apartment. I dumped the contents of the carton onto a plate, poured a couple of fingers of brown over some ice cubes and called out to the entertainment unit to play some jive samba.

It didn't take long playing with my comp to get the background of my client. She'd been born on Crockett to a modestly wealthy family, gone to a decent university there and gotten a degree in art appreciation. I hadn't known that you needed a degree for that, but then my parents hadn't been modestly wealthy. Several years out of college she'd married a man named Geoffrey Phillips, also from Crockett, also from modestly wealthy roots, who was several years older than her. At the time of his marriage, Phillips had been a rising young executive for TransGalactic. Now he was the senior vice president of passenger operations. Ten years earlier the couple had moved to Star City where TransGalactic maintained their headquarters. While Geoffrey attended to business, Mrs. Phillips had become prominent on the social scene, and was active in a number of philanthropic and cultural organizations. According to the press releases, the couple led a happy and productive life, but then they say that about most wealthy people who can't avoid the public eye. There was nothing in any of the gossip blogs that seemed plausible as the basis for blackmail.

Hari Fiskin, however, was another matter. He too had been born on Crockett, though his parents had not been even modestly wealthy. Interestingly, he had gone to the same university as Mrs. Phillips, though he had graduated a year earlier than she had. His degree was also in art appreciation. Did Crockett really need so many appreciators? Possibly not, because Fiskin had left Crockett shortly after graduation and had ended up on Star City where he operated an art dealership. The address of the shop was a good one within walking distance of some of the better hotels and on a block with other businesses catering to well heeled travelers. The dealership seemed legitimate, but when I examined the tax returns for the previous several years, the sales figures didn't seem to amount to enough to justify the rent on that block. Now, conducting business off book is nothing new on Star City where the general philosophy is if you can successfully avoid taxes you deserve to, but an art dealership might also provide a convenient front for less savory transactions. The question was what kind? The public record provided no answers.

Part of being a successful private investigator is knowing the right places to ask questions. What I needed was gossip and innuendo, and I knew just where to get it. I gave a quick glance at the time. It was late enough for the party to have started but early enough that my source would probably still be coherent enough to answer some questions.

Eighteen years earlier, Jack Feldman had written a basically unreadable novel that had been the talk of the galaxy for about three months. In the aftermath he'd moved to Star City where he'd become the center of the art colony based out of the Souk. As far as I knew, he hadn't written anything since, which is probably just as well. What he had done in the intervening years was become the focus of the poseurs and want-to-be artists that drifted in and out of the Souk allegedly in search of their muse, but mostly just looking for sex, parties, and recreational pharmaceuticals. What the non-human residents of the Souk thought of the lot of them would be interesting to know, but they wisely keep it to themselves.

Fortunately, the Souk is within walking distance of my apartment. I put on my most Bohemian outfit, which consisted of a cream colored shirt and a jacket that was just a shade too light of a blue for normal wear. Those who knew me wouldn't care, those who didn't, well they didn't matter.

It had been a few years since I'd hung out with the artsy crowd. That had been back in the days when Marcus Fitzroy was still working on his first novel, *The Sun Never Rises*. It had been Marcus that had provided my introduction to the scene. I still knew a few people from those days, though, at least by sight. I was hoping to run into one of them and get him to steer me to Feldman.

I'd completed about half a lap of the Souk when I saw a face I recognized even if I couldn't remember the name. The face was surrounded by yellow hair that was too straight and too long, and she was wearing tight black pants and a baggy white shirt which would have been alright if she would have lost a little weight. There was a skinny guy that was ten years her junior in tow who I didn't recognize. She called herself a poet, though I'd never read any of her works. Both of them looked like they were mildly high on something.

"Hey, it's the P.I. guy. How's it doing?"

"Well enough. How's the poet thing going?"

"You know—I'm still waiting for inspiration." She'd been waiting for inspiration for a few years now. I didn't know what she lived on, but that was par for the artists in the Souk. Most of them had no visible means of support and the rest lived on trust funds set up by their families, often with the condition that they stay on Star City and don't return home. Whatever the case, money just seemed to flow to where it was needed.

"Good luck with that," I said encouragingly.

"Thanks, man. This is Johnny," she belatedly introduced her companion. "He paints." That brought up some old memories that I would have preferred remained buried.

To change the subject I asked, "Where's the party?" There was no need to ask if there was a party. There always was one.

That was the whole reason for the existence of the artist's colony. There was usually only one, though, for logistical purposes.

"Over Popal's."

I knew the place. Popal's was a cheap restaurant run by a non-human from a planet on the fringes of human space. The food was palatable if spicy. Their specialty was greasy dumplings that were a favorite snack for people stumbling home. I'd have to remember to pick up a couple when I was done with Feldman.

"Thanks," I said. "Maybe I'll see you there." I was hoping to get the info out of Feldman and be long gone by then.

"Not for awhile. Johnny and me are going to do the nasty."

"Have fun," I said waving to them as they staggered down the street.

If I had just wandered past Popal's I wouldn't have needed directions to the party. I could hear music from a block away, some kind of weird non-human instrumental stuff in what was almost a minor key. It grated on my nerves. As I got nearer to Popal's I could see that the apartment on the floor above was full of people, some of whom were hanging out the windows in an effort to get some fresh air. This was definitely The Party.

I climbed the narrow stairs that ran next to the restaurant. The apartment door was open spilling out light and noise. No one protested when I entered. I'm not sure anyone even noticed.

The apartment was basically just one big room that ran along the front of the building, what is euphemistically called a studio. What furniture there was had been shoved against the walls. A table had been set up with various bottles of alcohol and there was a punch bowl with a red liquid that was emitting some sort of foul vapor. I wandered over, poured something from a bottle into a glass and looked around for Feldman.

He wasn't hard to spot. He was sitting in a chair positioned on a low platform in one corner. He was wearing some sort of garment that might have been intended as a toga, looking for all the galaxy like some ancient pagan god of drink. There were a couple of women on either side of him handing him tidbits of food. I honestly don't know how he does it, but he's been doing the same thing for almost two decades.

As I approached this throne, his dark bloodshot eyes came to a focus.

"Why if it isn't Frank Sladek. I haven't seen the sleuth of Star City in a dog's age. What brings you to this orgy?"

Jack Feldman really talks like that, even when he isn't drunk or high, which is not that often. That may be why he hasn't written anything in years.

"Just thought I'd drop by."

At that Jack turned to the younger of his companions and gave a lecherous wink. "I suspect our detective friend has some ulterior motive for his visit. Griselda, why don't you and Phoebe go amuse yourselves for a few minutes while I speak with the shamus." Phoebe pouted for a moment until Griselda whispered something in her ear, after which they both giggled and disappeared into the crowd.

"Could we maybe go someplace a little quieter?" I asked.

In response, Feldman got laboriously to his feet, crooked a finger at me to follow and headed out into the hallway. We went up a flight of stairs, and then one more until we found ourselves up on the darkened roof. The glow tubes had been turned down for the night, but you could see the lights on the other side of the cylinder which is Star City some three kilometers overhead. I know they're not stars, but there is something about the sight that always strikes me as majestic. In a corner of the roof, a couple that had spilled out of the party was making out, but they seemed too involved to notice us.

"So what is it, my boy?" Feldman asked. "You didn't descend into our pit of depravity just looking for a good time."

"You're right, Jack. I'm interested in some information on an art dealer named Hari Fiskin."

"And you thought I might provide you with it. Sorry to disappoint you my boy, but Fiskin is too much of a philistine to be associated with my circle of acquaintances, Frank."

"But you do know about him?"

"Well, yes. One *does* hear things."

Part of the art of investigation is knowing how to get information out of someone. With some people, a Crockett double sawbuck will loosen their tongues. With someone like Feldman that would have caused him to close up like a clam, which I understand is some kind of weird underwater creature. What Feldman needed was to be the center of attention if only for a few moments and to let him tell his story in his own way.

"Just what sort of things, Jack?"

"Well what sort of information are you interested in Frank?" Feldman asked with a chuckle.

"For one, I know he has an art dealership, but judging from his tax returns he shouldn't be able to pay the rent on that high priced shop of his."

"Very astute of you, my boy. Let's just say that some of the business conducted by Mr. Fiskin is for works of uncertain provenance."

"In other words, he acts as a fence for hot pieces of art."

"That is a rather pithy way of putting it, my boy, but essentially yes. Needless to say, such transactions are rarely recorded for tax purposes."

"That's quite interesting, Jack, but I'm more interested in whether Fiskin has any other businesses on the side. Say blackmail?"

Feldman eyes closed for a moment as if thinking. "That I'm less sure of. I'm afraid that we of the artistic persuasion rarely have enough resources to be worth blackmailing. Besides it's such a sordid business, don't you think?"

"Oh, I agree with you completely on that."

"Still, well, one *does* hear things. Fiskin does travel in what some people consider the best circles though I'm told he's not particularly welcome. I don't think that it's all snobbery. Several expensive pieces that were formerly in private collections belonging to women who are prominent socially have ended up in his possession without money changing hands, pieces that one would have thought the owners reluctant to part with."

"Sounds like a sweet racket. Get something to hold over a rich dame and take a work of art in return for his silence. Then he can sell the art at one hundred percent profit."

"Of course, these are rumors only," Feldman responded with a shrug.

"Of course, and trust me, no one will ever know who is spreading them."

"My trust in your discretion is absolute, Frank."

"Any idea where Fiskin might keep his secrets secret?"

"Not a clue. Though, I believe that he lives in an apartment above his shop. I'm not aware of him owning any other residence or place of business."

"You've been a big help, Jack. I'll remember."

"I'm sure you will, Frank, but remember, discretion is the better part of valor."

"Don't worry, Jack."

"Have you heard from Lucinda lately? I miss the dear girl. Sometimes I think she was the only one of us that had any talent."

Jack might know something about everything, but his sense of time leaves something to be desired. He has a tendency to remember things as if they happened yesterday long after they're gone. Lucinda had left Star City for Crockett years earlier, long enough ago that she had had time to make quite a career for herself. We didn't exchange Christmas cards.

"No, I haven't heard from her for quite awhile. I suspect we've both just been too busy."

"Pity. There was always a certain—chemistry with you two. As if the pair of you were in your own little world."

"Yeah, we had something." We'd had something, alright, until she saw a side of me that she wasn't sure she'd liked. She had known I couldn't change and had had sense enough to leave it at that.

"Well, I have a party to get back to. The children these days just don't know what to do without an older head to guide them. See you around, Frank."

Feldman descended the stair leaving me alone on the roof. I stood there for awhile watching the lights on the other side of the world twinkle and move in their silent dance. Then I went home. I stopped at Popal's for a couple of dumplings on the way.

In the morning, I decided it was time I made Hari Fiskin's acquaintance. I showered and had a decent sized breakfast. I find that it always helps to do these sorts of things on a full stomach. I was in no hurry. Those sorts of shops never open before 1000 and the fashionable clientele wouldn't make an appearance before 1100. After I had cleaned up the dishes I spent some time gazing at my wardrobe. As far as I knew, I'd never met Fiskin and I was counting on the fact that he'd probably never heard of me.

The real trick to a disguise is to keep it simple. Fake moustaches and wigs make for good scenes in videos, but up close they are hard to pull off. It's a lot easier to just pick a suit that fits the part. You can try combing your hair differently, but that's rarely worth the trouble.

I picked a suit that I'd found cheap in a second hand shop. It was nice material, good workmanship and didn't show much wear. The color was a little off, the jacket flared a bit below the waist, and the pant legs were just a shade too wide for local tastes, which was just what I wanted. The label inside said that it came from a tailor in The Escarpment, Farwall. I'm not quite sure what star Farwall orbits, but it didn't matter; as I put on the jacket I assumed the identity of a well-heeled traveler from that distant planet. A little work on my comm, and I phonied up the ID of Jake Bergen, planter. I'm not sure what it was that I was supposed to plant, but I was pretty sure that Hari Fiskin wouldn't care.

I took a look at myself in the full length mirror I keep in the bedroom. They say that clothes make the man. In this case, they made Jake Bergen.

Fiskin's shop was about what you'd imagine. It was in the middle of a block of similar stores all selling luxury goods. Assuming my role as bored traveler, I ambled up the street, pausing now and then to look at the displays. The front of the art dealership consisted of two display windows flanking the entry. A discrete sign over the door announced that it was "Fiskin's." I pretended to examine the displays; what I was really studying was the security system. It looked first rate.

One of the display windows held a sculpture, at least I think that was what it was, in a style that was probably described as "primitive." Personally, I thought that it looked like a something a four year old might do with a lump of clay, but then that's just me. The other window held a number of pieces of jewelry unsuitable for the human body. A placard claimed that they were the works of a Lizardman with an unpronounceable name. They weren't half bad.

After a moment I entered the shop. The only other customers were a mother and her teenage daughter. The mother looked Terran, the daughter looked bored. I couldn't blame her.

It looked like Fiskin believed in the principle that less is more. There were only about twenty pieces of two dimensional art hanging on the walls. A half dozen plinths and platforms strewn around the gallery held pieces of sculpture. I guess the idea was that the sparseness would be taken as an indication of quality and allow Fiskin to jack up the prices.

I admit that I don't know a lot about art, but I had picked up enough during my time with Lucinda to know that most of the stuff was crap, pieces that Fiskin had picked up from some poser in the Souk for the price of a stiff drink. The few that looked like something were probably fakes.

I found myself drawn to an oceanscape, three moons over a sea of phosphorescent waves.

"An interesting work, isn't it," an oily voice said in hushed tones.

I looked around at the speaker. It was Fiskin. He was short, maybe six or seven centimeters below my height, and thin, though he was developing a paunch. He was wearing a mauve shirt under a lemon yellow suit, and had longish blonde hair that he had slicked back from his forehead. I wasn't sure if he liked it that way or he did it just because it screamed "art dealer."

"Unusual," I agreed.

"It's an unattributed work of Lucinda, the great artist from Crockett. You know, of course, that she spent some time here on

Star City just before she became famous. When she departed she left a number of unsigned works behind with friends."

He was right about that. I had three of them, but they were all signed. One of them was the original of the painting on the wall. It hung over the head of my bed. Lucinda had hung it there herself to "brighten up the place" as she put it during the time she'd been sleeping in the bed. I knew the one on the wall was an imitation. In the original, the three moons are each a different size and the colors where the waves break are brighter. Besides, Lucinda would never have painted the same scene twice.

"It must be very valuable," I said.

"Oh, quite. After all, it is one of a kind."

I just nodded my head.

"Were you looking for anything in particular, Mr.—?"

"Bergen. Jake Bergen. I'm just here on a layover for a couple of days between Farwall and Crockett. No I'm just browsing. Mind if I look around a bit?"

"Oh, please, feel free. I'll be in my office if you have any questions." He turned on his heels in a peculiar motion and disappeared into his office. He left the door open, probably to make sure I didn't stuff a two meter long picture into my pants pocket, but that suited me fine. The office was the most likely place for Fiskin to keep a safe, and I wanted to get a look at it. I spent several minutes examining an especially hideous piece of abstract sculpture. By positioning myself strategically, I was able to get a good look at the office interior. There was indeed a large safe against the back wall. I took an image of the sculpture with my comm which included the door of the safe in the background. I got a pretty good idea of the layout of the rest of the shop, as well. In addition to the office and the gallery, there appeared to be storage space and a small workroom.

After fifteen or so minutes Fiskin came back out.

"Are you interested in the sculpture? Isn't it a fine piece? An alien primitive. I can give you a good price."

"I haven't decided yet."

"Do you have something else in mind? I have a number of more, shall we say, select pieces, that are not on display. If you gave me some idea of what you were looking for, there might be something I could suggest."

"Unfortunately, I'm running late. I have an engagement for lunch. Perhaps I'll be back before I leave."

"Any time, Mr. Bergen. Here's my card in case you want to make a private appointment. I'm available most of the time. I live in the apartment just above the shop here."

Taking the piece of pasteboard I said, "I'll keep that in mind."

Blackmailers, by definition, are not honorable people. If they were, they wouldn't be blackmailers. It's been my experience that it is almost impossible to buy them off. No matter how much you pay them, sooner or later they will come back asking for more. That leaves only two approaches for dealing with them. One is to frighten them so badly that they depart for regions unknown. The other is to deprive them of the leverage they hold over their victims by whatever means possible. No matter what his character, Fiskin hadn't struck me as someone who would frighten easily. That left the other option.

I'm no burglar. Sure, I can break into an office if I have to, but safe-cracking and getting past security systems is something best left to professionals. Star City doesn't run much to breaking and entering. Most of the people that have things that are worth stealing aren't the kind of people you want to be caught stealing from. There are, however, a few specialists in that line who have been successful, by which I mean they are still alive.

I contacted the one I knew. Professionally he went by the name "Jimmy." I didn't know his real name. As far as I knew, no one did. I gave him the address of Fiskin's shop and asked him to do a recon. I transferred the image I'd taken of the safe front, as well. Things must have been slow, because it only took him a few hours to get back to me.

"By passing the security should be a piece of cake. It's most aimed against a smash and grab, though frankly, I don't know any self respecting thief who'd want the stuff on display. The good thing, though, is that there's only one sensor on the door to the alley. That should be easy enough to bypass."

"And the safe?"

"Don't make me laugh. It might have been state of the art—
fifty years ago—but today, it's archaic. Shouldn't take me more
than a few minutes. When do you want to do it?"

"Soon. Tonight, if possible."

"I'm free. Say 0100?"

I agreed. We arranged a rendezvous.

At 0100 I was waiting at the tram stop closest to the shop. I
didn't know Jimmy by sight, but right on schedule a lean figure
carrying two bags got off the tram. Without a word, he handed
me one of them and we headed towards Fiskin's shop.

We turned into the alley that ran the length of the block
behind the shop. It was dark, but Jimmy didn't seem to notice.
We'd gone a dozen or so paces down the alley when he stopped
me. He pulled something out of the bag and handed it to me.
"Put this on."

"This" turned out to be what they call a "bunny suit," a plastic
coverall that covered the wearer from head to toe. I looked
enquiringly at Jimmy.

"You don't want to leave any DNA behind, do you?"

I shook my head. Following Jimmy's lead I pulled the suit on.
It went over my shoes, had built in gloves, and a hood that
covered your head. It was hot and uncomfortable, but my
confidence in Jimmy's abilities went up a notch.

He didn't seem to have any difficulty determining which door
lead into Fiskin's shop. He did something with a little box he
pulled out of his bag and a few seconds later the rear door to the
shop was open. We entered, shutting the door behind us.

"Like I said, not really state of the art," Jimmy explained once
we were inside.

We found ourselves in the storeroom. The room was dark,
but Jimmy had a lamp that provided just enough red light for us
to make our way through the crates and pictures that cluttered
the room. He paused at the door that led to the gallery in the
front.

The main lights were off in the gallery, but the displays in the front windows were lit up enough to provide light for the entire gallery.

"You stay here and keep a lookout while I open the safe."

The lock on the office door didn't slow Jimmy by more than a few seconds. He slipped inside. I was surprised when he reappeared after a few moments.

"There's something that you need to see."

"What?"

"Just come along. It'll be easier than explaining."

It didn't take more than a glance to see what he meant. The door to the safe was swung open. Lying in front of it was Fiskin's body. There was a neat, black hole in the rear of his skull, the kind a laser pistol makes when fired at close range. Someone had waited until Fiskin had opened the safe and then killed him. It wasn't clear whether Fiskin had turned his back on his killer because he had known him, or because he'd been standing there with a laser pointed at him. It didn't really matter. Either way, Fiskin was dead.

"What now?" Jimmy asked. It was a good question.

I pushed past him to look over the contents of the safe. There were a couple of ledger books, several small cases of the sort people keep high end jewelry in and a stack of currency. It looked to be about twenty thou in small denomination Crockett bills. There was also an empty space where it looked like something had been but wasn't now. I opened the jewelry cases, but the only thing they held was jewelry. The ledgers, as far as I could tell were just that, ledgers. Their contents might have been interesting to the police, but they didn't look like they contained blackmail material.

"I take it that what you were looking for isn't here?" Jimmy asked.

"Not that I can see. Any chance there's another safe hidden somewhere?"

"Maybe. Want me to look?"

"Please," I said with exasperation. Jimmy might know his business, but he wasn't a big picture sort of guy. While he looked for a safe, I gave my attention to the desk. It held the sort of things you'd expect a desk to hold. There were invoices, office supplies, a book of comm addresses, even a half-empty bottle of Crockett scotch. I felt like having a belt, but refrained. I didn't want to leave any DNA behind.

"Any luck?"

"There's no other safe. Not in this room, at least. Nothing that looked like it might be a hiding place, either."

"Fiskin had an apartment upstairs. Maybe what I'm looking for is up there."

There was a stairway in the storage room that led up to the next floor. Fiskin had done well for himself. It had been nicely furnished. The art that had hung on the walls was the real thing, not like the junk in the shop below. Of course, now, most of it had been trashed. So had the furniture. Someone had tossed the place looking for something. They'd been pretty thorough about it, too. I doubted that we'd find anything.

"What do you think happened?" Jimmy asked.

"My guess is that someone tossed the place while Fiskin was out. He came back unexpectedly and they got the drop on him. They persuaded him to open the safe, and, well, you saw what happened then."

"Do you think they got what you were looking for?"

"They weren't after money or jewels. They left those in the safe."

"Speaking of those, are we just going to leave them?" I could hear the eagerness in Jimmy's voice.

"That's not what we came for."

"You're the boss, Frank," he said with a shrug.

"We've been long enough. Let's get out of here."

"Works for me."

On the way out Jimmy fixed it so that it would look like we'd never been there. I transferred a pile of credits to him and then we went our separate ways.

I woke up to the sound of my comm ringing. It was just after 1000. I'd had maybe four hours of sleep. The call ID said it was Margaret Philips.

I answered the comm, "Frank Sladek."

"Mr. Sladek. I just heard." She sounded panicky.

"Heard what?"

"That Hari Fiskin is dead. It was on one of the newsfeeds. His body was found this morning in his shop. He'd been murdered."

"You don't say," I commented.

"You didn't have anything to do with it, did you Mr. Sladek? I didn't ask you to kill him."

"I haven't killed anyone, Mrs. Philips, at least not recently."

"You weren't involved?" she asked, sounding dubious.

"No, Mrs. Philips, I wasn't involved. I suspect that, given what I've discovered about Fiskin, that your situation was not unique. Perhaps one of the other victims took a more direct approach to the problem."

"I'm not sure that I understand what you're saying, Mr. Sladek."

"I guess that what I'm trying to tell you is not something I feel comfortable discussing over a comm link. It would be better if we could discuss this someplace face to face."

"If you think that's best."

"I do, Mrs. Philips."

"Alright. Where should we meet?" She had regained some of her composure. "I'd rather it weren't that saloon we met the first time."

"I can understand that, Mrs. Philips. The Blue Moon isn't to everyone's taste. How about the Café Parisienne? Say about 1230?"

"Yes. I think I can manage that."

"Until then, Mrs. Philips." The link went dead.

One of the contradictions of my business is that the best places to hold private conversations are often the most public. The Café Parisienne was a fashionable outdoor restaurant facing a large, open square within a few blocks of some of Star City's top tier hotels. During the lunch hour thousands of people crossed the square; few of them bothered to look at the dozens of diners at the café. Any that did would be easy to spot.

By judiciously picking one's table, you could find a spot where no one could come within fifty meters of you without being observed. As yet, I had no reason to think that either Mrs. Philips or I was suspected of having anything to do with Fiskin's death, but it didn't pay to take chances.

I arrived early, slipped the waiter a Crockett fin to let me pick the table and then ordered a coffee, they only serve the real thing and not joe, and a pastry. It had just been delivered to the table when Mrs. Philips arrived.

"Can I order you anything? A coffee, perhaps?" I asked as she sat down.

Mrs. Philips took the hint. "Yes, that would be lovely, Frank. And perhaps one of those pastries, as well."

I nodded to the waiter, who smiled and left. As far as he was concerned we were just old friends, or lovers, perhaps, meeting for a light lunch. Perhaps this was done without the knowledge of the lady's husband, but then, that was none of his concern.

"Just what did they say on the newsfeed, Mrs. Philips?"

"Only that Hari had been found dead in his shop early this morning. Evidently a cleaner discovered the body. The police suspect foul play."

"I suspect they are right. He'd been shot in the back of the head with a laser."

"Just how do you know that, Mr. Sladek?" Mrs. Philips said sharply. "There were no details in the newsfeed."

"I was there."

"But you said that you had nothing to do with his death. Did you kill Hari, Mr. Sladek?"

"No, I didn't. He was already dead when I got there."

"I don't understand."

"I thought it likely that Fiskin kept any items that were incriminating in a safe in his office. I suspect that there were a variety of such items incriminating a number of people. It seems that Fiskin had quite a sideline going in blackmail. Anyway, I thought that the quickest way to resolve your problem would be to pay an afterhour's visit to the shop and retrieve the item. Unfortunately, when I arrived, I found Fiskin dead, shot from behind while kneeling in front of the safe."

"And the memory stick? Do you have it?"

"No. The safe was empty, at least of anything of that nature. There was some cash and several expensive items of jewelry still in the safe, so it wasn't an ordinary robbery, but as far as I could tell, anything in the way of letters or photos—or memory sticks had been removed."

"But if you didn't kill him, Mr. Sladek, who did?"

"That's a good question. The short answer is that I don't know. As I mentioned, it appears that Mr. Fiskin was blackmailing a number of people. It's possible that one of them killed him or paid to have him killed, and removed anything that might be used for the purposes of blackmail with the intention of destroying it later."

"But you don't think so, do you, Mr. Sladek?"

"It was a very professional job, Mrs. Philips, and I speak from some experience in these matters. It's quite possible that whoever killed Fiskin intends to continue the blackmail game."

"I see—" Mrs. Philips said resignedly. "What do you suggest we do about it, Mr. Sladek?"

"For the moment—nothing. I doubt if the killer will make any immediate demands on you. That wouldn't be wise, given that the police are looking for him. Besides, if he were desperate for money he could have taken the cash from the safe. Your best move is to do nothing. In the meantime, I'll be looking for him."

"But how are you going to discover who it is?"

"There was no sign of a forced entry. That means one of two things. Either the killer is a professional thief and a good one, or he was someone Fiskin knew and trusted, at least to some extent. Either way, there are a limited number of suspects."

"You sound sure of yourself, Mr. Sladek," Mrs. Philips said.

"Oh, I am. This, after all, is what I do, find things—and people."

"And I suppose this will cost me, Mr. Sladek?"

"I can't afford to work for free. But we can leave the matter rest as it is, if you'd prefer."

"No. I don't think I can do that."

"Don't worry, Mrs. Philips. I've already told you my rates. I won't gouge you. I'll even give you a discount. Twenty-five hundred and that includes expenses. I'll even pay for the coffee."

"You are a rogue, Mr. Sladek," she said with just the hint of a smile.

"That's what I like to see. Don't worry, Mrs. Philips, I'll keep my word."

"Somehow, Mr. Sladek, I think you will." She seemed to relax with that, as if, once she had put herself in his hands, she knew there was no turning back.

At that point we were interrupted by the waiter who made a big show of placing the coffee and pastry in front of Mrs. Philips. She smiled and thanked him. He asked if there was anything else he could bring us. I said I wasn't sure. He smiled, winked at me, and then left.

"You know, you never did tell me what Fiskin had over you. I won't press you, but it might help me find it if I knew what I was looking for."

She looked at him, as if appraising just how far she *could* trust him.

"Very well. You'll probably find out sooner or later, anyway." She took a deep breath.

"I knew Hari back on Crockett. We were at university together, both students in the art department. I don't know if you know what artists are like—"

"I've met a few—" I responded. I didn't see the need to tell her just how well.

"To get back to my story, we were young, foolish, and irresponsible. We were also committed to flouting conventions— as if that was anything new, but as I said, we were young and foolish. It was Hari, really. He was always the instigator, the ring leader."

"Were you lovers?" I asked.

"No," she answered with a laugh. "Hari wasn't interested in women. But we were close friends. We engaged in a number of what could be called pranks. Nothing serious, really, not even particularly clever, though of course we thought so at the time."

"I gather that one of them was serious, though, or turned out that way?"

"You could say that. Have you ever heard of the apemen of Crockett, Mr. Sladek?"

"Some kind of furry creature that looks a little like a man, aren't they?"

"They are more than that, Mr. Sladek. They are very intelligent creatures, really. Sort of like man's ancestors were a million years ago. They were making tools and using fire before humans settled on Crockett. Who knows what they might have evolved into, given time. Of course that won't happen now that humans have colonized the planet. Now they are just another endangered species confined to a reserve, their numbers dwindling with every year. They don't need tools or even fire anymore, either, because we, in our kindness, supply them with whatever food and shelter they need." Mrs. Philips sounded bitter.

"When I was at university, the apeman cause was a hot one. There were protests for apeman rights, and setting aside one of the continents just for them. Of course, that would never happen.

"Hari got it into his head that the movement needed a big stunt to prove that the apemen were intelligent. He wanted to make a video. Unfortunately, he talked me into helping him." She paused then.

"We snuck onto the reserve, caught one of the poor creatures by himself, and I pretended to seduce him. Nothing really happened. The poor fellow didn't have a clue what was going on, but Hari was very clever in the way he shot the video and made it look like a lot more was going on than really was. In the end, it ended up looking like cheap pornography. It was never shown, of course. I'm not sure that Hari ever really intended it for public consumption. After that, we went our separate ways. I met my future husband, we married, and we came here."

"I take it that it would be embarrassing if this video got out?"

"It would be worse than that, Mr. Sladek. The video is disgusting. Not just for what it suggests happened, but for what we put that poor creature through. People would be revolted, and I don't blame them. Even if only my husband became aware of the existence of that video—well, my marriage would be finished. Can you understand?"

"I try not to judge people, Mrs. Philips. I've done plenty of things in my life that I'm not proud of. As far as I'm concerned, this conversation never happened."

"I'm trusting you with my life, Mr. Sladek. I want you to understand that."

"I understand, Mrs. Philips, I do."

"If you'll excuse me, then, I must be off. I've got another appointment."

"Of course," I said as I stood.

She picked up her things and started to walk away. As she did, I noticed a man who had been sitting on a bench in the square get up and start to follow her.

I signaled the waiter for the check. He responded promptly with the bill. For the price of two coffees and two pastries I could have eaten at the diner on my corner for a week. I dropped a Crockett double sawbuck and hurried after Mrs. Philips.

She was headed to the nearest stop for the circumferential tram. Her tail was about half a block behind her. I was about the same distance behind him. He was so busy trying not to lose sight of Mrs. Philips that he wasn't looking back.

She took up a position to get on the head of the tram. Her follower moved to get on at the rear. As the tram approached and slowed, he kept his eye on her to make sure that she got on before he boarded. She got on, but as her tail was about to step up, I stuck a knuckle into his back and said:

"Why don't you wait for the next one, Rik?"

I knew the tail. His name was Rik Lane and he was the house dick at a hotel called the Landfal. He isn't the brightest guy or the most honest, but he was mostly harmless.

"I don't know what you mean, Frank," he said as the tram took off.

"It's just that it's been awhile since we've seen each other. What you been up to? Still the house dick at the Landfal?"

He turned, not sure if my being there was just a coincidence.

"Yeah. They got me on nights, now."

"Convenient."

"I don't know what you mean," he said puzzled.

"Let's you pick up some extra work during the day."

"I don't know what you're talking about, Frank."

"You were tailing Mrs. Philips. The woman who got on the last tram. Tall, blonde, well dressed, about thirty-five. I had coffee with her back at the square."

"You got me wrong, Frank."

"Do I, Rik? I don't think so."

"OK. So maybe I was trying to pick up some extra cash. You know the job at the Landfal don't pay so good. But it's not like I'm doing anything wrong."

"I know that, Rik. I just want to know who you're working for. That's all."

"Ah, Frank. You know I can't tell you that."

"You don't want to cross me on this, Rik. Trust me," I told him pleasantly. I think that worried him more than if I'd come on heavy.

"OK. I'm working for her husband. He wants to know who she's been seeing. He thinks she might be cheating on him. But now that I know she was meeting with you—"

"She can't be cheating on him with me, because I'm just a two-bit private dick and she's way too classy for me. That's what you mean, isn't it Rik?

"No. I didn't say that Frank," he said nervously. Rik can be awful nervous for a house dick.

"That's OK, Rik. I'm not mad. Say, the next tram is just about here. You'd better get on it. You wouldn't want to lose Mrs. Philips, would you?"

I stepped back from the boarding platform. Lane looked at me, looked down the tram line, and decided he'd better do as I had suggested. I waved to him as the tram pulled away.

So Geoffrey Philips suspected his wife of having an affair. At the time I thought, just what I needed, another complication.

Of course, that was just a prelude to things getting worse. I was on my way home, debating whether to stop at the corner diner for something to eat, when I suddenly found Latimer walking next to me. Latimer is a detective sergeant on the homicide squad. We have a relationship that can best be described as interesting. His partner, Rossetti, took up a position on the other side, and a couple of steps back. It couldn't have been a coincidence. Latimer knew where I live and had to have been waiting for me.

"What's up? Do you and your shadow have something on your mind, or are you just slumming?"

"Cut out the wisecracks, Sladek," Rossetti parried.

"Can it, Rossetti," Latimer spat out. He has about as much use for his partner as I do.

"So what is it, Latimer?"

"I just need to ask a few questions, Frank. About last night."

"Last night? What's so special about last night?"

"An art dealer named Fiskin got himself killed. I was just wondering if you knew anything about it."

"What makes you think I would?" I didn't know what angle Latimer was playing. If he really had had something on me he'd have yanked me down to the station and let me stew in an interrogation room for a couple of hours. The fact that he hadn't, made me think that he didn't have anything conclusive. Of course, the fact that he was asking me questions at all meant that he thought he had something to tie me into Fiskin's murder.

"Fiskin was knocked off last night in his shop. Sometime around midnight. We did a check of the surveillance cameras in the area. Funny thing, Frank. Your mug shows up at the tram stop closest to Fiskin's place at 0100 last night."

"Where was this?"

"Glenway station."

"Last night at 0100?"

"Yeah."

"Could have been. I was on a job."

"At 0100?"

"You know the kind of hours I keep, Latimer."

"What kind of job was this, Frank?"

"I was tailing a guy."

"Oh? Who?"

"I don't know if you know him. He goes by the name Jimmy. At least professionally. He's supposed to be some sort of high class expert at circumventing security systems."

"In other words a burglar?"

"Only if he takes things."

"So you were tailing this Jimmy. Why?"

"A client of mine was concerned that his security was being breached."

"And just who is this client, Frank?" Latimer asked.

"That's sort of privileged information."

"Yeah, sure," Latimer responded. Actually, it was kind of a grey area. Some of the people who hire me aren't the kind of people a cop like Latimer wanted to cross. He let it slide for the moment.

"So, this Jimmy, you were following him?"

"Yeah, sort of."

"What's that supposed to mean?"

"I'd heard that he was going to be getting off at that station a little after 0100. I decided to wait for him."

"And did he show?"

"Yeah. He actually did."

"So what happened, then, Frank?"

"I followed him for a bit."

"And then?"

"He lost me."

"You *lost* him, Frank?" Latimer asked.

"It happens," I replied with a shrug.

"It's 0100, there's maybe one guy on the street, the guy you're tailing, and you lose him?"

"Like I said, it happens. It was dark. Maybe he ducked into an alley."

"So you didn't see if this Jimmy went to Fiskin's shop?"

"No. Like I said, he got off the tram, I followed him for a bit, and then he gave me the slip. Maybe I'm losing my touch."

"Maybe, Frank," Latimer said, like he didn't believe it. "Funny thing, though, Frank. There's a camera on the street outside Fiskin's shop. Guess what shows up yesterday morning? A shot of a guy that looks just like you, except he's wearing some off world suit like he's in disguise. He looks at the window display and then he goes inside. Know anything about that, Frank?"

"Oh, that was me, Latimer. I'd heard through the grapevine that this Fiskin had a picture that he was shopping around as an unattributed Lucinda. I was curious."

Latimer knew about my history with the artist.

"Was it? I mean a Lucinda?"

"Nah. It was a fake. I know, because the original is hanging over my bed. You should maybe look into that, Latimer."

"It's a little late for that."

"Oh?"

"Yeah. Fiskin is dead, remember."

"Right. Say, you don't think I killed this Fiskin character because he was trying to shop around fake art work attributing it to an ex girlfriend, do you? It's been a long time. Besides, anybody who knew anything would know it was a fake. The colors were all wrong, for one thing."

"Yeah, sure. But you *did* talk to Fiskin?"

"Yeah. I heard his spiel. He was very careful, though. He didn't come right out and say it was a real Lucinda. He just implied it and left the rest to my imagination. Say, maybe he pedaled some other piece of fake art to some poor sucker who found out and came back for revenge."

"That's certainly one theory," Latimer said.

"So you were aware that this Fiskin was selling fake art?"

"We've had our eye on him," Latimer admitted.

"You know, while I was there in the shop, I got the impression that this Fiskin guy wasn't playing straight. And I don't just mean the fake art. He mentioned something about having some choice pieces in the storage room in the back. He sort of implied that they were the real deal, but of dubious provenance if you get what I mean?"

"What the hell do you mean," Rossetti broke in.

"He means that this Fiskin was acting as a fence for stolen art work, dummy," Latimer explained to his partner.

"Not so much stolen, as parted with against the owner's will," I clarified.

"Just what do you mean by that?"

"Someone I was talking to hinted that Fiskin was doing a bit of blackmail on the side, but taking his payoff in art rather than cash. A lot harder to trace that way."

"For not knowing this Fiskin you seemed to know a lot about him, Frank," Latimer commented.

"That's kind of my stock and trade, isn't it?"

"But you won't tell me your client's name."

"You know I can't, Latimer," I answered.

He didn't like the answer, but Latimer wasn't going to push it, not without more of a reason.

"So you're telling me that you weren't in Fiskin's place around midnight?"

"I'm telling you that I didn't kill Fiskin. Scouts honor."

"Any idea who did, Frank?"

"Not a clue," I answered. It was, after all, the truth. "There is one thing, though. If Fiskin really was a blackmailer, maybe whoever knocked him off got his hands on whatever Fiskin was holding over people."

"That would be one theory," Latimer said. "Is that what you think, Frank?"

"Me? Me personally, I think it's time for dinner. Will that be all?" Rossetti glared at me.

"For the moment, Frank. Just don't leave town." The latter was a joke

"Have I ever, Latimer? Where else is there?" We both knew that I'd never been off of Star City. Neither had Latimer for that matter.

"Are you guys done, or are you going to harass me over a bowl of stew?"

"Beat it, Latimer. I just hope, for your sake, that you told me the truth."

"Close enough, Latimer. Close enough."

The case was getting messier by the minute. Not only did I have to figure out who had killed Fiskin and what they intended to do with the information that Fiskin had been using to blackmail people, but I'd have to fend off Geoffrey Philips while I was at it. It was pretty clear, too, that Latimer knew, or at least suspected, more than he'd let on. Latimer's honesty was relative. If he had proof that I was involved somehow in Fiskin's death, he wouldn't blink at pinning the murder on me if no better suspect emerged, just to clear the case.

The problem was that I didn't have a clue as to who had knocked off Fiskin and emptied the safe. As far as Latimer went, I *was* involved in Fiskin's murder, even if only peripherally. I didn't see how I could do anything to improve the situation with either, at least in the immediate future. That left Mr. Philips, but maybe there was something that I could do to take him out of the picture.

It was still early enough that I might catch him at his office. I didn't need to look up the address. Geoffrey Philips was head of TransGalactic, and TransGalactic ran half of the starliners that docked at Star City, the starliners that were the whole reason for Star City's existence. Everyone knew TransGalactic, and their office was one of the major features of the local skyline, if skyline is the appropriate term to use for buildings built on the inside of a hollowed out rock.

TranGalactic occupied prime real estate, not quite as prime as the top hotels maybe, but close enough to be convenient to the docking ring for passenger ships that occupied the top of Star City.

I walked in and found myself in an impressive lobby two stories high that took up the lower level of the building. There were kiosks for booking tickets, desks for processing customer complaints, and stations for various other services. Access to the elevators that lead to the upper levels where the offices were, was guarded by a long counter manned by a half dozen receptionists.

I presented myself to one of these, an attractive young lady who looked just a trifle bored behind a smile that appeared frozen on her face.

"I'd like to see Mr. Philips, please," I said, stating my business.

"Do you have an appointment?" she asked in a voice that said she knew I didn't, and that without an appointment there was no way I would be allowed to see Mr. Philips.

"No, I'm afraid I don't have an appointment, but I'm sure that Mr. Philips would be interested in seeing me. You see this is a personal matter."

"I see," the receptionist said dubiously. "And your name is—?"

"Sladek. Frank Sladek. Mr. Philips doesn't know me. Just tell Mr. Philips that Mr. Lane sent me."

"That would be very irregular, Mr. Sladek."

"I appreciate that, Miss Volner," I said, reading her name off of a name plate sitting on the counter. "However, I think on this occasion, it would be best if you made an exception."

"I could call security, Mr. Sladek."

"You certainly could, Miss Volner, but I don't think that would be in your best interests."

"Very well. Please wait a moment." She pressed a button and suddenly I found myself in a bubble of silence unable to hear the bustle of the lobby—or anything Miss Volner said. I knew that she was saying something, though, as I could see her lips move. There was a pause, more lip movement, an unconscious nod of the head, and then Miss Volner pressed another button.

The silence collapsed as quickly as it had descended.

"Mr. Philips will see you now, Mr. Sladek. Please proceed and take elevator Number 2." She pointed at a bank of elevator tubes that rose from the lobby.

I didn't bother to find out what would have happened had I tried to take elevator 1 or 3. I suspect that I would have found myself quietly but efficiently escorted from the building.

There were no controls when I entered elevator Number 2. They weren't needed. Miss Volner had programmed my destination, avoiding the embarrassing possibility of my getting off at the wrong floor.

The door closed behind me, and I felt that unique sensation one gets when ascending in an environment where the illusion of gravity is provided by centrifugal force. After a few moments, the sensation ceased and the wall of the elevator opened onto a lobby that if smaller in scale was much more luxurious. A voice from the ceiling announced: "You have arrived at Mr. Philips' office." I took the hint and stepped out of the elevator. The door closed behind me, cutting off any line of retreat.

A pleasant young woman who could have been a clone of Miss Volner except for the fact that she was a brunette to Volner's blonde instructed me, "Please take the door on the left, Mr. Sladek. Mr. Philips will be waiting."

Following the directions, I went through the door and found myself in a corner office that was as large as my apartment. There was a desk as big as a dining table with its back to one of the windows. I'd seen images of Geoffrey Philips on the newsfeeds and it was him who was sitting behind the desk.

"Mr. Sladek, is it? I presume that this has something to do with my wife."

"Indirectly. I'm here to clear up a misconception on your part."

"And what is that, Mr. Sladek?"

"That I am having an affair with your wife."

"And why might I think that?"

"Because you have been having your wife followed by a hotel detective by the name of Rik Lane. He watched us have lunch at the Café Parisienne today."

If Philips was surprised, he wasn't showing it. "Might I ask why, if you aren't having an affair with my wife, you had lunch with her?"

"You can ask. The answer is that I'm a private detective employed by your wife. I was giving her a report on the investigation."

"Just why would my wife need to hire a private investigator, Mr. Sladek? Assuming, that is that you really are one."

"Oh, I'm legit, Mr. Philips. You can check with Lane. He knows me."

"That doesn't answer my other question."

"You'll have to ask your wife about that, Mr. Philips."

"It can't be because my wife suspects me of infidelity, Mr. Sladek. I've given her no cause. I happen to love my wife. Besides. If you'd been following me I'd know about it. Even if I didn't spot you, I have security that would have."

"I haven't been following you, Mr. Philips."

"Then what have you been investigating for my wife?"

"As I said, you'll have to ask her. I just came so you could call off Lane. He was annoying me and he's not very good at the job."

"Not as good as you, Mr. Sladek?"

"No, not as good as me."

I could see the circuits in Philips' head working. I wasn't playing by the rules as he knew them. He was a big man. People usually did what he told them. Finally, he seemed to reach some conclusion.

"It's blackmail, isn't it?"

"What makes you think that, Mr. Philips?"

"Margaret hasn't been the same the last few months. I could tell that something was weighing on her mind. I also noticed that several pieces of jewelry, expensive jewelry were missing. She didn't think that I knew, but I did."

It suddenly struck me that Philips really did love his wife, loved her enough to let her try to work her problems out by herself so as to maintain the illusion of their perfect life. The funny thing is I was pretty sure that she loved him, too.

"Tell me, Sladek, who is it. Who's been blackmailing my wife."

I noticed that he hadn't asked with what.

"I can't tell you that, Mr. Philips. What I can tell you is that you don't have to worry about him anymore."

"And why is that, Mr. Sladek?"

"Because he's dead."

I'd come out with the fact because I wanted to see his reaction. It was what you'd have expected of a man, a man who wasn't guilty of Fiskin's murder. It was a look of surprise and something else; revulsion.

"Did you kill him, Mr. Sladek? Is that what my wife hired you for?"

"Why does everyone keep asking me that question? No, I didn't kill him, and as far as I know, your wife didn't have any part in his death, either. You'll probably be able to figure it out if you put two and two together, so I'll tell you who it was that was killed. It was a man named Hari Fiskin, an art dealer, and someone who knew your wife back on Crockett. I don't know who killed him, but I do know that your wife wasn't the only person he was blackmailing, so there are probably plenty of suspects."

"I knew Hari, vaguely, back on Crockett. I guess I'm not surprised—" his voice tailed off as it hit him. Suddenly, "Why did you come here, Mr. Sladek? If Fiskin is dead, what really brought you to me?"

"I want you to lay off with the surveillance of your wife. It's only complicating things. My best advice to you, is to just let things blow over. And with luck, they probably will. But in the mean time, I've got enough complications in my life without having to look over my shoulder to see if a two bit amateur detective like Lane is trying to tail me. It's a waste of effort and, frankly, a waste of your money."

"Do you really think it will blow over? Without involving my wife?"

"Maybe. With luck. If not, I'll take care of it because I'm involved already. It will be better for everyone if you don't do anything."

"I see. Mr. Sladek, I'll take your advice—for the moment. I'll call off Lane, as well. I'd like to thank you for coming—"

"Don't think anything of it, Mr. Philips. I'd better be going."

"Yes, I understand."

As I rode in the elevator down to the lobby I thought about Philips. He was like a lot of big men, used to getting his way, but there was something honorable about him, as well. He really did love his wife, not as a possession, but as a person. I had to admire him for that. Under different circumstances, I might even have liked him. But of course, that's not how it ended.

I picked up some take out on my way through the Souk and headed back to my apartment. I wasn't sure what to do next, but I knew that I'd have to do something, if only to keep Latimer off my back.

I poured out a couple of fingers of brown, added some ice, and asked the entertainment system to play some background music as I ate my dinner. The system was set to shuffle and the song came up, the song that had been playing in the Blue Moon the day Margaret Philips had walked in. I was about to flip to the next song when I caught the words:

They say there's a woman for every man,
That it's all part of some great big plan,
They'll try to fool you if they can,
With love, with love.

It was clear that Geoffrey and Margaret Philips thought they were made for each other. I considered my own love life, what there was of it. There'd been a point with a woman when I thought maybe we were that way. It hadn't worked out, though, not at the end. She'd left on a starliner which seemed to be the common fate of the women I got involved with, that or they ended up dead. I called out to the system to switch to another song. It picked an instrumental, slow and seductive with no words to set one to thinking.

There things sat for several days. If Latimer was making any progress with his investigation of Fiskin's death, he was letting me in on it. He wasn't hassling me, either, which I took as a good sign. It came as a surprise, then, when I received a message from Geoffrey Philips saying that he wanted to meet.

The place he chose was a cocktail bar about a third of the way spinward around the circumference from the TransGalactic offices, close enough by tram to be convenient, but far enough that it was unlikely that anyone he knew would spot him. It was obvious that Philips was being careful.

The bar was one of those places that caters to travelers and tourists staying at the better hotels, all shiny metal and lights. To reinforce the notion that this was Star City, the transit hub of human space and not someplace back at home, images of various celestial marvels decorated the walls and ceilings. I've looked out the windows of the Promenade, the big viewing gallery of the passenger docking ring, and space didn't look anything like those images. Mostly, it's just empty and dark.

At 1700 or so, a place like that would fill up with people having a drink before dinner or after a day of shopping, but it was the middle of the afternoon and there were maybe three people at the long bar besides the single bartender. Philips wasn't one of them. When I ordered a glass of brown on the rocks, the bartender gave me a look like he'd never heard of it. I guess they didn't get many locals in a joint like that. He fished around his bottles and finally came up with a nearly full bottle of Old Star City, by which is meant aged in the finest stainless steel for at least a month. He plopped a couple of ice cubes into a tumbler, and poured a couple of centimeters of amber liquid from the bottle.

"You want seltzer with that?"

"Nah. I take it straight."

"That'll be six credits." At the Blue Moon, the same drink would have been two. From a corner vending machine, a liter bottle would be five. I dropped three two credit coins on the bar and added a quarter for a tip. The bartender gave me a dirty look, but I didn't care.

I was saved from it getting ugly by Philips showing up. He ordered a Crockett Scotch and soda, and suggested we move to a booth after the bartender brought him his drink.

We picked a booth off in the corner. I sat on the side that gave me the best view of the room. I wasn't sure what Philips was planning. If he noticed, he gave no sign. I sipped my drink and waited for him to start the conversation.

"I need your help, Mr. Sladek," Philips said. He wasn't nervous, but I could sense a certain tension in him.

"I'm already working for your wife, Mr. Philips, or at least I was."

"This won't conflict with that. You said that whoever killed Hari Fiskin emptied the contents of his safe, and that included whatever Hari was using to blackmail my wife. Is that correct?"

"As far as I could tell. It seems likely."

"And you don't know who it was?"

"No. It *is* possible that it was one of Fiskin's other victims, of course."

"But you don't think so, do you?"

"No. It was a professional job. The murderer waited until Fiskin got the safe open and then drilled him in the back of the head. It was a clean shot. Not an amateur. Now maybe it was one of the victims, but the dirt in that safe must have been worth quite a bit. Enough to make killing Fiskin worthwhile. Has your wife been contacted by someone?"

"No, Mr. Sladek. I have."

"I see. Care to give me the details?"

"I received a text message. From an untraceable source, and trust me, Mr. Sladek, TransGalactic has quite good tools for that kind of thing. The message said that the sender had something that could prove very embarrassing to me and my wife, and that if I didn't give him ten thousand dollars Crockett it would be sent to where it could do the most damage. It gave instructions for handing over the cash."

"Are you going to do it? Pay off the blackmailer, I mean?"

"I'm not sure. That's why I came to you, Mr. Sladek. I take it you have experience in these sort of matters."

"Some," I admitted.

"Do you know what this blackmailer is holding over my wife?"

"The message didn't say?"

"No."

"I haven't seen the item, but I have a general idea of what it is."

"But you aren't going to tell me, are you?"

"I suggest you ask your wife, Mr. Philips."

"I can't do that, Sladek. If I did, she would know that I knew. That kind of thing can poison a relationship, even one as close as that of Margaret and myself."

He was right, of course. I'd seen it before. Sometimes something like that strengthens the bond between a man and a woman, but more often than not it serves as a wedge of suspicion that slowly pushes lives apart. I had to admire Philips for not wanting his wife to know. It still might not make a difference, though. He'd still know.

"So, are you going to pay the blackmailer off?"

"You know as well as I do, Mr. Sladek, that never works. Sooner or later they come back asking for more. And more after that."

"Yes, that's the way it usually works, Mr. Philips."

"That's why I came to you. What do *you* recommend?"

"You could go to the police—"

"You know the local police better than I do, Mr. Sladek. Would you trust them not to use the information themselves?"

"No, I guess I wouldn't. That leaves you with two options as I see it. You can pay him off and hope for the best, or you can take action to identify who the blackmailer is."

"What good would that do?"

"Well, for one thing, he murdered Fiskin. That would give you leverage. The police are looking for the murderer. If you knew who he was, you could threaten to give him away. You might be able to negotiate for the item that he holds.   If that didn't work, well, there are other steps that might be taken."

"You refer to the blackmailer as a man.   Are you sure of that?"

"No, I'm not.   That was just a figure of speech I guess.   But it takes a certain type of cold blooded individual to stand behind someone and shoot them with a laser at close range as was done to Fiskin.   I've known women who could do that, but not many."

I think it was dawning on Philips just what he was getting involved in.   He looked at me as if I was some kind of dangerous beast.   I've gotten that look before.

"I see.   What, then, do you think I should do?"

"How is the payoff supposed to be handed over?   I assume you weren't just given an account to transfer the money into."

That's actually the smart way to do these things.   There are all sorts of ways to cover you tracks that way, if you know what you're doing and have the right contacts.   The reality is that most blackmailers aren't that smart.   They try to get clever with all sorts of complicated schemes.   That's what tends to get them.

"I'm supposed to get the money in Crockett dollars, used, unmarked bills of medium denominations, twenties and fifties."

It's a strange thing.   With credit sticks and computer transfers and all the other electronic banking services, there still is a place for cold hard cash.   For some reason, people put more faith in some piece of plastic film produced by a planetary government a hundred light years away than in banks.   Not that I blame them, necessarily.   A Crockett blueback is good anywhere humans go and some places beyond, and is a lot harder to trace than some bits in a computer.   Ten grand in double sawbucks was a handful, but not unmanageable.

"I'm supposed to put the money in a bag and place it in a planter behind the bench at a tram stop on the east line tonight just before 2000."

"Do you have the money?"

"Yes.   That's not a problem.   You're suggesting I go through with the payoff, then?"

"Yes. You'll make the payoff. I'll be there to see who makes the collection."

"Won't you be spotted?"

"I'm not Rik Lane, Mr. Philips. Besides, I don't have to get close. All I have to do is take a picture of him. Once we have that, we can decide how to proceed."

"You make it sound simple, Mr. Sladek."

"Oh, it's not simple. It's not even guaranteed that I'll be successful. But as you said earlier, I've had quite a bit of experience in this sort of thing. I suggest you make the payoff and leave the rest to me. Forget that I'm even going to be there."

"I'll do that, Mr. Sladek. You've taken a weight off my mind, but just how much is this going to cost me?"

"My standard rate is one hundred twenty dollars Crockett plus expenses per day. I don't expect the expenses to be much on this job, but you never know. If you like, I'll give you a detailed invoice upon completion. I normally get two days pay in advance. Let's just say two fifty."

"Will you accept a credit transfer?"

"Why not? I've got nothing to hide."

We did the bit of magic with our comm units and the money was transferred between accounts.

"If you'll excuse me, Mr. Philips, I have some preparations to make before tonight. I'll let you know what I find out."

I got up and left him staring at his drink. He hadn't touched it during our conversation, a waste of good booze.

On my way home, I took a detour to check out the drop site. It was about what I had expected. The tram stop was along one side of an open plaza that occupied most of the block. The sight lines were good, and anyone approaching the bench could be easily observed from several locations, including an open air café that occupied the side of the plaza opposite the stop. If I were planning a pickup, I'd park myself in the café, order a nice cup of joe, and sit sipping it while waiting for the drop to be made. After that, it would be a simple matter to pay the bill, pickup the dropped object and board the next tram. Trams run like clockwork, so the whole thing could be timed so that the pickup could be made so that anyone watching wouldn't have a chance to catch the same tram. After that, you could get off in a stop or two and disappear into the crowd. It would be almost foolproof.

The only fly in the ointment, which is one of those sayings that I've never really understood, is that I wasn't interested in disrupting the pickup or retrieving the cash. All I wanted to do was identify the person making the pickup. If I could manage that, I could leave the clean up till later.

An idea started to form in my head. I'd need an accomplice to pull it off, but I didn't think that would be a problem. A couple of comm calls arranged things. I caught the next tram headed in the right direction and headed back to my apartment.

For what I had planned I needed some special equipment. The back of my bedroom closet has all sorts of goodies stashed away on shelves behind a false back. I pressed the stud that released the panel and grabbed what I wanted, a high quality imager from Crockett; the kind that professionals and well healed tourists use. It has a long distance lens and super high resolution. It wasn't the kind of thing that you could conceal, but that was the point. I checked the power pack and memory card to make sure everything was in order.

The next item was wardrobe. I changed into a comfortable pair of slacks, and topped it off with an open necked shirt. It was a little flashier than what I'd normally wear. OK, it was a shiny sort of bluish silver metallic fabric, just the sort of thing that a certain class of traveler would wear for a night on the town in a place like Star City. As an afterthought, I added a gold chain around my neck. For good measure, I put a little gel in my hair and combed it straight back. I took a look at the effect in the bathroom mirror and had to smile. I looked like the kind of obnoxious tourist who talks too loudly in bars.

One of the reasons I'd chosen that particular shirt was that it was worn outside the slacks. That provided a perfect hiding place for the needler that I stashed in the small of my back. If things went as planned I wouldn't need it, but I wasn't going to take any chance of ending up like Fiskin.

I arrived at the plaza a little after 1700. My guess was that whoever was going to make the pickup had already positioned himself in the café. I didn't bother to look. There'd be time enough for that later. Instead, I made a big deal of looking impatient, checking the time on my comm several times.

My accomplice arrived on the next tram. Brendal worked as a desk clerk at one of the mid-level hotels. I'd met her while I was doing some surveillance for the hotel. She's got expensive tastes, but her job doesn't pay that great, which is why she's always willing to pick up a few credits on the side as long as it doesn't involve too much. She's attractive in a low key sort of way, nice to look at, but not quite striking enough to make it pay. That seems to be alright with her. She likes a good time, but not too wild. She's smart enough to follow directions without asking why, which is why I've worked with her more than once.

I'd asked her to wear a dress that would attract attention, but she'd outdone herself. What there was of it was a shocking red that complemented her blonde hair and tanned skin. She had on a pair of twelve centimeter heels the same color as the dress and some bangley sort of bracelets on her right arm. She looked cheap in an expensive sort of way which was perfect for what I wanted.

"Look at you, Frank," she said in a brash voice. "I hardly would have recognized you."

"You look pretty good, yourself," I said with a smile.

"This better be worth it, Frank. I went to a lot of trouble," she said, flicking her hair at me. That was one of the things I liked about Brendal. She could really throw herself into a part.

"Like we agreed, fifty dollars Crockett for a half hours work. If things work out right, I'll even buy you a drink."

"So what do you want me to do?"

"I'm going to take your picture. Lots of them. I'm going to ask you to pose in various places. All you have to do is look beautiful."

"You say the nicest things, Frank. What's it all for?"

"Let me worry about that, Brendal. Why don't you stand over there for starters. Try to look sassy."

She did a good job of it. For the next half hour I took images of her using every building around the plaza as a backdrop. Along the way I managed to get a good head shot of everyone sitting in the café, all of the wait-staff and anyone else who seemed to be loitering around the plaza too long. All the while, looking like a traveler on layover with a flashy girlfriend, a new toy, and maybe one cocktail too many. For good measure, I managed to catch Philips as he made the drop.

A couple of minutes later, a man sitting at the café got up, laid a couple of bills on the table, and walked over to the tram stop. I got a few extra shots of him as he waited, though I didn't think I needed them. Just as the tram pulled into view he reached behind the bench and pulled the bag holding the money out of the planter where Philips had put it. I doubt if anyone but me noticed. The tram stopped, he got on, and disappeared down the line.

I smiled. "Let's go get that drink, Brendal. You've earned it."

"It's about time, Frank. I was starting to feel like an idiot. There's only so many poses a girl can manage."

I had images of the guy who had handled the pickup, but they really weren't necessary. I had recognized him as soon as I had spotted his profile sitting in the café. Wally the Weasel is hard to miss. I'm not sure what kind of animal a weasel is, some sort of carnivore on Earth, I think, but my guess is that it has a long pointy nose and close set beady eyes. That pretty much sums up Wally the Weasel's face. For that matter, it's a fair description of his personality.

The problem was that the Weasel wasn't a big time player, not the kind to kill someone for a big score like the contents of Fiskin's safe. He certainly wasn't someone that you'd turn your back on, even if he had a pistol; especially if he had a pistol. Wally was strictly a small time crook. He wasn't even good enough to be a con-man. He was, however, just the kind of talent that might be used to limit the exposure of the main player. The big question was, who was behind it all? There was only one way to find out, and that was to ask Wally.

I bought Brendal her drink. I even bought her a second one. We had a few laughs playing the tourist couple. Then I walked her home, the perfect gentleman. We were both happier that way.

In the morning I set about finding Wally. The Weasel has what is technically called "no permanent residence." What that means is that he kind of floats around from one flop to another based on his cash flow of the moment. I had no idea of where he might be staying, and with whatever he'd been paid for the previous night's work, he might well be in the process of moving to better accommodations.

Fortunately, he had a couple of regular hangouts. I asked around a bit, making it sound like I might have a bit of work for Wally so as not to arouse suspicion. I'd actually used him a couple of times when I needed an extra pair of eyes, so my looking for him wasn't that out of the ordinary. Somebody suggested Geezer Park. It seemed as likely as any, so I headed over.

It's not really named Geezer Park, but that's what everyone calls it. The real name is Geisert Park, named after some forgotten minor public official from Star City's past. It's not really much of a park, either, just an open space with a few trees and benches and chunks of lawn that are more dirt than grass. Old timers congregate there during the day to play chess and pinochle on folding tables they set up. There are public rest rooms, and a food cart cruises by around noon most days. Such is retired life on Star City.

It's not just retired folk that hang out there, either. There are always some of the temporarily unemployed and a few of those permanently without work looking for a place to pass their idle moments. Depending on your definition, the Weasel fit into one of these latter categories.

I wandered through, trying to look nonchalant; stopping to kibitz a game of checkers that looked like it was pretty cutthroat.

I spotted Wally sitting on a bench with a brown bag holding a bottle. Wally was looking pretty pleased with himself.

I sat down next to the Weasel. It took a couple of moments before a flicker of recognition lit up his small, dark eyes.

"Hey, Frank. Been a while. Want a snort?" he said, offering me the bag.

"Nah. It's a little early in the day for me. But feel free to have one yourself if you want."

"Don't mind if I do." He lifted the mouth of the bag to his lips and took a swig from the bottle inside.

By way of conversation I commented, "Business must be alright if you're drinking this early."

"Can't complain, Frank."

"So who were you working for last night?"

Wally looked at me, his eyes almost crossing as he attempted to focus. "I don't know what you mean, Frank."

"Don't play games with me, Wally. I saw you make a pickup last night. You fetched a bag that someone had just dropped into a planter at a tram stop uptown. Tell me that wasn't a pickup."

"So what if it was? What's it to you, Frank? Can't a guy earn a little honest money?"

"Oh, I was just curious, Wally. That's all."

"Don't kid me, Frank. I wasn't born yesterday. When Frank Sladek comes around askin' questions he ain't doin' it out of idle curiosity."

"OK. You got me, Wally. It turns out I *am* interested in where that bag ended up. Interested enough that I might be willing to pay, say, a sawbuck, for the name of who paid you for the job."

"You know I can't do that, Frank. That would be a breach of my professional ethics. Hell, I wouldn't even do it for a double sawbuck."

I didn't want to seem too eager, but Wally seemed to be encouraging a bidding war.

"How about a double sawbuck and a fin?" I took a Crockett twenty-five dollar bill out of my wallet, and showed Wally the color of the money.

"I don't know. My client might not want it to get out. He looked like he could get pretty mean about things like that."

"Meaner than me?" I asked in such a way that Wally couldn't be certain if I was joking or not.

"Come on, Frank. I thought we were pals. You don't have to pull any rough stuff on me."

"All I'm looking for is a name, Wally. Just a name."

"He said it was Lucas."

"Just Lucas? That's not very specific."

"OK. Lucas French. That's what he said. It might not be real, though."

"That's a possibility, I suppose."

"He was from out of town, though." On Star City, "out of town" is a euphemism for another star system, you go beyond the cozy confines of our little rock and you find yourself in the hard vacuum of space. Wally continued, "I could tell. Crockett I think."

"Where'd you meet him?"

"He found me. But we met once in the lobby of the Landfal Hotel. I think he might be staying there. I'm not sure, though."

"It's something, Wally. Anything else you can tell me?"

"No, not really. Like I say, he found me and asked if I wanted to make some easy money. When I said yes, he said to come to the Landfal for the details. He said he'd give me a hundred bucks if I picked up a bag for him. Told me how to do it. He had it all planned out. Real professional like. I got fifty up front and another fifty when I handed over the bag."

"Where was that?"

"Another tram stop. I was to go down a couple of stops and get off. He came in on an up tram, got off, made the exchange and took the next circumferential. I was to walk off in the opposite direction and catch a down tram on the next line."

Wally was right. It had the hallmarks of being planned by a professional. This Lucas French was no fool if he were the brains behind it.

"That it? Did he tell you what was in the bag?"

"Just money. That's all. I ain't got a clue what it's all about. Do you, Frank?"

"Maybe. But take my advice, Wally. It's nothing you want to be involved in." I slipped him the 25 and bid him and his brown bag good day.

After I left Geezer Park I headed to the Landfal Hotel. The Landfal is a respectable enough place, but it isn't what you'd call a luxury hotel. Most of the guests are commercial travelers with not too liberal expense accounts. The rooms are small but clean, there's a cheap restaurant on the second floor and a decent bar at street level. It also has a large lobby which is usually bustling with people checking in and out. I wandered in like I belonged, took a seat in a quiet corner and pretended to read a discarded newssheet.

I'd been there maybe fifteen minutes when Rik Lane took the seat next to me.

"Hey, Frank. What's up? You here on business?" Lane asked as if he wasn't sure he wanted to hear the answer.

"Me. Nah. I'm just reading the paper,"

"You're not still mad about the other day, are you?"

"Why should I be, Rik? You were just doing a little job on the side. You had no reason to think that I'd be involved, did you?"

"No. Of course not, Frank."

"Good. Then as far as I'm concerned we're all square."

"Glad to hear it, Frank."

"There is one thing, though—"

"What's that?"

"I'm looking for a guy that might be staying here. His name is Lucas French, though that might not be what he's checked in under."

"If you don't mind my asking, what's your interest in this guy, Frank?"

"Routine stuff. Insurance. Just verifying some facts." We both knew I was lying through my teeth, but it might provide Lane some cover if things blew up.

"Let me check," Rik said as he played with his comm.

"There's a Lucas French staying in room 833. The room sensor shows that he's out.

"Too bad. I guess I'll have to come back later. The thing is, I'm not sure what this French guy looks like. You wouldn't happen to have an image of him, would you, Rik?"

It's not something they publicize, but most hotels have hidden cameras at the check-in desks that take pictures of guests when they register.

"I'm really not supposed to give out information like that, Frank."

"You might make an exception in this case, Rik, seeing as we're working for the same client. Did I mention that I'm working for Geoffrey Philips now? Maybe if I mentioned that to the hotel manager—" I was pretty sure that the hotel hadn't approved Lane's moonlighting.

"I don't think that will be necessary, Frank. I'm always willing to cooperate with a fellow detective." He played with his comm again and an image came up. I pointed the camera lens of my own comm to capture French's picture. I know there are better ways to transfer images, but they tend to leave a trail.

"Thanks, Rik. I appreciate it." I held out my hand with a double sawbuck in it. Lane shook it palming the bill. As far as anyone in the lobby could tell, we were just a couple of businessmen who had just closed a deal.

"Mind if I finish reading the newssheet?"

"Go right ahead. Now, if you'll excuse me—?" Lane said as he stood.

"Be seeing you."

I hung around the lobby for another hour pretending to read the sheet. After that I pretended to play with my comm. As a detective, you get real good at that kind of thing.

It was late afternoon when I finally spotted French as he entered the lobby. It looked like he was heading up to his room, but something must have spooked him. Maybe he had me made, maybe it was just some sixth sense working, but without breaking stride, he crossed the lobby and walked out the side exit.

I had to dodge a luggage cart as I followed him. By the time I made it to the street, he was a block away. I didn't want to tip my hand by running after him, and kept that distance until he turned a corner. I sped up then, but it didn't do me much good. There was a tram stop up at the end of the next block. I saw French's face looking back as the tram pulled away. He was looking straight at me.

I walked back to the Landfal and asked Lane to keep an eye on French's room and to give me a call when he returned. After that I called Geoffrey Philips with the news. I considered giving Latimer a call as well, but thought better of it.

Two days later Rik Lane called to tell me that French had never come back to his room. He'd only reserved it through the previous day. We used that as an excuse to check it out. We might as well not have bothered. The room hadn't been touched since housekeeping had changed the sheets two days earlier. All we found was an empty suitcase, a change of underwear, and a toothbrush and some toothpaste in the bathroom. French hadn't stashed the ten grand or any of the items he was using for blackmail in the room. It was possible that he'd just shifted to another hotel and I might find him, but the chances were he'd found himself a safe place to hide. I slipped Lane another twenty for his help. For the moment there wasn't much else I could do.

Things were quiet after that for a while until I received a call from Margaret Philips early one evening. She was upset, but not yet in a panic.

"Mr. Sladek, I'm afraid I need your help again."

"What's happened? Have you been contacted by the blackmailer?"

"No—but I think my husband may have been. I'm afraid that he might be about to do something foolish."

"What makes you think that, Mrs. Philips?"

"I'd rather not try to explain it over the comm. Could you come over? Right away?"

Whatever had happened, I was already involved. Besides, their money had been good so far.

"I can be there in fifteen, twenty minutes."

She gave me the address, and then ended with a breathy "Thank you," that made me want to hurry. I wasn't sure what the situation was, but I slipped a laser pistol into a shoulder holster and dropped my needler into a pocket for good measure.

The place the Philips lived in was about what you'd expect, a top floor unit in a luxury apartment building a few blocks from the TransGalactic building. There was a live doorman at the lobby who must have been told to expect me. Other than looking down his nose at me, which wasn't easy considering he was ten centimeters shorter, he passed me through without comment and pointed out the elevator. The lobby was all marble and polished woods; the elevator was more wood and shiny brass. I made a bet with myself that unlike the one in my own building the elevator probably worked all the time. It was a short ride up eight floors to a foyer with pale beige carpet two centimeters thick. There were only two doors off of it. A neat brass name plate proclaimed which of the doors belonged to the Philips.

There must have been a camera, though I hadn't spotted it, because I didn't have to knock. Instead Margaret Philips opened the door to greet me.

"Please come in, Mr. Sladek," she said as if this was a social call and I had been invited to cocktails. She was dressed in tight white pants and a high necked red sweater that did nothing to conceal her figure and was just the right shade to set off her blonde hair. Her high heeled shoes brought her eyes almost level with mine.

As she shut the door behind me, I found myself in a living room that must have been as large as my entire apartment. It had been tastefully done out in muted tones. The only splashes of color came from several large paintings on the wall. From what I could tell, they were all real and first rate, and there weren't too many of them to make the walls appear crowded. The same could be said of the furniture which was arranged in several seating groups that left plenty of open floor space. It looked as if it had been designed for hosting intimate cocktail parties for twenty or thirty people, which it probably had.

From the front door, you could see all the way through to a wall of glass that opened up onto a small patio. From what I could see, the view was as spectacular as you could find locally. From the patio, I imagined that there would be an unobstructed view all the way to the far side of the cylinder that was Star City.

"Can I offer you a drink, Mr. Sladek?" Margaret Philips asked in a voice that would have been sultry if there hadn't been a note of tension in it.

"I understood the matter was of some urgency."

"Please, Mr. Sladek. I find myself in need of a drink, and I dislike drinking alone."

"In that case, Mrs. Philips, I'd love a drink."

She walked over to a cabinet set against one wall that contained a wet bar. I noticed that she didn't have a machine to dispense drinks, but mixed them herself. She poured several centimeters of an amber liquid into a glass. I didn't recognize the label, but I was pretty sure it wasn't a local vat grown brown. Using tiny silver tongs she added several precise cubes of ice from a bucket on the counter with practiced motions. It reminded me of a video I had seen portraying an ancient tea ceremony of some long lost civilization on earth. For good measure, she added a splash of carbonated water from an elaborate flask with a nozzle.

Handing the glass to me, she said, "Whisky and soda on the rocks, Mr. Sladek. I hope you approve."

"I'm sure it's just fine, Mrs. Sladek."

"Please call me Margaret."

"Margaret." I didn't know if it would be appropriate to say she should call me Frank. Things seemed to be getting intimate in a hurry.

I stared at one of the paintings on the wall while she mixed her own drink, something more complicated that involved a chrome shaker of ice. The painting was by Lucinda, a nocturnal beach scene in blues, blacks and silvers. There was only one moon, hanging impossibly large just over the surf. I was pretty sure it was one of her more recent ones, from after she had left Star City.

"I see you are admiring the painting," Margaret said. She was holding a long stemmed glass with a conical bowl containing a clear liquid. I noted with approval that the liquid neither bubbled nor glowed. "It's of a beach on Crockett that I used to swim at. I have to admit it never looked so good or romantic. It's by Lucinda."

"Yes, I know," I responded softly.

"Oh?"

"I knew her for a short time when she lived on Star City. Of course that was several years ago before she became famous."

"It sounds like there is a story there—"

"Frank."

"—Frank."

"You were worried that your husband might be going to do something foolish—" I said, changing the subject before it went somewhere I didn't want to go.

"Yes. He received a comm call just before I called you. He stormed out of here, and when I asked what he was going to do he refused to answer. I think he may have taken a pistol with him."

"What makes you say that?"

"Perhaps it would be better if I showed you." She led me to a room off the living room, evidently Geoffrey Philips' study. It was all dark woods and was dominated by a chrome and wood desk that took up much of the room. Books filled several bookcases, and there was a large painting of a starliner hanging on the wall behind the desk.

Sitting on the desk was an open case. It had been custom made for a laser pistol, a large one, probably a Kunstler 75. The pistol was missing.

"Geoffrey usually keeps that case locked in the safe." She went to one of the pictures on the wall which swung out to reveal the door of a safe. It was a good model, very secure.

"Does your husband know how to use a laser?"

"Oh, yes. Back on Crockett he was an avid hunter. He still tries to get back once or twice a year for a hunt."

I've never understood the mystique of hunting. It seems unfair. Maybe it's because we have no animals roaming the wilds of Star City because there are no wilds. Maybe it's because I've hunted men, and been hunted in my turn. Even if Philips knew how to handle a weapon, it's one thing to shoot an animal, it's quite another when the animal can shoot back.

"Do you have any idea where your husband went?"

"No, I'm afraid not. As I told you, he received a call, he was in here, and then he left in a hurry. When I came into his study I saw the case on the desk. That's when I called you."

"Are calls recorded?"

"It came in on his personal comm. He took that with him."

I looked over the top of the desk, looking for a clue. Geoffrey Philips was evidently one of those pathologically neat individuals. With the exception of the pistol case, everything was in its place perfectly aligned, the desk set, the blotter, the lamp. Even the notepad was set at a perfect ninety degree angle. I looked at the notepad. The top page had been torn off in a hurry leaving a jagged edge that jarred with the rest of the desk.

"Was your husband in the habit of jotting things down?"

"Now that you mention it, yes."

There was a trick I'd seen in an old play, Shakespeare maybe or Christie, I can't remember. I took a pencil from the desk set and rubbed it sidewise over the notepad. To my surprise, an address appeared where the pen had pressed into it from the sheet above.

"Do you recognize this address?" I asked Mrs. Philips.

"No. It's not familiar to me. It's not one of our friends, I'm sure."

I was pretty sure, too. The address was quite a ways down Star City, a part of town quite different from the one we were in.

"I think I'd better check this address out, Margaret, and in a hurry."

"Of course. In the state he's in, Geoffrey might do anything. He has a temper, I'm afraid, and he still is very much in love with me. Please take care of him, Mr. Sladek." The way she said that, it wasn't clear that the feeling was still mutual.

I let myself out after draining my glass. It seemed a shame to treat good whisky that way, but it couldn't be helped.

The address Philips had written down was a couple of kilometers down city from where he lived. It wasn't in New Minglewood or even the Souk, but it wasn't what one would call one of the better neighborhoods. Most of the buildings were apartments and rooms rented out to transients on a short term basis. By its very nature, Star City has plenty of those, and that was the part of town where they tended to live, at least until they could move up or down, or just out.

I took a tram down to the closest stop and then walked the rest of the way. It was almost 2000, but there were still plenty of people out on the street. The accommodations locally weren't the kind that encouraged staying at home. Mostly people were just standing around talking to each other, occasionally passing around a bottle or a smoke stick. There was a crowd on the corner watching a hustler play three card monty trying to lure in suckers. You'd think that after several millennia people would get wise to the old cons, but they don't. I noticed, though, that most of the onlookers were just that, watching but not participating. I guess for most of them it was just cheap entertainment watching the huckster juggle the cards and hurling insults as he tried to con someone into playing. I knew how it was done; I'd done it as a kid.

If there had ever been security on the entrance to the building, it hadn't functioned in decades. The pencil trick hadn't revealed the apartment number, just the address, but there was a label for an F. Lukas over one of the mailboxes, apartment 6C. Just my luck as the elevator wasn't working, either.

I started the long climb up a narrow flight of stairs. Each floor after the first seemed to be laid out the same way, two apartments, A and B, in the front, C and D along either side, and E and F in the back. When I got to the sixth floor I pulled the needle gun out of my jacket pocket. I needn't have bothered. I'd gotten there too late.

When I tried it, the door to 6C wasn't latched. Standing to the side, I gave it a little push so that it swung open. As I glanced inside, I spotted a pair of feet lying toes down. From the expensive shoes I assumed it was Geoffrey Philips. Stepping inside, I saw that I was right. There was a burn mark in his back where a laser had burned its way through his body. Sitting in a chair was another body that I didn't recognize, presumably French. Philips had either been a good shot or lucky, the beam from his laser pistol had caught French in the eyes. What Philips hadn't been was fast. The way I figured it, French had gotten in the first shot which hadn't killed Philips right away. Philips had made his shot and then collapsed. I checked to make sure, but both were dead when I felt for a pulse.

I didn't have much time to decide what to do. There didn't seem much point in trying to cover things up. With a little persuasion Latimer could probably be convinced that French had killed Fiskin allowing him to close the case. After all, it was the truth. I made a quick search of the room, which didn't take long. French had been traveling light. It was possible that he'd just taken the room to meet with Philips or his other victims. As far as I could tell, he hadn't brought any of the items he'd taken from Fiskin's safe to the apartment. I did, however, find a key on him, the sort that is used for lockers. I pocketed it, called Latimer, and sat down to wait.

"Geez, Frank, what is it with you and corpses?" the detective said when he pushed open the door. "The medical examiner should put you on commission. Care to tell me what happened?"

"I'll tell you what I know. I wasn't here when it happened. Mrs. Philips, the wife of Mr. Philips, that's him on the floor, called me earlier tonight. She'd called because she was afraid her husband was going to do something rash. When I went to her apartment, I found that her husband had written down this address. I didn't think it was the sort of place a man like Philips would normally be involved with."

"Who's this Philips?" Latimer interrupted.

"Geoffrey Philips, he's the local head of TransGalactic."

"You certainly can pick 'em, Frank," Latimer said shaking his head. "What did you do next?"

"Well, Mrs. Philips thought that her husband might have taken a laser pistol with him. There was a case for a Kunstler 75 sitting on his desk with the pistol missing. I thought it might be a good idea if I tried to head him off. I guess I got here too late."

"Do you think? Who's the other stiff?"

"I'm not sure, but I think he was going by the name Lucas French, probably arrived recently from Crockett. I suspect, but can't prove, that he's a blackmailer. I also suspect, but can't prove, that he's the one that killed Hari Fiskin."

"You seem to be doing a lot of suspecting, Frank."

"Yeah, well I know someone was blackmailing Mrs. Philips. She hired me to find out who. It was probably Fiskin. My guess is that French here knocked Fiskin off and decided to assume the blackmail business except that he chose Mr. Philips as the victim. That probably was a mistake."

"You have a talent for understatement, Frank," Latimer said sarcastically.

"Yeah, well, Philips came here planning to end things once and for all. Problem was, French was expecting him and got off the first shot. Philips took a little time to die, just enough to fire a shot back."

"Convenient, Frank. What makes you think French had anything to do with Fiskin's death?"

"Not much, except they both came from Crockett originally. That and the fact that French started blackmailing the Philips right after Fiskin was killed."

"Any idea what French had on Mrs. Philips?"

"No, she never told me. I didn't ask."

Latimer just grunted. Rossetti popped his head in, looked at the two bodies and just whistled. "I questioned the other tenants. No one saw nothin'."

"Big surprise."

"Want I should book Sladek?" Rossetti asked eagerly.

"Shut up, Rossetti. We know where to find Frank if we need him."

"Do you need me for anything more, Latimer? Someone has to go and break the news to Mrs. Philips."

"No. You can go. Just don't—"

"—leave town," I said completing the sentence.

"Get out of here, Frank, before I change my mind and let Rossetti book you."

I left.

As I waited for the up tram I examined the key I had taken from French. It had the TransGalactic logo and a number. I was pretty sure it was for a locker at a terminal, probably the one here on Star City. When the tram came, I rode it all the way up to top of the city where the starliner terminals are.

The whole reason for Star City's existence is to serve as the transit hub for human space where travelers can make connections. Depending on schedules, this usually results in a layover which can be anything from a few hours to a week or more. People who have layovers that are more than a few hours but less than a day need a place to stash carry-on luggage while they wait, hence the lockers.

I was pretty familiar with the layout of the terminal. It didn't take me long to find the bank of lockers that matched the key. It was two meters high and maybe twenty long. I inserted the key in the jack and pressed a button to energize it. A few meters down the bank a door popped open. Looking inside, I spotted a soft sided bag with a carrying strap. I pulled it out, slung the strap over my shoulder, slammed the locker door shut and walked out of the terminal.

Fifteen minutes later, I was back at Mrs. Philips apartment.

"I could use a drink, Margaret. You'd better pour one for yourself, as well."

"Is Geoffrey—?"

"Yes, I'm afraid I didn't get there in time. Your husband is dead. So is a man named Lucas French. I'm pretty sure he's the one who killed Fiskin."

"I see," she said slowly, turning her head away from me. "And the memory stick?"

"I haven't had time to look, but I suspect it's in that bag over there." I pointed to where I had dropped the bag next to the front door. "I suspect that there are other things in there as well. For other people."

She turned her face back to me, looking me in the eyes. "You must think me a horrible person, Frank, worrying about that at a time like this."

"I try not to judge people, Margaret. It only gets in the way."

"Geoffrey loved me. I'm not sure that I can say the same, at least not in the same way as he did. Maybe I did once, though, as time goes by I'm less sure of that. Don't get me wrong. I didn't hate him. I wasn't unhappy being Mrs. Philips. I just don't think I would have died for him. I don't think Geoffrey ever had doubts like that. Does any of that make sense, Frank?"

"Sure. People change. It happens all the time. Why don't you let me fix that drink for you?"

"Thank you, Frank. You're right, I could use a drink."

I went over to the bar, put some ice cubes in two glasses and poured the whisky over them. I didn't bother with the seltzer, just a splash of water. When I turned back, she had put the bag up on a table and was taking the contents out. There were a bunch of memory sticks, a few envelopes, and a packet of bills. She was holding one of the memory sticks in her hand.

"Find what you were looking for?"

"Yes, I think I have."

"Good. Here's your drink."

She tossed off a good portion of it. "What should we do with the rest of this?" she said waving her hand towards the pile on the table.

"We could try to return it to the relevant people, but that might be a long and messy undertaking."

"What do you recommend?"

"There's a disposal chute a few blocks from here. I could dump the whole lot into it."

"Would you do that for me?"

"Sure. It's not a problem."

"You don't have to include the money. I imagine a man like you could use the money?"

"I won't lie to you, I could."

"Then take it, Frank. I don't want to see it. And dispose of this as well. It's better destroyed." She tossed the memory stick in her hand onto the pile.

"If you're sure?"

"If you don't mind, Frank, I think I'd like to be alone now."

"Of course."

I bundled the items on the table back into the bag. The money I stuffed into my pocket. After that I let myself out. Margaret had gone out onto the balcony and was looking up at the twinkling lights in the sky which were just people on the other side of the city.

I kept my word and dumped the bag into the disposal. As I walked home I thought of one of the last verses of the song that had kept playing the last few days:

It's the truth, or so I found
Love's just a con to keep you hangin' round
But when you're dead and in the cold, cold ground
What's love, what's love?

I wondered what thoughts had run through Geoffrey Philips head as the life left his body. I'd never know.

Margaret Philips decided to leave Star City and go back to Crockett. She said that with her husband dead there was nothing more to hold her here. I guess I could understand that. Like so many people on Star City, she hadn't been born here; there certainly was no reason for her to die here.

She asked me to see her off. I had no reason not to. I watched her walk up the boarding ramp to the airlock. Unlike many of the passengers, she didn't turn and wave.

For the hell of it, I went up to the Promenade, the viewing platform of the docking ring. It's one of those strange things that most of the people on Star City, the ones who were born here and who will die here, never see a starship arrive or depart. I have. It's impressive in its own way.

The starliner Margaret was on was one of the big ones, nearly a kilometer long and a hundred meters in diameter. About an hour after they had shut the airlock, the ship separated from the docking ring and slowly drifted away. As it did so, and not for the first time, it struck me that this was how most of my relationships with women ended, with them leaving on a starliner, that is those that weren't dead.

I watched for a while, but after fifteen minutes or so I got bored and left. When I got back to my apartment I poured myself a drink and turned on the entertainment system. As the light from the glow tubes that run down the center spine of Star City dimmed for the evening, the last verse of the song played.

So I sit here and I drink my beer,
And I wonder what I'm doing here,
I guess I'm one of those people who jeer
At love, at love.

It wasn't beer that I was drinking, but the rest seemed to fit.

AUTHOR AFTERWORD

I didn't start to write the stories in *Blackmail Under a Dark Star* around a theme, that's just the way it ended up. Frank Sladek, as is the case with most good fictional detectives, has a flaw in his character. In his case it has to do with his relationship with women. Whether they love him or hate him, sooner or later they take the first ship off of Star City; either that or they end up dead. Neither possibility lends itself to a long term relationship

There is, of course, nothing original in this. The tragic interplay between hard-boiled detectives and dames can be traced back to Hammett's *The Maltese Falcon.* Detective stories aren't meant to have happy endings. At best, they end in a stalemate, wherein the protagonist maintains a fragile status quo until the next broad walks thought his door and threatens to upset the balance of the universe.

It wasn't really my intention when I started to write this series to cast Sladek in this mold; it was just a natural evolution of the character. The first story in *Star City Stories* started out as a ray-gun shoot-em up. It was really only as I wrote two other stories in that book, "The Sun Never Rises" and "Fear of Falling" that the pattern was set, but once it was, there was no turning back.

The five stories in *Blackmail Under a Dark Star* cover a number of different situations, the blackmailed woman, the woman scorned, the woman murdered, etc. None of these is particularly novel in that respect, but each provides an opportunity to say something about Sladek and the women around him. It like the blues, the chords are always the same, but it's the story that you tell with them that is important.

Lurking in the background of all of this is Lucinda, an off stage presence that hangs over Sladek's head like a black cloud. For those readers unfamiliar with *Star City Stories*, Lucinda was introduced in "The Sun Never Rises." Initially, she was just supposed to be a woman Sladek meets at a party, but the character, as they have a tendency to do, took on a life of her own. Possibly the only woman who ever really loved Sladek, and whose love was reciprocated, she eventually comes to the conclusion that she can't live the reality of Sladek's life, and she, like all the others, takes the first starliner leaving Star City. Unlike the others, Lucinda, would go on to become an artist famous across human space. The best indication that Sladek has never gotten over her is that he has three of her paintings hanging in his apartment, including a not terribly flattering portrait of himself positioned prominently in the entryway.

"Blackmail Under a Dark Star" was the first story in this collection that I wrote, and it sort of set the tone for the rest. I followed it with "Night on the Town." I was trying to be a little more light hearted with that one, but maybe I shouldn't have started it with Sladek waking up in a strange bed with a corpse. "The Big Score" came next, and was perhaps the most openly cynical of the five stories. The premise owes something to Chandler's *The Little Sister*. "Lies That Are Told" started as a caper story, but became more of a comment on the aftermath of love. I wrote the song that is featured in the story one bright sunny morning while walking my dogs. Go figure. The last story written was, "The Blue Skin Girl," in which Sladek takes on the role of knight errant that the literary critics of detective stories are so fond of.

A word about the title. Technically, this collection should probably have been called *Blackmail and Murder Orbiting A Brown Dwarf.* I think you'll agree that I made the right choice.

Blackmail Under a Dark Star is science-fiction mainly because it takes place a thousand years in the future, hundreds of light years from Earth, and the bartenders have four arms, but in reality, I could just have easily set these stories in Las Vegas in the 50's just by changing some of the details. But I didn't. I hope you enjoy them anyway.

Greg Fowkles

Special Preview!

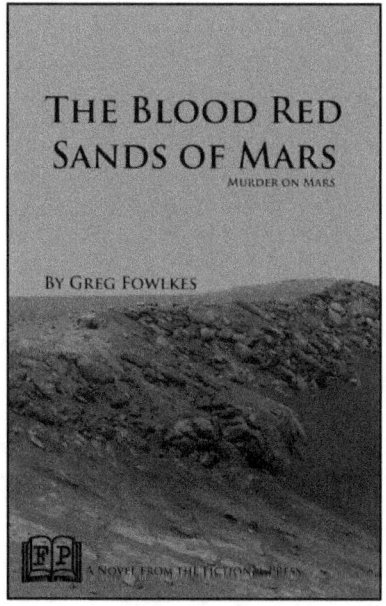

The Blood Red Sands of Mars

By Greg Fowlkes

Book One from the Murder on Mars Series

Now available from The Fictional Press
www.TheFictionalPress.com

THE BLOOD RED
SANDS OF MARS

The wind was blowing again against the west wall of the hut. He could hear the grains of sand abrading the thin aluminum skin that protected him from the outside. Through the window, half frosted from the continuous onslaught of sand and dust, he could see clouds of dust obscuring the sky. The sky was a pastel pink, a color no sky had any right to be. The wind, despite its 120 kph. velocity, made only a thin howl as it blew over the half buried cylinder of the hut.

McKernan lay on his cot trying not to admit that he was awake. It was a losing battle. After a few minutes he surrendered and glanced over at the clock sitting on the crate next to his bed. The dim red digits of the LED display read 7:58. It was too early to get up, too late to go back to sleep. He rolled over, shivering at the cold. The temperature couldn't have been more than ten degrees Celsius inside the hut. For the twentieth time he thought to himself that he would have to fix the heater before winter—if he could get the parts. Either that, or put in more insulation—if he could find that. The cold finally forced the decision to get up.

Standing, he felt the cold plastic floor beneath his bare feet. With his foot he fished the worn and patched pants from beneath the cot and pulled them on. He dug underneath his pillow and came up with a switchblade knife that he stuck in his pocket before drawing on the turtleneck sweater that had lain next to his pants. The cold feel of the cloth did nothing to dispel the cold from his body. From the crate he picked up a shoulder holster with a small automatic pistol and put it on. McKernan drew the weapon, worked the slide once, and after examining it perfunctorily, placed it back in the holster. Satisfied, he pulled on a worn pair of leather boots and placed another knife in a sheathe between his skin and the boot top.

Dressed, he went over to the shelf that served as counter and table. He put a pan of beans onto the heating unit and got a soysteak from the small refrigerator that held up one end of the shelf. The steak went into the frying pan on the other heating element. An egg would have been nice, but at the current price of three dollars apiece it was an extravagance that he would have to put off for a while.

As the food cooked he drew a liter of water from the spigot in the corner of the hut and watered the plants in the garden under the window. The carrots and tomatoes were doing nicely. He smiled briefly because it would be good to have fresh vegetables for a change. The big, leafy oxygen plants were doing well, too. He would be able to cut down on his oxygen ration this month and save some money.

He took the beans off the heating element and replaced them with the coffee pot. The beans were still half cold, but he wasn't in the mood to hassle with them. He only had the two heating elements, and he didn't want to have to wait for his coffee. He forced down the beans and then wolfed down the steak. It almost tasted like real beef, but then maybe his memories were fading. As usual, the coffee tasted terrible and tepid, too. The air pressure in the hut was too low for water to boil properly.

He finished his meal and scraped the remnants of food into the pressure vessel that served as a compost heap. The gauge on its neighbor showed that he had almost half a tank of methane. He'd be able to sell that soon and use the money for something useful, like a still. Completing his rounds, the gauges on the life support systems showed that everything was still working at keeping him alive. He went back to the pots and scrubbed them clean with sand. That, at least, was plentiful and cheap.

He checked his watch against the clock. It was time to get going. Pulling on his jacket he went to the airlock at the corridor end of the hut. After checking the gauge to make sure that there was pressure on the other side, he undogged the latches and stepped through. Closing the door behind him, he repeated the process with the outer hatch, latching both doors behind him. The outer door he locked with a heavy padlock.

He had entered a low tubular corridor made of the same aluminum foil and plastic foam construction as the hut. The walls, however, were even thinner, and no pretense was made of heating it. He could see his breath condensing in front of him as he began to walk down its length. It was a hell of a way to live, he reflected, not for the first time. But then, it had been hell living in L.A. where he'd been born, with brown air, rats, a chronic shortage of water, and overcrowded tenements. He had made his choice, but sometimes it seemed as though life was a continual shiver.

The corridor was pierced at regular intervals by hatches identical to his own. The huts behind the hatches were identical, too, except for the modifications the owners had made to make them more livable. This part of the city was old, dating back a couple of decades to the first days of the settlement when it had been part of a scientific base. The scientists had departed, at least from that corridor, and been replaced by those who had the money to buy or rent the huts from the Trust Authority. Maintenance was pretty much left up to the residents.

Along the sides and overhead ran the pipes and conduits that pumped in the gases, liquids, and power necessary for sustaining life. The whole system looked as jury rigged and fragile as it actually was, though surprisingly few people died whenever the system failed. Martians were a cautious lot. One didn't talk much about injuries. Accidents on Mars didn't leave many.

A hundred meters down the tube he came to an airlock. Going through the same ritual that he had used on his front door, he went through to another length of corridor indistinguishable from the one he had just left. Continuing on, he passed through two more airlocks until he entered a corridor that sloped downward. The hatches were farther apart, and larger. Signs overhead indicated the businesses or functions that were carried out behind them. The air was warmer because the corridor was buried beneath the sand which provided insulation. At the end of the tunnel was a larger airlock set into a wall of fused silica bricks, the first substantial piece of construction he had met that morning.

Passing through the portal was like entering another world, which in a way he had. This was the public Mars, the planet seen by the corporation men and the officials of the Trust Authority. It was also the planet seen by tourists, the brave new colony, man's first outpost on another planet. The tourists didn't really care to see the hut town. They were part of the same world as the corporation men and the government types. It still took a great deal of money or power to reach Mars.

The difference was more than one of degree. For one thing, the temperature was a comfortable twenty. For another, the walls were flat and met the floors and ceilings at right angles, unlike the inflated skins of the huts and corridors. With a little imagination it could almost be an enclosed shopping mall on earth, though the presence of fused silica blocks was more prevalent than any architect would allow.

The most important difference, however, was the sight of people scurrying along. He hadn't met anyone in the outer corridors. People rarely lingered there because of the cold. Now, McKernan could see at least twenty people and it was still fairly early. No airlocks interrupted this corridor. Extending for two hundred meters in either direction, it was twenty meters wide and ten high, the largest enclosed volume on the planet. Arrayed along its length were the offices and store fronts of the corporations that owned Mars, as well as the more prosperous saloons and bordellos.

One day the Trust Authority promised that the whole city would be like that, with apartments and condominiums for the ordinary workers, but neither the Authority or the corporations had yet come up with the money. For the moment all that existed was the one street of a few blocks.

McKernan headed towards the Authority's offices which dominated one end of the mall, but turned aside at the last moment when he noticed that a small, dark doorway was open. He knew that he should resist the temptation, but he was not in a very disciplined mood. He went through the doorway into the darkness beyond.

Finnegan's was the only real, honest bar on Mars. There were any number of saloons and even a cocktail lounge in the Mars Sheraton, but only one quiet, dark place where a man could drink in peace. McKernan felt the need for some of that peace at the moment.

He sat down on one of the stools before the only mahogany bar on Mars. Finnegan, himself, was behind the bar, though in fact he almost always was, no matter what the hour. The bartender looked up and greeted the newcomer, "Good morning, Constable. Beer or whiskey?"

"It's too early for beer. It's too early for whiskey, but give me a shot, anyway."

Finnegan poured out a shot glass of amber liquid and placed it before McKernan and then stood back polishing a glass while he studied the man opposite him.

McKernan knocked back half the glass before he spoke. When he did, there was a bitter edge to his voice. "Sometimes I wonder if it's worth it, Finnegan. I could be back on a planet fit for human life."

"Could you, now, Constable?" Finnegan said, putting down the glass and picking up another in equally gleaming condition. "If mother earth was such a bed of roses, why are you here?"

He breathed on the glass and examined it against the light for a moment, then looked at McKernan with the same intentness. "You're here because you're not the sort to live off the dole or to spend your life with another man being your boss. Instead you'll spend your life trying to make this planet a fit place to live and retire in twenty years with a nice pension. Now drink up and get to work, laddy."

"Yeah, sure. Sorry to burden you with my problems. Early morning depression, I guess. See you." He finished off the shot and left five dollars in Authority script on the bar.

The bite of the whiskey so early in the morning didn't really help his disposition, but it did give him enough courage to make it to the office. The morning ritual at Finnegan's was becoming too much of a habit. His three years on Mars were beginning to show.

The jail wasn't in the brick part of the Authority building, but in the complex of pneumatic architecture that sprawled behind it. The huts were old—older than his own—but dated back to the days when governments had not begrudged a few billions for exploration, back before space had to show a profit. For that reason, they were sound and well insulated, though a bit tacky looking.

The jail consisted of two huts joined together, one for offices, the other for the two makeshift cells and storage. Ferris was the only one there when he walked in, a young kid, younger than he had been himself when he had come to Mars. He was still impressed enough with his responsibilities and had not yet been worn down by the grim realities to take his job in any way but seriously.

Ferris greeted him with a solemn, "Good morning, sir," with a stress on the sir. As a three year veteran of Mars, Ferris looked on his boss with more than a touch of awe.

"Anything exciting happen overnight?" McKernan didn't really expect much. A few fights in the saloon district, a knifing maybe if things got out of hand. Petty thievery, or perhaps not so petty. He looked at Ferris and saw a flash of excitement in his eyes that the younger man was trying hard to suppress in order to match the hard bitten image he had of his superior.

"Yes, sir. We've got a murder on our hands."

"Another knifing down at Thelma's?" he asked, naming an infamous saloon and bordello that figured in a quarter of all the police reports.

"No. A prospector was found out on his claim yesterday, over on the far side of Olympus Mons. He was shot, Inspector."

That was bad, McKernan thought. People on Mars weren't supposed to have guns. With the thin skins of most buildings and a hostile atmosphere outside that would support life exactly as long as you could hold your breath, they were dangerous, and not just to the targets. The Authority had made them illegal and the corporations had been more than willing to agree. They weren't easy to get—not something that could be picked up casually or made, like a knife. Even without the details it sounded like the work of a real criminal and not just a squabble over a claim or a woman.

"Okay. Let me have the report. I'll take a look at it."

He took the folder from Ferris who looked a bit crestfallen. He probably expects me to go rush off to the outside and track down the murderer like an Indian scout, McKernan thought. He'd learn in time. Mars was a big planet and a dangerous one, but because of its nature there were also very few places that a man could run to and none where he could hide indefinitely.

He was leafing through the report when he came to his door. For the thousandth time he read, "Inspector Erik McKernan, Chief Constable." Mother would have been proud, he thought sardonically. She had hated the L.A. cops like all the other residents of the barrio. He went through the door into the little cubicle that was his real home. There, sitting at his desk, he began to read the report, sketchy though it was, to look for some explanations.

The Blood Red Sands of Mars c is available now from The Fictional Press. Find it on TheFictionalPress.com, or buy it on Amazon.com!

BOOKS BY GREG FOWLKES

From the Wizard at Law Series:
The Laws of Magic
Trial by Magic

From the Murder on Mars Series:
Blood Red Sands of Mars
A Death at Station Alpha
A Corpse in Hut Town
Murder at the Mars Club

From the Fictional Detective Series:
The Fictional Detective
A Fictional Detective Trifecta

Star City Stories: Space Opera Noir Featuring Frank Sladek

The Uncorrupted Corpse

Tequila Visions

Cargo From Paradise

Ice Viking

FROM THE WIZARD AT LAW SERIES BY GREG FOWLKES

THE LAWS OF MAGIC

Egil Njalsson was an aspiring lawyer. A lawyer with a difference. Not only had he passed the bar, but he had an undergraduate degree from the most prestigious school of magic in the country, the California Institute of Thaumaturgy. Needless to say his caseload and clients tended to the unusual. Like witches; or vampires. And the opposition, well they were likely to be demons. But Egil Njalsson had sworn an oath to uphold the law of the land, and... *The Laws of Magic*!

TRIAL BY MAGIC

Egil Njalsson is just another practicing attorney. Except, that is, for the occasional unusual client. Such as the ghost who retained his services using e-mail. Or the wolf who has been cursed by an Indian shaman to turn into a human during the full moon. Or the Leprechaun who is facing the loss of his saloon. Even when the clients are human, they have unusual problems like the Creole chef accused of making a rival a zombie or the scientist accused of transmuting a man into a statue of silicon. Yet somehow, Egil manages to resolve all his client's problems whether legal or magical. Of course it helps that he is a wizard as well as a lawyer.

Trial by Magic includes five new tales from the same world as *The Laws of Magic*.

FROM THE MURDER ON MARS SERIES BY GREG FOWLKES

BLOOD REDS SANDS OF MARS

On Mars the wind was rising. The grains of sand could be heard abrading the thin aluminum skin that was the only protection against the outside. On the far side of Olympus Mons a prospector lies dead in the sand. Inspector Erik McKernan, head of the handful of men that make up the small Martian police force must find the killer while threading the maze of corporate and international politics that govern the planet, and he must do it while trying to survive . . .*The Blood Red Sands of Mars!*

A DEATH AT STATION ALPHA

Station Alpha, a remote Martian research facility isolated by a planet wide dust storm. When one of the scientists is found murdered, it falls to Inspector McKernan to determine which of the remaining twelve people at the station wielded the fatal weapon. But, as the crime was committed in a locked laboratory with no possible access and all the suspects would seem to have unbreakable alibis, it will take all his skills as a detective to solve the puzzle of *A Death at Station Alpha*. Thirty years in the making, the long awaited sequel to *The Blood Red Sands of Mars*.

A CORPSE IN HUT TOWN

Hut Town is the remnants of the original Martian settlement; a collection of inflatable buildings abandoned by the Trust Authority and the mining corporations and now occupied by those catering to the baser needs of miners and construction workers in for a spree. But when a corpse is found in one of the service tunnels, Chief Inspector McKernan is called in.

He has plenty of questions. Who's body is it? How did they die? How did they get to Mars in the first place, and why weren't they missed? And the most important one on the Inspector's mind— are there any more bodies down there?

MURDER AT THE MARS CLUB

The Mars Club was the sanctuary of the rich and powerful on Mars, so when one of the members is found dead, Chief Inspector is called in to solve the case as discretely as possible. Will the solution of the case prove to be the one man he'd least like to implicate?

FROM THE FICTIONAL DETECTIVE SERIES BY GREG FOWLKES

THE FICTIONAL DETECTIVE

Mystery writer Ezekial O. Handler has been killed in a suspicious car crash. Private detective Frank Slade has been hired by Handler's beautiful girlfriend to investigate. Handler, seemingly with a premonition of his death, has left a trail of clues. Can Slade discover the murderer, or will he instead uncover a secret that will shake his existence to the core?

A FICTIONAL DETECTIVE TRIFECTA

The Fictional Detective has gotten out of the Private Investigator game. Instead, he's trying to write hard-boiled masterpieces such as *Death Buys a Condo*. But despite the fact that the door of his office now says WRITER, some of his clients haven't gotten the word. And a strange lot of clients they are. A man that only contacts him during séances because, well, he's dead; a female impersonator who has inherited a house that's just a little too haunted for the market, and a small time gambler who's trying to end an affair with Lady Luck.

Three All New Novellas featuring the Fictional Detective!

The Fictional Press
www.TheFictionalPress.com

The Fictional Press is a small, independent press specializing in the publication of fictional works by emerging authors. If you are interested in bringing your fictional works to life in print as well as electronically, contact us! We can help!

Find out more at www.thefictionalpress.com.